The Hypertension Reference Book that:

- Explains what hypertension is, its causes, and how it affects the body.
- Warns you when you or someone in your family is most likely to have a hypertension problem.
- Helps you to better understand your doctor's treatment, including "stepped-care" drug therapy.
- Gives you the latest facts on the effectiveness and risks of diuretics, vasodilators, and other treatments for hypertension.
- Provides detailed information on how you can help manage the disease at home—through diet, maintaining optimum weight, physical fitness, abstinence from alcohol, and more.
- Informs you about hypertensive emergencies and the strategies your physician uses to manage them.

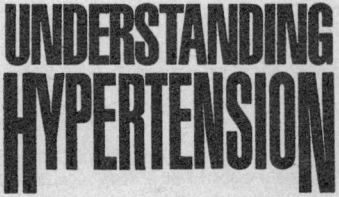

UNDERSTANDING HYPERTENSION

ATTENTION: SCHOOLS AND CORPORATIONS

WARNER books are available at quantity discounts with bulk purchase for educational, business, or sales promotional use. For information, please write to: SPECIAL SALES DEPARTMENT, WARNER BOOKS, 666 FIFTH AVENUE, NEW YORK, N.Y. 10103.

**ARE THERE WARNER BOOKS
YOU WANT BUT CANNOT FIND IN YOUR LOCAL STORES?**

You can get any WARNER BOOKS title in print. Simply send title and retail price, plus 50¢ per order and 50¢ per copy to cover mailing and handling costs for each book desired. New York State and California residents add applicable sales tax. Enclose check or money order only, no cash please, to: WARNER BOOKS, P.O. BOX 690, NEW YORK, N.Y. 10019.

UNDERSTANDING HYPERTENSION

CAUSES AND TREATMENTS

Adapted from *A Clinical Guide to Hypertension*

TIMOTHY N. CARIS, M.D.

WARNER BOOKS

A Warner Communications Company

Medicine is an ever-changing science. As new research and clinical experience broaden our knowledge, changes in treatment and drug therapy are required. The authors and the publisher of this work have made every effort to ensure that the treatment and drug dosage schedules herein are accurate and in accord with the standards accepted at the time of publication. Readers are advised, however, to check the product information sheet included in the package of each drug they plan to administer to be certain that changes have not been made in the recommended dose or in the indications and contraindications for administration. This recommendation is of particular importance in regard to new or infrequently used drugs.

WARNER BOOKS EDITION

Adaptation copyright © 1986 by Warner Books, Inc.
Copyright © 1985 by PSG Publishing Company, Inc.
All rights reserved. No part of this publication may be reproduced or transmitted in any form or by any means, electronic or mechanical, including photocopy, recording, or any information storage or retrieval system, without permission in writing from the publisher.

This Warner Books Edition is published by arrangement with PSG Publishing Company, Inc., 545 Great Road, Littleton, Massachusetts 01460

Warner Books, Inc.
666 Fifth Avenue
New York, N.Y. 10103

 A Warner Communications Company

Printed in the United States of America

First Warner Books Printing: June, 1986

10 9 8 7 6 5 4 3 2 1

To my wife, Ann,
and to my daughter, Nina,
for their encouragement,
support, and understanding.

CONTENTS

Chapter 1: Basic Facts About Hypertension   1
    What Is Blood Pressure?   1
    How Blood Pressure Is Measured   4
    When Is Blood Pressure Too High?   6
    Who Is Affected and How?   7
    Rating the Severity   9
    Is the Hypertension Primary or Secondary?   10
    The Natural Course of Essential Hypertension   11
    Inheritance and Lifestyle   17

Chapter 2: How Changes In Body Functions Lead to Essential Hypertension   19
    Changes in Blood Flow (Hemodynamics)   20
    Regulation by the Central Nervous System   21
    Regulation by the Peripheral Nerves and the Kidneys   25

Chapter 3: How Essential Hypertension Is Diagnosed 38
Clues Found in the Patient's History   40
Clues Found in the Physical Examination   44
Clues Found in Laboratory Studies   49
Debatable Procedures for the Initial Evaluation   52

Chapter 4: Finding and Treating the Causes of Secondary Hypertension 56
Problems Related to Endocrine (Hormonal) Function   57
Problems Related to Renal (Kidney) Function   68

Chapter 5: How Effective Is Treatment? 77
The Veterans Administration Cooperative Study   79
The U.S. Public Health Service Cooperative Study   82
The Australian National Blood Pressure Study   83
The Oslo Study   84
The Hypertension Detection and Followup Program (HDFP)   85
Conclusions   88

Chapter 6: Using Nondrug Treatments for Essential Hypertension 90
Low-Sodium Diet   91
Weight Reduction   93
Exercise   94
Reducing or Eliminating Alcohol Consumption   96

Reducing or Eliminating Tobacco Smoking 97
Dietary Supplements 97

Chapter 7: Planning a Drug-Treatment Regimen 101
The Stepped-Care Approach 104
Single-Drug Therapy (Monotherapy) 106

Chapter 8: Diuretics 112
Diuretic Agents 114
Sodium and Water Excretion and Other Metabolic Effects 118
Lipid Changes Associated with Diuretic Therapy 128

Chapter 9: Sympathetic Inhibitors 130
Reserpine 131
Methyldopa (Aldomet) 134
Clonidine (Catapres) 137
Guanabenz (Wytensin) 139
Beta-Adrenoreceptor Blockers 140
Prazosin (Minipres) 150
Labetalol (Normodyne, Trandate) 152
Guanadrel (Hylorel) 152

Chapter 10: Vasodilators, Converting-Enzyme Inhibitors, and Calcium-Channel Blockers 155
Vasodilators 155
Converting-Enzyme Inhibitors 161
Calcium-Channel Blockers 163

Chapter 11: Hypertension in Elderly Patients 167
    Essential Hypertension   168
    Hypertension *de Novo*   176
    Pure Systolic Hypertension   176

Chapter 12: Mild Hypertension   180
    Is Treatment Beneficial?   180
    Strategies for Treatment   183

Chapter 13: Hypertensive Emergencies (Hypertensive Crises)   188
    Accelerated Hypertension   189
    Intravenous Therapy in Emergency Situations   191
    Hypertensive Encephalopathy   196
    Malignant Hypertension   199
    Severe Hypertension Complicating Other Conditions   200
    Postcrisis Blood Pressure Control   204

LIST OF TABLES

1.1 U.S. Classification of Hypertension by Diastolic Pressure Level   10
1.2 Primary (Essential) Versus Secondary Hypertension   11
2.1 Cardiovascular Responses to Stimulation of Adrenoreceptors   22
2.2 Autoregulation in Essential Hypertension   27
2.3 Inhibition of Cellular Sodium (Salt) Transport in Essential Hypertension   30
2.4 The Renin-Angiotensin-Aldosterone (RAA) Axis   32
3.1 Causative Factors Found in Studies of Patients with Hypertension   39
3.2 Clues from the Patient's History Suggesting Secondary Hypertension   40
3.3 Funduscopic Changes in Hypertension   45
3.4 Clues from the Physical Examination Suggesting Secondary Hypertension   47

3.5	Minimal Laboratory Tests in Initial Evaluation of the Patient with Hypertension	50
4.1	Potential Causes of Secondary Hypertension	57
4.2	Common Mechanisms for Cushing's Syndrome	60
4.3	Physiologic Effects of Catecholamines	64
4.4	Urinary Findings in Pheochromocytoma	67
4.5	Characteristics of Renal Arterial Dysplasia	69
4.6	Abnormal IVP (Excretory Urogram) as a Predictor of Surgical Correction of Renovascular Hypertension	71
4.7	Clinical Indications Suggesting Renovascular Hypertension	72
5.1	Episodes of Illness (Morbid Events) in Patients with Diastolic Pressures Averaging 115 to 129 mm Hg (VA Study)	80
5.2	Episodes of Illness (Morbid Events) in Patients with Diastolic Pressures Averaging 90 to 114 mm Hg (VA Study)	81
5.3	Complications in Patients with Moderate Hypertension Compared to Patients with Mild Hypertension (VA Study)	81
5.4	Mortality and Morbidity in the Australian Blood Pressure Study	85
5.5	Mortality After Five Years in the Hypertension Detection and Follow-up Program (HDFP)	86
5.6	Mortality from Mild Hypertension Compared to All Subjects in HDFP	87
5.7	Mortality Rates by Age Group in HDFP	87
5.8	Mortality Rates by Race and Sex in HDFP	88
6.1	Converting Grams of Salt to mEq Sodium	91

6.2	Recommended Low-Salt Diet for Patients with Essential Hypertension 93	
6.3	Common Beverage Equivalents of 30 ml of Ethyl Alcohol 96	
7.1	Normal Compensatory Mechanisms That Maintain Blood Pressure at Setpoint Level 103	
7.2	Sympathetic Inhibitor Drugs 105	
8.1	Sulfonamide-Derivative Diuretics 115	
8.2	Areas of the Renal Tubules Where Diuretics Act 120	
8.3	Potassium Chloride Preparations 125	
8.4	Commercially Available Salt Substitutes Containing Potassium 126	
9.1	Characteristics of Reserpine (Rauwolfia Alkaloid) 133	
9.2	Characteristics of Methyldopa (Aldomet) 136	
9.3	Characteristics of Clonidine (Catapres) 139	
9.4	Characteristics of Guanabenz (Wytensin) 140	
9.5	Characteristics of Beta-Blockers 142	
9.6	Effects of Beta-Adrenoreceptor Blockade 143	
9.7	Outcome of Norwegian Multicenter Study 147	
9.8	Outcome of Beta-Blocker Heart Attack Trial 148	
9.9	Characteristics of Prazosin (Minipres) 150	
9.10	Characteristics of Guanadrel (Hylorel) 153	
10.1	Characteristics of Hydralazine (Apresoline) 158	
10.2	Characteristics of Minoxidril (Loniten) 160	
11.1	Stroke Recurrence Rate Related to Level of Diastolic Pressure Attained by Antihypertensive Treatment 169	

11.2 Drop in Systolic Pressure After One Minute Quiet Standing in 494 Subjects 65 Years or Older 171
13.1 Frequently Encountered Hypertensive Emergencies 188
13.2 Response to Oral Loading with Clonidine in 34 Patients 190
13.3 Comparison of Accelerated Hypertension, Hypertensive Encephalopathy, and Malignant Hypertension 200

LIST OF FIGURES

1.1 Factors that determine blood (arterial) pressure 3
2.1 Neural mechanism of essential hypertension 24

FOREWORD

Understanding Hypertension: Causes and Treatments originated as a text for physicians. Its purpose was to provide a concise review of current knowledge about high blood pressure that physicians could use in designing individual diagnostic and treatment programs for their patients. High blood pressure is not the same in everyone. Its causes vary, and treatment should be tailored to fit the cause as well as the patient's tolerance and response to pharmacologic (drug) and nonpharmacologic (nondrug) measures. Treatment should also be compatible with the patient's lifestyle and any unrelated medical problems he or she might have.

Once the original text was published, some patients and friends thought it was *almost* comprehensible to nonphysicians! This version contains the same general information found in the professional text, but I have avoided medical jargon wherever I could. I have, however, included medical terms that you as a patient are likely to encounter during the lifelong process of treating your condition. These terms are *italicized* and are defined at least the first time they are used—more often where this strategy seemed indicated.

Medical professionals continually use these terms, and it is a good idea to learn them.

This volume is *not* intended to be a guide for diagnosing or treating yourself. Partly for this reason, no dosages are given for the drugs that are discussed. Dosage recommendations are continually changing, and prescription should be left to your physician's judgment in accordance with current practice and your individual situation.

This book *is* intended to help you understand the significance of high blood pressure, the risks and underlying causes associated with it, the logic that leads the physician to prescribe various diagnostic approaches, and the rationale behind the treatment programs that are prescribed. I hope that it will answer the questions that you may forget to ask while you are in your physician's office and that it will serve as a reference between visits.

This volume is dedicated to my wife, Ann, who has continued to encourage and support me in my writing efforts. In addition, my sincere thanks go to Mrs. Lynda Barton for her cheerful cooperation and expertise in preparation of the manuscript. I am grateful to Dr. Frank N. Paparello, president of PSG Publishers, and the staff at Warner Books, Inc., for their assistance and guidance. Finally, I should like to express special thanks to Lillian R. Rodberg, whose expertise as the manuscript editor has been of great value. Her adaptations have made the text more comprehensible.

Timothy N. Caris, M.D.

CHAPTER 1

BASIC FACTS ABOUT HYPERTENSION

PERHAPS you have had high blood pressure (hypertension) for some time. Or perhaps the condition has been recently diagnosed. In either case, understanding some basic facts about body structures (anatomy) and function (physiology) will be helpful in understanding the measures your physician prescribes for bringing your blood pressure to appropriate levels and keeping it there.

WHAT IS BLOOD PRESSURE?

To live and function normally, every cell in every tissue and organ in the body requires that nutrients and oxygen be brought to it and that its metabolic waste products be carried away. In humans, as in all mammals, oxygenation and waste removal are accomplished through the *cardiovascular system*: the heart, arteries, and veins. The heart pumps a stream of blood high in oxygen and nutritive substances through the arteries to perfuse (spread through) each cell. The left ventricle, the largest, most muscular chamber of the heart, first fills with oxygenated, nutritive blood, then contracts rhythmically to spurt blood into the aorta, the main trunk of the arterial tree. Major arteries branch off the aorta to reach each organ of the body. As these main branches enter the organ, they divide into smaller and smaller "stems and twigs": smaller arteries, arterioles, and, finally, numerous thin-walled capillaries that are distributed profusely throughout every portion of the organ. The oxygen and nutrients diffuse (pass through) from the capillaries into the cells. Meanwhile, waste products diffuse from the cells into the capillaries, which join to form small veins that branch "in reverse" to form larger and larger veins and through which the blood eventually returns to the heart. The process then begins all over again.

You can see that the flow of blood depends on the pumping action of the heart. A measurable pulsatile pressure within the aorta and the larger arteries is directly related to each contraction of the left ventricle. This *intraarterial pressure* declines slightly and gradually as distance from the heart increases. In the smaller subdivisions and in the arterioles, the pressure diminishes considerably, and fluctuations in pressure are damped out because these tiny tubes are highly resistant to flow. By the time blood reaches the capillaries, it is under much lower pressure. Similarly, the venous channels are also a low-pressure system.

The term *blood pressure*, then, refers to the pressure in the arteries, which is the product of the volume of blood pumped by the heart (*cardiac output*) and the peripheral resistance of the arterial tree—especially the arterioles. If either or both of these two factors rise, blood pressure rises also. This relationship may be expressed by the equation P (pressure) = Cardiac output × Total peripheral resistance. Several major factors influence each of these determining elements (Fig. 1.1).

Cardiac output is the product of *stroke volume* (the quantity of blood ejected by each left ventricular contraction) and *heart rate* (the number of contractions per minute). In addition, the branches and twigs of the venous and arterial "trees" are not a network of rigid conduits; they are

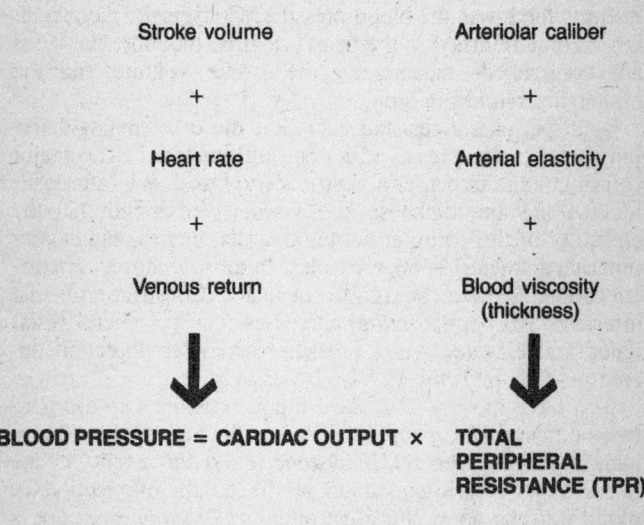

Figure 1.1 Factors that determine blood (arterial) pressure.

capable of distending and constricting. The veins can distend to great capacity. By its contraction (narrowing) or dilatation (widening), the dynamic reservoir determines how much blood returns to the heart. The greater the volume of blood maintained in the peripheral venous circulation—that is, the more the veins are dilated—the less the return or preload to the heart, the less the stroke volume, and consequently, the lower the blood pressure. Conversely, the greater the volume returned to the heart—that is, the more the veins are constricted—the greater the stroke volume and the higher the blood pressure.

Total peripheral resistance (TPR), the other major determinant of blood pressure, is also multifactorial. The major contributors to intraarterial resistance to blood flow (afterload) include (1) the thickness and viscosity of blood, (2) the elasticity of the aortic and arterial walls, and (3) the caliber (internal diameter) of the arterioles. In most instances, arteriolar caliber is the most significant factor. Constriction of the arterioles (*vasoconstriction*) increases total peripheral resistance and elevates blood pressure; arteriolar dilatation decreases TPR and lowers blood pressure.

You have most likely heard blood pressure expressed as two numbers—for example, 120 systolic and 80 diastolic or simply "120 over 80." *Systolic pressure* refers to the intraarterial pressure attained at the height of ejection of blood into the aorta and great arteries. *Diastolic pressure* is the pressure that is maintained in these vessels after the left ventricle relaxes and the valve between the aorta and left ventricle closes.

Blood pressure does not remain at a constant level. It fluctuates during exercise, anxiety, and pain, and with various physiologic demands on the body. The blood pressure level that is used diagnostically is that which is obtained after a short period of rest and relaxation.

HOW BLOOD PRESSURE IS MEASURED

In the early 1700s, Stephen Hales, an English clergyman, devised a means of measuring arterial pressure in horses and other animals. His technique, however, was not suitable for use in humans. He inserted a brass tube into a main artery, tied it in place, and used the flexible trachea of a goose to link it to a vertical glass tube. Hales noted that a horse's blood rose to a height of nearly nine feet within the glass tube.

In 1828 a French medical student, Jean Leonard Poiseuille, utilized a U-shaped glass tube containing mercury to measure blood pressure. Using this heavy material (about 14 times the weight of water) at the head of the blood column considerably reduced the length of the tubing needed, making the measuring device much less cumbersome than Hale's. The mercury manometer measured blood pressure in terms of how many millimeters the mercury rose within the glass tube. Today, over 150 years later, blood pressure is still expressed in millimeters of mercury (mm Hg). However, Poiseuille's method still required puncture of the artery.

Then in 1896, the Italian physician Scipione Riva-Rocci developed the concept of using a wide inflatable arm cuff to measure systolic pressure, eliminating the need for arterial puncture. He reasoned that the pressure required to stop flow of blood in an artery by circular constriction would be equivalent to the arterial (systolic) blood pressure. The rubber cuff was connected to a bulb for pumping air into it and to a graduated manometer filled with mercury which would indicate the pressure. Riva-Rocci palpated the pulse of the radial artery at the wrist while inflating the cuff. When pulsations were no longer palpable, the pressure indicated by the mercury column reflected systolic pressure in millimeters of mercury (mm Hg).

Finally, in 1905, Nicolai Korotkoff, a Russian physician, described a method for calculating diastolic pressure also. Korotkoff's method is still in use today. First, he would determine systolic pressure by the Riva-Rocci method. He would then increase the pressure to a slightly higher level (about 20 mm Hg is recommended presently) and apply a stethoscope to the antecubital fossa (the inner part of the arm in front of the crook in the elbow). While listening through the stethoscope, he bled out the cuff pressure slowly and continuously by allowing the air to escape under control. Pulsations would be heard just as the cuff pressure dropped below the systolic pressure in the artery. These pulsations (named Korotkoff's sounds in his honor) gave a more accurate systolic pressure. At the point where the sounds disappeared completely, the artery was no longer occluded by the pressure in the constricting cuff. The pressure in the manometer at that point reflected the arterial diastolic pressure.

WHEN IS BLOOD PRESSURE TOO HIGH?

Two American physicians, T. C. Janeway[1] and his father, did pioneering work in demonstrating that blood pressures above a certain level can be dangerous. Father and son cared for almost 8,000 patients between 1903 and 1912. The younger Janeway recorded blood pressure levels in most of them. He noted that 11 percent of these stood out from the rest in having systolic pressures of 165 mm Hg or more. He also observed these patients did not live as long as those with lower pressures. Janeway concluded that systolic pressures of 165 mm Hg or higher were pathological (injurious) and called the disorder "hypertensive cardiovascular disease."

Unfortunately, the medical profession at large was not impressed. As a matter of fact, many doctors believed that increasing height of blood pressure was a beneficial compensatory mechanism. They had noted that arteries tended to become constricted as people aged, and it seemed reasonable to believe that higher pressures were necessary to sustain adequate blood flow in aging arteries. Physicians feared that lowering blood pressure by medical intervention might lead to inadequate perfusion and deterioration of such vital organs as the heart, brain, and kidneys. This theory of compensation was shaken, however, by a study reported by Irwin Page in 1934.

Using the urea clearance test developed by Donald Van Slyke, Page demonstrated that blood flow to the kidneys was not significantly changed when the blood pressure of hypertensive patients was lowered.[2]

By 1940, the concept that high blood pressure (*hyperten-*

sion) was harmful had been accepted. Its relation to stroke, heart failure, kidney failure, and heart attack was recognized. Between 1950 and 1960, it was established that the lives of patients with severe, rapidly progressive hypertension could be significantly prolonged by drug therapy. The drugs used at that time, however, produced highly undesirable side effects when used long term. Both physicians and patients were reluctant to use them for milder forms of hypertension. Fortunately, through continued research by individual investigators, research institutes, medical schools, and pharmaceutical companies, additional antihypertensive drugs have been developed. Not only are they more effective than earlier medications in treating high blood pressure, but they also cause fewer and less severe side effects, and their effects are more predictable. As these new drugs were coming into use, studies were reporting how large a portion of the population was at risk because of hypertension. These findings, together with the newly available effectiveness of treatment, focused attention on this disorder. It may be said that the modern era of hypertension began in the 1970s.

WHO IS AFFECTED AND HOW?

Health care professionals use the term *prevalence* to refer to the number of cases of a condition in a given population at a given time. In the early 1960s the U.S. Public Health Service conducted a National Health Examination Survey. The results, published between 1964 and 1966, give an indication of the magnitude of hypertension as a health problem.[3] Using World Health Organization (WHO) criteria (blood pressure at 160 mm Hg or greater systolic and 95 mm Hg or greater diastolic) this random sampling found 9 percent of white U.S. adults and 22 percent of black adults suffering from hypertension. (These readings are commonly stated as 160/95 mm Hg.) If when hypertension is defined as pressures of 140/90 mm Hg or greater, it is estimated that 20 to 25 percent of the U.S. adult population has elevated blood pressure. Several other regional health surveys have confirmed the national findings.[4]

Hypertension and Risk of Illness

At about the same time, published reports appeared from several studies in which adult populations were followed longitudinally—that is, the same patients were studied for considerable time periods. The National Cooperative Pooling Project published a comprehensive report in 1970[5] including the observations of: (1) the Albany civil servant project, (2) the Chicago Peoples Gas Company project, (3) the Chicago Western Electric Company project, (4) the Framingham study, and (5) the Minneapolis–St. Paul study of business and professional men. These studies indicated that hypertension is the most important risk factor for the development of strokes. Individuals with high blood pressure are four times as likely to suffer stroke as those with normal pressure.[6]

Hypertension is the major cause of heart failure: 75 percent of adults who develop this problem have high blood pressure in the background.[7] It is also important to realize that heart failure in a person with hypertension is especially dangerous. Only 50 percent of such patients survive five years after the initial recognition of heart failure. Incidentally, hypertensive patients whose electrocardiograms (EKG or ECG) demonstrate increased heart muscle mass (hypertrophy) of the left ventricle have been found to be extremely vulnerable to developing congestive heart failure—at ten times the risk of hypertensives whose EKGs are normal.

Of the various predisposing risk factors for developing coronary artery disease and heart attack, high blood pressure is one of the most important.[5] Pooled data from various studies indicate that 66 percent of patients who suffered coronary heart disease had a background of blood pressure levels of 140/90 mm Hg or higher.

Hypertension and Risk of Death

Since Janeway's report in 1913[1], it has been known that patients with high blood pressure tend to die earlier than those with normal blood pressure. For decades, life insurance companies have been emphasizing the fact that high blood pressure, even when elevated only slightly, correlates well with increased risk for premature death.[8] Sir George Pickering showed that the higher the blood pressure, the shorter the longevity.[9] Even within what is considered to be a normal range, increasing rates of blood pressure correlate with decreasing longevity. Those with blood pressures of 140/90 mm Hg are not likely to live as long as those with 135/80, who are not likely to live as long as those with 120/80 and so on.

Not only is hypertension more prevalent in blacks, it is also more severe. Higher mortality related to high blood pressure is apt to occur more in blacks than in whites and more often in men than in women. When mortality rates for hypertension are analyzed according to age, it is obvious that for blacks with high blood pressure at a young age, the risk is extremely high. Before the age of 50, the death rate from hypertension is about six to seven times higher in blacks. After the age of 50, the death rate drops to two and one-half times higher in blacks.

RATING THE SEVERITY

Knowledge regarding the prevalence and significance of hypertension has been evolving over the past 50 years, and major contributions to this area have been made independently throughout the world. No wonder, then, that opinions vary. What level of blood pressure are considered abnormal? What constitutes mild, moderate, and severe hypertension?

We know that blood pressure is a continuum in which risk increases as pressure levels increase. The diastolic pressure is generally believed to be the more significant. In the United States, the classification shown in Table 1.1 is generally accepted; that is, a diastolic range of 90 to 104 mm Hg is considered mildly hypertensive, 105 to 114 is considered moderately hypertensive, and 115 mm Hg or over is considered severe.

TABLE 1.1
U.S. Classification of Hypertension by Diastolic Pressure Level

Stratum	Diastolic range (mm Hg)
Mild	90–104
Moderate	105–114
Severe	115 and over

IS THE HYPERTENSION PRIMARY OR SECONDARY

The causes of persistently elevated blood pressure vary among individuals. In some cases, hypertension may be traced to an abnormality of body function. When a specific cause is identifiable such as kidney disease, decreased blood supply to the kidney, a tumor of the adrenal gland, or constriction of the aorta the patient is said to suffer *secondary hypertension* (see Chapter 4). If the underlying cause can be corrected or eliminated, blood pressure may return to normal levels without further therapy. In the vast majority of patients with high blood pressure, however, no such specific cause can be found. Hypertension without a discernible cause is called *idiopathic, primary,* or *essential hypertension*.

Gifford[10] thoroughly evaluated 5,000 consecutive hypertensive patients with emphasis on detecting hypertension secondary to identifiable causes. A secondary cause of hypertension was found in only 11 percent of the patients studied, and only 6 percent had a potentially curable secondary cause for their elevated pressures (Table 1.2). Subsequent similar studies all confirm that about 90 to 95 percent of patients with high blood pressure suffer essential hypertension.

TABLE 1.2
Primary (Essential) Versus Secondary Hypertension in 5,000 Consecutive Patients

Diagnosis	Percentage Affected
SECONDARY HYPERTENSION	**(11.0%)**
Tumors of the adrenal gland	1.0
Constriction (coarctation) of the aorta	1.0
Decreased blood supply to the kidney (renovascular hypertension)	4.0
Chronic kidney disease	5.0
ESSENTIAL HYPERTENSION	**89.0**

Source: Data from Gefford, R. W. Jr.[10]

THE NATURAL COURSE OF ESSENTIAL HYPERTENSION

The ways in which essential hypertension manifests itself were well-known long before effective treatment was available. Such early researchers as Bechgard,[11] Perera,[12] and Leishman[13] collectively studied nearly 2,000 patients for long periods ranging to 22 years. All agreed that patients with hypertension tend to die prematurely of coronary artery disease, strokes, congestive heart failure, or kidney failure.

The Insidious Nature of Hypertension

Early in the course of their disease, patients with essential hypertension have recurrent findings of elevated blood pressure. These episodes are interspersed with varying periods when pressures are normal. This labile (fluctuating) phase may begin as early as the twenties. Finally, by the patient's midthirties to early forties, hypertensive levels become practically constant. Fixed high levels of blood pressure that appear before age 25 or for the first time after the age of 50 years are *usually* due to essential hypertension, but studies should be done to determine whether an underlying cause exists. Secondary hypertension most often occurs under these circumstances.

During the early years of essential hypertension, the patient most likely has no symptoms. Damage to various organs, such as the kidneys may be progressing, but hypertensive patients spend most of their adult lives symptom free and unaware of their problem unless it is revealed by examination. Specific symptoms generally do not appear until the elevated pressures have gradually ravaged the arteries or overwhelmed the heart muscle of the left ventricle, causing it to fail. The insidious nature of the damage caused by hypertension has led to its being called "the silent killer."

Consequences of High Blood Pressure

Atherosclerosis. Studies in humans and in animals demonstrate a distinct relationship between increased levels of blood pressure and the development, acceleration, or aggravation of atherosclerosis in large- and medium-sized arteries. *Atherosclerosis* is a process by which lipid material (cholesterol), fibrous tissue, and calcium deposits accumulate in the lining of the arteries. As the process continues, the arterial channel (lumen) is progressively obstructed, and tissue depending upon that vessel for its blood supply receives insufficient oxygen and nutrients. If the artery becomes completely blocked, the tissue dies.

The theory that high intraarterial pressure leads to atherosclerosis is supported by the fact that the pulmonary artery, which leads from the right ventricle of the heart into the circulatory tree of the lungs rarely becomes atherosclerotic. Pressures in the pulmonary artery are normally low—much lower than those in the aorta. If pressure in this artery is significantly raised, however—for example, because of chronic lung disease or by chronic left ventricular failure—it does develop atherosclerotic changes. In other words, atherosclerotic lesions (*plaques*) are a major consequence of high blood pressure. When arteries providing essential blood supply are obstructed by such lesions, major organs such as the heart and brain may suffer.

In addition, hypertension causes obstructive lesions in small arteries and arterioles. These are similar to the atherosclerotic lesions of the larger arteries, but may be distinguished from them by microscopic inspection and by biochemical analysis. One major difference is that excessive lipid (fat) cholesterol accumulates in atherosclerotic lesions but not in the hypertensive lesions of the small arteries and arterioles. Obstruction of the smaller arterial structures occurs in various organs, but is most pronounced and significant in the kidneys. The complex microscopic circulation of the kidneys may be severely damaged.

Coronary Artery Disease. The coronary arteries are the major sources of blood supply to the heart muscle itself. These vessels are very susceptible to atherosclerosis, particularly in individuals who have high blood pressure. If the obstructive plaques are so large or numerous that normal coronary blood flow is partially impeded, the patient may have no symptoms at rest but may be incapacitated during exercise. With exertion, the heart is called upon to work harder and to propel greater quantities of blood. The reduced blood flow within the coronary arteries may be inadequate to supply the increased oxygen and nutrient needs of the hard-working heart. A sickening, deep, pressure-pain discomfort behind the breastbone (*angina pectoris*) will develop, forcing the patient to cease activity. If the atherosclerotic process goes on to a complete occlusion (blockage) of a coronary artery, the part of the heart muscle that depended upon it for its blood supply dies. This condition, technically known as *myocardial infarction*, is commonly called a heart attack.

As already mentioned, hypertension is one of the most important predisposing risk factors for developing coronary artery disease. Of course, not all individuals who suffer coronary disease have high blood pressure. Other risk factors include heredity, cigarette smoking, obesity, high blood cholesterol levels, and diabetes. Nevertheless, two-thirds of patients with coronary heart disease have been found to have a background of blood pressure levels of 140/90 mm Hg or higher.[5]

Left Ventricular Hypertrophy and Failure. In individuals with hypertension, the contracting muscular left ventricle must generate a higher pressure within itself before it can overcome the higher than normal diastolic pressure in the aorta to open the valve between these two structures. Only then can blood be ejected forward into the aorta and the arterial system. This increased effort leads to high oxygen consumption of the heart muscle (*myocardium*). A series of biochemical phenomena then leads to an increase in size (*hypertrophy*) of each of the myocardial heart muscle fibers. The increase in muscle mass that results is termed *left ventricular hypertrophy*. Initially, the increased mass serves as a compensatory mechanism, providing increasing strength of contraction. As time progresses, however, this beneficial effect gradually wanes. Ventricular performance deteriorates and finally fails, with a marked decrease of blood propulsion into the aorta. The degree of left ventricular hypertrophy is related to the severity and duration of the hypertension.

A large, long-term study done in Framingham, Massachusetts,[6] showed that hypertension was the major cause in 75 percent of all cases of congestive heart failure (left ventricular failure) in adults. Despite appropriate therapy, 50 percent of those who developed failure died within five years, and about 20 percent died during the first year after this complication appeared.

Cerebrovascular Accident (Stroke). The Framingham study indicated clearly that hypertension was the most significant risk factor for developing stroke.[6] About 60 percent of strokes occur because the atherosclerotic process occludes an artery supplying blood to the brain. The portion of the brain that depended on that artery for its blood supply dies (becomes infarcted) and is functional no longer. The severity of atherosclerosis in arteries supplying the brain correlates directly with the height of blood pressure levels.

About 20 to 25 percent of all strokes are *hemorrhagic*; that is, they involve bleeding into the brain. Although hemorrhage is involved in only one-fifth to one-fourth of cases of stroke, it is associated with half the stroke deaths. Prolonged high pressure in the brain's arterial system leads to spotty destruction of the middle layer of the wall (*intima*) in small arteries located within the brain substance. The damaged portion of the vessel balloons out like the weakened area in the wall of a rubber inner tube. This localized bulging (*aneurysm*) tends to stretch and stretch and finally rupture. The pressure exerted by the bleeding within the tight confines of the skull destroys the surrounding brain tissue so that it can no longer function. These microaneurysms which were described first by Charcot and Bouchard in 1868, are referred to as *Charcot-Bouchard aneurysms*.

About 10 to 15 percent of strokes are embolic; that is, they involve migrating blood clots. Small pieces of clot or pieces of the atherosclerotic plaque that only partially block a major artery to the brain break off and are propelled forward into smaller arterial branches and twigs. These emboli eventually wedge into and occlude a smaller vessel. Brain tissue supplied by that branch then becomes infarcted.

Dissecting Aneurysm of the Aorta. In hypertensives, the increased pressure within the arteries (*intraluminal pressure*) not only enhances atherosclerosis within the aorta but also may cause *necrosis* (cell death) of the middle layer of its wall. Atherosclerosis, medical necrosis, and hypertension combine in some patients—particularly older hypertensive black males—to produce a lesion called a *dissecting aneurysm*. A rent develops in the damaged lining of the aorta within or near an atherosclerotic plaque. The usual forward flow of blood under pressure works itself into this tear and then continues into the deteriorating middle layer, dissecting (separating) the inner and outer walls. Bulging in of the inner layer may block the aortic channel. Bulging out followed by a tear in the outer layer produces a massive hemorrhage. If this complication is recognized early, the patient's life may be saved by medical treatment to lower blood pressure quickly followed by surgery to repair the damaged aorta.

Renal (Kidney) Insufficiency. In studying a group of untreated patients with hypertension, Perera[12] found that 42 percent began excreting significant amounts of albumin in their urine (*albuminuria*). This development is indicative of blood-vessel damage within the kidney. These patients survived for a mean of only five years after the albuminuria appeared. In other, later studies, microscopic examination of kidney tissues (*renal biopsy*) showed that 65 to 85 percent of patients with moderately severe to severe hypertension had sclerosis of the renal arterioles (*nephrosclerosis*). Enough such cases have been studied to indicate that the high blood pressure antedates the nephrosclerosis. Similar lesions have developed in laboratory animals only after they have been rendered hypertensive. From these findings we can conclude that these degenerative changes of the arterioles and the accompanying damage to the kidney tissue are the direct consequences of high pressure on the arteriolar walls. As a rule, these renal changes occur slowly and often have no serious effect on the patient's condition. It has been estimated, however, that approximately 10 percent of patients suffering from essential hypertension will eventually develop some degree of kidney failure (renal insufficiency).

Accelerated Hypertension. A very small proportion of patients wih essential hypertension go on to develop accelerated hypertension (see Chapter 13). When diastolic pressure is elevated persistently to a high degree (130 to 150 mm Hg), a severe inflammation of the arterioles (*arteriolar vasculitis*) ensues. It is characterized by necrosis of blood vessels in the kidneys, spleen, pancreas, and brain, in the retina of the eye, and probably in other tissues and organs. The syndrome is characterized by persistent extreme high levels of blood pressure, retinal hemorrhages and exudates, and progressive kidney failure. Before effective treatment was available, death usually occurred within the year due to renal failure, left ventricular failure, or cerebral hemorrhage.

INHERITANCE AND LIFESTYLE

It long has been recognized that essential hypertension tends to occur in families. Observations made on identical twins suggest strongly that such familial clustering is related to genetic rather than environmental differences. Although they may have lived apart in very different environmental situations for many years, similar blood pressure levels were found in both members of each pair. When blood pressures were monitored in adopted and natural children and these were compared with the levels in the adoptive and natural parents, there was a striking correlation between the blood pressures of the children and those of their natural parents. There was no correlation of blood pressures between adopted children and their adoptive parents. Zinner[14] examined 721 children from 2 to 14 years of age in 190 families. He found that blood pressure tended to be higher in children whose mothers were hypertensive. Others have noted that if both parents have elevated blood pressures, the risks are especially great in the children.

Although susceptibility to essential hypertension may be largely genetically predetermined, it does not necessarily follow that all individuals with a family background of this disorder will become afflicted. It appears that predisposition plus a triggering factor may be needed in many instances. These factors include salt (sodium) in the diet in excessive amounts, obesity, alcohol ingestion, lack of physical fitness, and probably others that are poorly understood or as yet unrecognized.

REFERENCES: CHAPTER 1

1. Janeway TC: A clinical study of hypertensive cardiovascular disease. *Arch Intern Med* 1913; 12:755–798.

2. Page IH: The effects on renal efficiency of lowering arterial blood pressure in cases of essential hypertension and nephritis. *J Clin Invest* 1934; 13:909–915.

3. US Dept of Health, Education and Welfare: Hypertension and hypertensive heart disease in adults, United States, 1960–1962, National Health Survey, National Center for Health Statistics Series 11: No. 13, 1966.

4. Inter-Society Commission for Heart Disease Resources: Guidelines for the detection, diagnosis and management of hypertensive populations. *Circulation* 1971; 44:A263–A272.

5. Inter-Society Commission for Heart Disease Resources: Atherosclerosis Study Group and Epidemiology Study Group: Primary prevention of the atherosclerotic diseases. *Circulation* 1970; 42:A55–A95.

6. Kannel, WB, Wolf PA, Verter J, et al.: Epidemiologic assessment of the role of blood pressure in stroke: the Framingham study. *JAMA* 1970; 214:301–310.

7. Kannel WB, Castelli WP, McNamara PM, et al.: Role of blood pressure in the development of congestive heart failure. *N Engl J Med* 1972; 287:781–787.

8. Lew EA: High blood pressure, other risk factors and longevity. *Am J Med* 1973; 55:281–294.

9. Pickering G: Hypertension. Definitions, natural histories and consequences. *Am J Med* 1972; 52:570–583.

10. Gifford RW Jr: Evaluation of the hypertensive patient with emphasis on detecting curable causes. *Milbank Mem Fund Q* 1969; 47:170–186.

11. Bechgard P: Arterial hypertension: A follow-up study of one thousand hypertonics. *Acta Med Scand* 1946 (suppl); 172:358.

12. Perara GA: Hypertensive vascular disease; description and natural history. *J Chronic Dis* 1955; 1:33–42.

13. Leishman AW: Hypertension: Treated and untreated; a study of 400 cases. *Br Med J* 1959; 1:1361–1368.

14. Zinner SH, Levy PS, Kass EH: Familial aggregation of blood pressure in childhood. *N Engl J Med* 1971; 284:401–404.

CHAPTER 2

HOW CHANGES IN BODY FUNCTIONS LEAD TO ESSENTIAL HYPERTENSION

WHAT basic abnormality in the body's blood pressure control mechanisms leads to high blood pressure? This question remains an enigma. Any number of specific causes of secondary hypertension have been discovered (see Chapter 4), but we still do not completely understand what abnormal changes lead to the origin (pathogenesis) of essential hypertension—the type that affects the vast majority of hypertensive patients. The body depends on a variety of complex mechanisms to maintain normal arterial pressures. Page,[1] one of the early leaders in U.S. study of hypertension, felt that these physiologic mechanisms are interrelated and interdependent. Normally they remain in equilibrium; that is, if any one mechanism malfunctions, the others adjust to compensate. If compensation is inadequate for any of a number of reasons, hypertension results.

Hypertension is probably not related to the same initial malfunction in all patients. The condition may occur because of various disorders of any of the controlling mechanisms, singly or in combination. The clinical manifestations of hypertension are very similar, however, regardless of its initial cause.

There is reason for optimism that the pieces of the puzzle may be coming together. Current research has clarified how malfunction of various control mechanisms might play a role in producing hypertension. Several likely hypotheses are discussed in this chapter to give you a background for understanding current medical thought as it relates to diagnosis and treatment. Detailed discussion of the research underlying these theories is beyond the scope and purpose of this book.

CHANGES IN BLOOD FLOW (HEMODYNAMICS)

The study of *hemodynamics* is concerned with the movement of blood through the body and the forces involved in that movement. From the previous chapter, you know that blood pressure, no matter what its level, reflects the relationship between cardiac output and total peripheral resistance. It is the product of these two factors. If either rises above normal, or if they both do, abnormally high levels of blood pressure result.

When essential hypertension initially develops, the hemodynamic profile is usually one of high cardiac output and normal total peripheral resistance. In addition, the resting heart rate increases, the volume of blood ejected into the aorta with each left ventricular contraction increases, and the left ventricle empties more rapidly. This combination of events strongly suggests that hyperactive heart function causes the elevated pressure.

As times progresses and the abnormally elevated blood pressure becomes fixed, the profile converts to one of normal cardiac output and an elevated total peripheral resistance. At this point, the elevation in pressure reflects constriction throughout the body's arteriolar bed. Arteriolar constriction is the major factor in causing a rise in peripheral resistance and an elevation of blood pressure. Finally, as the patient grows older, and particularly if the hypertension worsens, the hemodynamic findings change once more to lower than normal cardiac output and an even higher total peripheral resistance. A similar evolution of hemodynamic patterns has been demonstrated in spontaneously hypertensive rats and in other laboratory animals in whom high blood pressure was induced.

Although the scenario just described may apply to a large number of individuals who develop hypertension, there are exceptions. In some individuals, the high-cardiac-output hypertensive state may persist for years without further hemodynamic changes. Conversely, not all patients begin with a high cardiac output and normal peripheral resistance. Experimentally in both animals and humans, when cardiac output is prevented from increasing early in the development of hypertension, elevation of blood pressure continues to occur at the same rate and severity. In these instances, the major mechanism is that of arteriolar bed constriction.

The foregoing discussions explain, in broad terms, how the cardiovascular system maintains arterial pressure, and what hemodynamic changes occur as hypertension occurs. But what brings these changes about? What alters the normal physiologic mechanisms of control, and how? We do not yet know the full answer to these questions, but current knowledge suggests several possible routes with many common or overlapping steps. Some of the better understood concepts are summarized below.

REGULATION BY THE CENTRAL NERVOUS SYSTEM

Experiments have shown that stimulation of several areas within the brain raises or lowers blood pressure. Once the areas that raise blood pressure have been stimulated, the brain transmits impulses to the involuntary (autonomic) nervous system, which reaches throughout the body through a network of sympathetic nerve branches. The endings of these nerves nearly touch specialized receptor cells (*adrenoreceptors*) in the muscular layers of arteries, arterioles, and veins. There are similar adrenoreceptors within individual heart muscle fibers and in other types of cells in the body. At the *synapse,* where nerve ending and the receptor meet, the nerve ending releases the catecholamine, *norepi-*

nephrine (noradrenaline), which stimulates the adrenoreceptors so that the individual cells of the vessel walls respond by constricting or dilating. Which response occurs depends on which type of adrenoreceptor is stimulated.

TABLE 2.1
Cardiovascular Responses to Stimulation of Adrenoreceptors

Adrenoreceptor	Effector Organ	Response
Alpha	Arterial and venous tissue	Vasoconstriction
Beta-2	Arterial and venous tissue	Vasodilatation
Beta-1	Cardiac (heart) tissue	Increase in heart rate; increase in speed of blood ejection; increase in force of myocardial contraction

There are two types of adrenoreceptors, alpha and beta (Table 2.1). Alpha receptors are located primarily in the arteries, arterioles, and veins. Stimulation of alpha receptors leads to arteriolar and venous constriction (*vasoconstriction*). Stimulation of beta-2 adrenoreceptors leads to dilatation (*vasodilatation*). At usual norepinephrine levels, the two actions tend to cancel each other out; that is, the vessels are neither constricted nor dilated. Stimulation of the beta-1 adrenoreceptors, which are found mostly in the heart muscle (*myocardium*), leads to an increase in heart rate, increased speed of blood ejection from the heart, and an increase in the force of myocardial fiber contraction.

Evidence exists to indicate that sympathetic nerve activity increases early in the development of essential hypertension. Many patients show an increase in heart rate and increased myocardial contractility. Recently, more specific and sensitive tests have been developed for determining the levels of catecholamines (norepinephrine, epinephrine) in the blood.

Using these tests, researchers have found that the blood plasma of some hypertensives shows elevated levels of catecholamines—especially norepinephrine. These findings indicate enhanced sympathetic nerve activity.

Thus, stimulation of the central nervous system leads to increased norepinephrine levels; alpha-adrenoreceptor activity supersedes beta-2 adrenoreceptor activity so that arteriolar vasoconstriction occurs, increasing total peripheral resistance; and beta-1 adrenoreceptor activity in the heart muscle results in increased cardiac output. This sequence leads to elevated blood pressure levels (Fig. 2.1).

Goldstein,[2] reviewed 78 studies of plasma catecholamines in subjects with essential hypertension compared with normotensive controls (subjects with normal levels of blood pressure). He concluded that the preponderance of recent studies support the hypothesis that increased catecholamine concentrations occur in some patients with this disorder. Furthermore, he found that in young, consistently hypertensive patients elevated norepinephrine levels were present in virtually all studies. In addition, independent of age, if the hypertensive patient also had rapid resting pulse rates, elevated levels of epinephrine (adrenaline) were found consistently. The catecholamine epinephrine, which is secreted by the adrenal gland, also reaches the adrenoreceptors through the bloodstream. These observations strongly suggest that increased sympathetic neural activity plays a role in the development of hypertension in some patients and may contribute to sustaining this disorder in a smaller number.

Present thinking regarding nervous system activity as a major contributor in essential hypertension also has been summarized effectively by Dustan,[3] a leader in the study of hypertension. She writes:

> The evidence of a neural component in borderline and/or mild hypertension now seems firm. How this develops is unknown. Also we do not know the natural history of this increase, whether it is permanent or merely a phase that wanes when significant medial hypertrophy of the arterioles has occurred. We do know, however, that increased

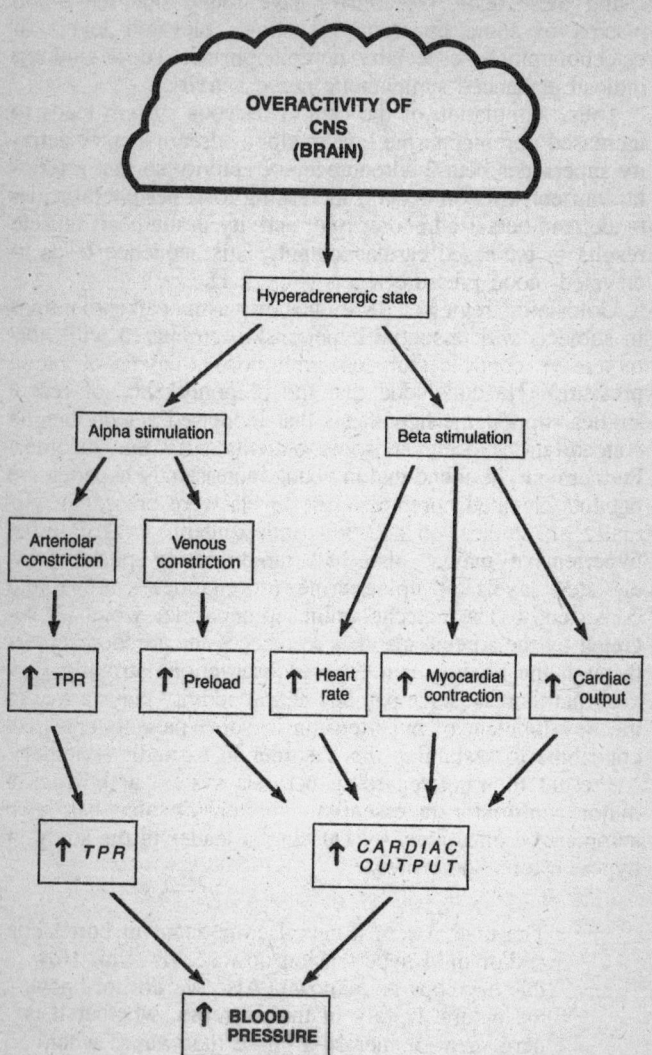

Figure 2.1 Neural mechanism of essential hypertension.

cardioenergic drive can be demonstrated in some patients with severe hypertension, so there is a possibility that some hypertension is neurogenic, both in its inception and its maintenance.

Some hypertensives are salt sensitive with significant blood pressure elevations occurring after salt loading. Other hypertensives, however, are salt-resistant. In normotensive individuals and in salt-resistant hypertensives, high salt intake does not cause much, if any, rise in blood pressure and is associated with a decrease in plasma levels of norepinephrine. Some salt-sensitive hypertensives, however, not only show distinct elevation in blood pressure with salt loading, but also show an increase in plasma norepinephrine levels. It may be that in genetically predisposed salt-sensitive individuals, high sodium intake is the first step, producing central nervous system stimulation and sympathetic nerve hyperactivity which in turn results in hypertension.

REGULATION BY THE PERIPHERAL NERVES AND THE KIDNEYS

The kidneys play an important part in maintaining blood pressure levels. Normally, their excretion of sodium and water into the urine is partially related to the level of arterial pressure. If blood pressure falls, the kidneys retain sodium and water until plasma volume expands again, cardiac output increases, and blood pressure rises to normal values. If arterial pressure rises above normal, the kidneys respond by increasing urinary output of sodium and water. As a result, plasma volume shrinks, cardiac output diminishes, and pressure drops to normal again.

Sometimes, however, this regulatory mechanism fails to compensate for increased pressures in the early stages of essential hypertension. That is, the kidneys retain sodium and water even at normal levels of arterial pressure. Plasma volume and cardiac output increase, and elevation of blood pressure follows. Eventually the kidneys become responsive again and excrete additional sodium and water from the level of a higher "setpoint." This underlying mechanism in which plasma volume and cardiac output are initially high, may result eventually in sustained high blood pressure with normal cardiac output and an increased total peripheral resistance—the usual hemodynamic findings in the majority of patients with established essential hypertension.[4,5] The process by which the initial failure of the kidneys to compensate leads to high blood pressure is related to internal regulatory mechanisms of the body tissues.

All body tissues are able to regulate local blood flow within themselves in accordance with their needs for oxygen and nutrients. If blood flow is inadequate to satisfy these needs, the arteriolar smooth muscles relax and the vessels dilate to permit more blood to flow through the tissue. If flow is excessive for tissue needs, the arterioles constrict. This process of local control of blood flow within tissues is called *autoregulation*.

In individuals whose kidneys do not adequately excrete sodium when pressures are normal, plasma volume, cardiac output, and flow of blood to the tissues increase. These signals initiate the autoregulatory process. The arteriolar bed constricts, peripheral resistance increases, and blood pressure becomes elevated. The kidneys respond to the rise in pressure by excreting sodium and water until the plasma volume and cardiac output are normal, but increased vascular resistance and hypertension persist (Table 2.2). In time, the arteriolar walls thicken and the local vascular structures narrow.

Keep in mind that increased neural activity may cause constriction of the efferent arterioles of the kidneys so that the kidneys' normal ability to excrete sodium and water under normal arterial pressure is impeded. This mechanism is described in the next section. In other words, the cascade of events just described—increased plasma volume, increased cardiac output, increased blood flow to the tissues, autoregulation, and the development of hypertension—would follow, having been initiated by a neural mechanism and not by a defect in the kidneys themselves.

TABLE 2.2
Autoregulation in Essential Hypertension

1. The kidneys retain sodium and water at normal arterial pressure levels:
    a. Extracellular fluid volume increases,
    b. Cardiac output increases, and
    c. Flow to peripheral tissues increases, producing autoregulation in peripheral tissues.

2. Autoregulation leads to:
    a. Increased total peripheral resistance and
    b. Increased blood pressure.

3. At higher blood pressure, the kidneys resume sodium and water excretion:
    a. Extracellular fluid volume returns to normal, and
    b. Cardiac output returns to normal.

4. But, increased TPR and elevated pressures persist.

5. If blood pressure drops, the whole cycle recurs.

Hypertension and the Structure of the Kidney

To understand several other mechanisms that might lead to essential hypertension, you need to know something about the *nephrons,* the functional units that make up the greater part of the kidney. A nephron consists of a blood vessel component, the *glomerulus* (plural, *glomeruli*), and a U-shaped tubular portion (the *renal tubule*). These structures are so small they cannot be seen without a microscope; each kidney, which is about the size of an adult fist, is composed of over a million nephrons.

The glomeruli might be pictured as the tiniest of tufts at the end of the renal arterial "tree." The renal arteries are the major branches off the aorta that supply arterial blood to the kidneys. As a renal artery approaches the body of the kidney, it divides into major branches. Within the substance of the kidney, these branches divide into still smaller arteries and these divide further into even smaller arteries, the interlobular arteries. These in turn give off *afferent* (incoming) *arterioles*. The afferent arterioles divide into a branching, spherical cluster or tuft of capillaries (the glomerulus) which then continue on and merge to form the *efferent* (outgoing) *arteriole*. The efferent arteriole proceeds and gives rise to another network of capillaries which surround the tubular part of the nephron. They then proceed to form the venous return from the kidneys; that is, the means by which the now cleansed and filtered blood returns to the circulation.

The second major component of the nephron is the *renal tubule*. It has a globular closed upper end, into which the glomerulus indents, almost surrounding itself. The tubule then continues as a U-shaped structure with a proximal descending portion, a loop, and then a distal ascending portion that eventually becomes a straight collecting tubule. Collecting tubules converge and finally empty into the ureter of the kidney and thereby into the urinary bladder, where urine is stored until it is excreted.

The single-layer capillaries of the glomerulus are well suited for filtration, which is driven by the hydrostatic pressure within them. Similarly, the thin-walled globular end of the tubule which surrounds the glomerulus is porous. The glomerulus, then, serves as an ultrafilter through which water, electrolytes such as sodium, and small organic molecules such as glucose, urea, and some metabolic waste products are passed into the tubule. Plasma protein and other larger elements in the blood do not normally pass through. The tubule is not simply a passive conduit. As the filtrate passes along the U-shaped structure, electrolytes, glucose, and some other essential products are conserved. They are reabsorbed through the tubular wall and back into the bloodstream through the surrounding capillary network. In addition, some additional substances are secreted into the tubule from this surrounding vascular bed as the filtrate fluid column continues on its path to the collecting system and eventually toward the urinary bladder.

The Concept of Natriuretic Hormone

One recently proposed mechanism for development of hypertension concerns the function of the renal tubules. Autoregulation is not involved in this mechanism.[6]

The enzyme sodium, potassium adenosine triphosphatase (Na^+, K^+ ATPase) is responsible for the active transport of sodium out from within cells. Excessive sodium intake in nonhypertensive humans inhibits the activity of this enzyme. A Na^+, K^+ ATPase inhibitor has been identified in human plasma, and its circulating concentration is related to sodium intake.[7] In the renal tubule, this inhibitor (*natriuretic hormone*) reduces the ability of the tubular cells to take up filtered sodium in the tubule's lumen and pass it through into the bloodstream via its adjacent capillaries. In other words, the hormone reduces the usual sodium resorption so that more sodium is excreted into the urine to make up for the excessive intake. This response, then, is a protective mechanism that helps prevent expansion of plasma volume, increased cardiac output, and a rise in blood pressure.

Researchers propose that some patients with essential hypertension have a renal defect that inhibits the expected excretion of sodium at normal blood pressure levels. As more sodium is retained, more water is retained; consequently, extracellular volume expands and blood pressure rises somewhat. Under these circumstances, increased production of natriuretic hormone is stimulated, and it may induce some increase in sodium excretion. Since these patients chronically retain sodium, circulating levels of natriuretic hormone remain continually high.

This greater level of natriuretic hormone not only affects the management of sodium by the renal tubular cells but also interferes with sodium transport out of other cells in the body. For example, some patients with essential hypertension have been shown to have abnormally elevated intracellular concentrations of sodium in both red and white blood cells. In one study, white blood cells from subjects with normal blood pressure were incubated in plasma from hypertensive patients. The normal cells responded by decreasing their natriuretic hormone activity, which dropped to about the same level as that in the hypertensive patients' white cells.

In patients with hypertension related to increased circulating natriuretic hormone, increased levels of intracellular calcium play a role in elevating blood pressure. The extrusion of sodium from within the smooth muscle fibers of the arterioles may be diminished, leading, through physiological mechanisms, to an increase in their intracellular sodium concentrations. Under such circumstances, the intracellular concentration of calcium will rise also. The latter leads to increased smooth muscle contractility, increased vascular muscle tone, arteriolar constriction, elevation of total pe-

---

TABLE 2.3
Inhibition of Cellular Sodium (Salt) Transport in Essential Hypertension

---

1. The kidneys retain sodium and water even though arterial pressure levels are normal:
   a. Extracellular fluid volume increases.
   b. The higher volume stimulates increased production of natriuretic hormone.

2. Nutriuretic hormone inhibits Na^+, K^+ ATPase activity so that:
   a. Less sodium is reabsorbed through the renal tubules,
   b. More sodium is excreted through the kidneys, and
   c. More sodium is concentrated in the smooth muscle cells of the arterioles.

3. Higher smooth-muscle intracellular sodium leads to higher intracellular calcium concentrations.

4. Increased intracellular calcium leads to:
   a. Increased contractility of the blood vessels,
   b. Increased muscle tone of the blood vessels,
   c. Constriction of the arterioles (arteriolar vasoconstriction),
   d. Increased total peripheral resistance, and thereby to
   e. Elevated blood pressure.

ripheral resistance, and increased blood pressure.[8] Thus, through inhibition of the cellular sodium transport by the natriuretic hormone, the initial result of a renal defect in sodium excretion leads to increased peripheral resistance and hypertension (Table 2.3) without the need to consider autoregulation.

It may be that each of the two concepts (autoregulation or natriuretic hormone) is operative in different groups of patients with essential hypertension. It is possible, also, that the two concepts are combined in still other patients.

The RAA Axis

Of the mechanisms by which the body regulates its various functions, the renin-angiotensin-aldosterone axis is one of the most intricate and complex. This so-called RAA axis regulates the balance of the electrolytes sodium *and* potassium as well as fluid balance. It also regulates pressor activity to increase blood pressure as needed. All these factors are major components of blood pressure stability in normotensives (persons with normal blood pressure). The same factors may also be significant contributors to essential hypertension. Because the RAA axis is intricately interrelated with the other control systems, it is difficult to determine whether it is a major cause of high blood pressure or an effect of other more basic causative mechanisms.

Renin is an enzyme that is secreted into the blood primarily by the juxtoglomerular cells found in the afferent arterioles of the renal glomeruli. A common cause for its release is lowered perfusion pressure within these arterioles. Pressure receptors in the arterioles recognize a diminished stretch of the walls. Through a beta-adrenoreceptor–mediated system, they stimulate release of the renin by the juxtoglomerular cells. Another mechanism that leads to increased release of renin is through a group of specialized cells known as the *macula densa*, which detects and reacts to decreases in plasma sodium concentration. Potassium deprivation also results in plasma renin release, as does stimulation of the central nervous system.

Renin acts on a substance in the blood called *angio-*

tensinogen, releasing the hormone *angiotensin I*. This hormone is relatively inactive physiologically, but as it passes through the circulation channels in the lungs, a converting enzyme acts upon it and produces *angiotensin II*. Angiotensin II is the key effector hormone of the RAA axis. It is a powerful pressor agent, and its immediate effect is to contract arteriolar smooth muscle, constrict the arterioles, and increase total peripheral resistance, with a resultant elevation in blood pressure. A second major effect is its stimulation of the outer portion of the adrenal gland (the adrenal cortex), triggering the release of the hormone *aldosterone*. The latter brings about increased sodium reabsorption by its effect on the distal tubules of the renal nephrons.

The resultant sodium retention produces an early effect and a delayed one. First, it increases the sensitivity of the arteriolar smooth muscles to the pressor effect of angiotensin II. As a consequence, the initial vasoconstrictive effects are strengthened further. Second, the aldosterone-produced sodium retention leads to expansion of plasma volume. Vaso-

---

TABLE 2.4
The Renin-Angiotensin-Aldosterone (RAA) Axis

1. Decreased perfusion pressure in afferent arterioles to glomeruli cause release of renin.

2. Renin + angiotensinogen = angiotensin I

3. Angiotensin I + converting enzyme = angiotensin II

4. Angiotensin II
   a. Is a powerful pressor agent, promoting arteriolar vasoconstriction.
   b. Increases aldosterone production, promoting plasma volume expansion.

5. Pressor effect (primarily) + expanded volume = blood pressure evaluation.

6. Increased blood pressure normalizes perfusion pressure of afferent arterioles of the kidney.

7. RAA axis becomes inactive.

constriction leading to increased peripheral resistance plus plasma volume expansion leads to increased blood pressure levels. Now the perfusion pressure in the afferent glomerular arterioles normalizes and the RAA axis becomes inactive (Table 2.4). It should be noted that angiotensin II also causes the release of catecholamines from the inner portion of the adrenal gland (the adrenal medulla), and also it acts directly in the central nervous system to increase sympathetic activity (see earlier discussion).

Patients with essential hypertension may be classified according to their levels of plasma renin activity. Such a classification consists of three major subgroups.

High-renin hypertension: approximately 15 percent
Low-renin hypertension: approximately 30 percent
Mid-renin hypertension: approximately 55 percent

High-Renin Essential Hypertension. Plasma renin activity tends to be higher in younger patients and is likely to decrease with advancing age. There is a correlation as well between increased sympathetic activity (increased catecholamines) and high plasma renin activity. In patients with high renin levels, essential hypertension is believed to be related to vasoconstriction caused by the overwhelming pressor effect of angiotensin II. Propranolol (Inderal), a drug that blocks the norepinephrine effect on beta-adrenergic receptors, inhibits the release of renin by the kidney. When administered to patients with essential hypertension, it induces a significant drop in blood pressure in those with the high-renin form, intermediate drops in those with the mid-renin form, and very little or no response in the individuals with the low-renin form. The amount of blood pressure lowering is related directly to the degree to which the renin level is reduced by propranolol. Since decreasing renin release leads to less angiotensin II and a diminution of pressor effect, these observations tend to support the belief that high-renin essential hypertension is predominantly a vasoconstrictive type. However, not all patients with this form of high blood pressure respond to propranolol therapy, nor is increased peripheral resistance the major finding in all such patients.

Low-Renin Essential Hypertension. Any number of studies have demonstrated that up to 30 percent of patients suffering essential hypertension have low plasma renin activity. A plausible explanation would be that a primary expansion of plasma volume (for example, in salt-sensitive hypertensives) leads to high blood pressure, increased perfusion pressure in the afferent glomerular arterioles, and suppressed renin release. These patients generally do have higher fluid volumes than hypertensives with mid-renin activity. Most low-renin essential hypertensives do not respond well to beta-adrenergic receptors. On the other hand, up to two-thirds of them benefit from diuretic drugs. Such therapy increases sodium excretion and volume depletion. Parenthetically, a similar beneficial response to diuretic therapy has been noted in approximately one-third of patients with mid-renin activity. It is justifiable to suspect that not all cases of low-renin essential hypertension reflect the same disease mechanism. Not all patients respond to diuretic therapy; nor do all have fluid and plasma volume expansion. Plasma renin activity decreases with advancing age in individuals with normal blood pressure levels as well as in those who have hypertension. Low-renin essential hypertension is more common in blacks at all ages.

It is possible that future research will identify a specific subgroup of hypertensive patients in whom plasma renin activity is a definite cause of what is now thought to be "essential" hypertension. But in a large portion, renin levels may well be indications of stages in the natural evolution of essential hypertension responding to metabolic and hemodynamic changes brought on by some of the mechanisms discussed earlier.

Vasodepressor Mechanisms of the Kidney. Fifty years ago, Grollman and Rule[9] noted that surgical removal of both kidneys in laboratory animals resulted in blood pressure elevation. This finding led to the theory that the kidneys might be a source of blood pressure-lowering elements (*vasodepressor elements*) that played a role in maintaining blood pressue at normal levels. Earlier, researchers had reported that certain compounds derived from fatty acids and found in male seminal fluid exerted a significant influence on smooth muscle contractility and blood pressure levels. Because these compounds were initially thought to originate in the prostate gland, they were called *prostaglandins*. Subsequently, various prostaglandins have been found to originate in almost every organ of the body.

Prostaglandin E_2 (PEG_2) and prostaglandin A (PGA) dilate the arterioles, lowering peripheral resistance and thereby blood pressures. Both are found in the kidney. PGE_2 is inactivated as the blood carrying it passes through the lungs (the pulmonary circulation) so that its actions probably are significant in the arterioles within the kidney. PGA, however, passes the pulmonary circulation barrier successfully. When it is administered intravenously, it lowers blood pressure in patients with essential hypertension. Under these circumstances, one must consider the possibility of prostaglandin deficiency, no matter what the cause, as a possible mechanism producing essential hypertension in some patients.

Urinary *kallikrein* is an enzyme synthesized by the kidney. It reacts with bradykininogen which is carried in the bloodstream to form *bradykinin*, an arteriolar vasodilator. The effect of bradykinin in dilating the arterioles and thereby lowering blood pressure may be direct, or it may be at least partially related to the kinin's ability to stimulate synthesis of prostaglandins. In addition, angiotension and aldosterone can stimulate release of renal kallikrein, thus suggesting a relationship with the RAA axis. Blood pressure has been lowered in some patients with mild to moderate essential hypertension by oral administration of kallikrein. These and other findings suggest that abnormalities of the renal killikrein–kinin system might play a role in the development of essential hypertension in some patients.

To sum up, then, the changes in physiologic mechanisms that lead to the development of essential hypertension continue to puzzle us. We are beginning, however, to recognize factors that are associated with this disorder. Progress has been made in understanding more clearly the role of various processes that are involved in the maintenance of normal blood pressure levels and which might contribute, if faulty, to the development of hypertension. Many of these mechanisms share parts of common ground and may even overlap. A single common thread through onset and subsequent development of this disorder continues to elude us. This thread may not exist at all. At times, there appears to be complete entanglement of all these factors in some patients, but in differing patterns.

It is not unreasonable to expect that additional knowledge which we are bound to gain will permit us to dissect out and identify a number of subgroups among those now labeled as having "essential" hypertension. Fortunately, our current understanding is sufficient to provide physicians with a pathway through which we might approach the diagnosis and treatment of our patients with some degree of logic and rationale. The following chapters attempt to provide a reasonable guide for physician and patient as they approach treatment of hypertension from the perspective of current knowledge.

REFERENCES: CHAPTER 2

1. Page IH: Pathogenesis of arterial hypertension. *JAMA* 1949; 140:451–458.

2. Goldstein DS: Plasma catecholamines and essential hypertension. An analytic review. *Hypertension* 1983; 5:86–99.

3. Dustan HP: Physiologic regulation of arterial pressure. An analytical review. *Hypertension* 1982; 4(suppl 3):62–67.

4. Guyton AC, Coleman TG, Cowley AW Jr, et al.: Arterial pressure regulation. Overriding dominance of the kidney in long-term regulation and in hypertension. *Am J Med* 1972; 52:584–594.

5. Guyton AC: The relationship of cardiac output and arterial pressure control. *Circulation* 1981; 64:1079–1088.

6. MacGregor C, deWardener H: Is a circulating sodium transport inhibitor involved in the pathogenesis of essential hypertension?, in Fregly MJ, Kare MR (eds): *The Role of Salt in Cardiovascular Hypertension.* New York, Academic Press, 1982, pp 331–343.

7. deWardener HE, MacGregor GA, Clarkson EM, et al.: Effect of sodium intake on ability of human plasma to inhibit Na^+-K^+ adenosine triphosphatase in vitro. *Lancet* 1981; 1:411–412.

8. Blaustein NP: Sodium ions, calcium ions, blood pressure regulation and hypertension: a reassessment and a hypothesis. *Am J Physiol* 1977; 232(3):C165–C173.

9. Grollman A, Rule C: Experimentally induced hypertension in parabiotic rats. *Am J Physiol* 1943; 138:587–592.

CHAPTER 3

HOW ESSENTIAL HYPERTENSION IS DIAGNOSED

HIGH blood pressure is often discovered during routine physical examination (preemployment, insurance, or health screening programs) or when a patient consults a physician for some unrelated problem. Consequently, the initial evaluation usually occurs in the doctor's office. Remember that a single reading of elevated blood pressure does not constitute a diagnosis of hypertension. An additional two or more measurements should be obtained at separate visits on different days. If the blood pressure levels persist at 140/90 mm Hg or more, an initial diagnostic workup is warranted.

Some physicians still feel that they must definitely exclude every conceivable correctable cause by testing before they can safely offer a diagnosis of essential hypertension. Yet a complete battery of diagnostic studies to rule out all causes of secondary hypertension is time consuming and costly. It may require a hospital stay. Some tests carry some risk to the patient. Several studies indicate clearly that the vast majority of patients with persistently elevated blood pressure do not have an identifiable cause but suffer essential hypertension instead (Table 3.1). These findings have

TABLE 3.1
Causative Factors Found in Studies of Patients with Hypertension

Diagnosis	Percent of Patients Affected					
	Gifford[1]	Kennedy et al.[2]	Iimura[3]	Boch & Hilden[4]	Berglund et al.[5]	Ferguson[6]
Pheochromocytoma	0.2	0	0.2	0.2	0	0
Cushing's syndrome	0.2	0	0	0	0	0
Hyperaldosteronism	0.5	0.3	0.9	0.4	0.1	0.8
Coarctation of the aorta	1.0	0	0	0	0.1	0
Renovascular stenosis	4.0	6.1	0	5.0	0.6	2.8
Chronic renal disease	5.0	17.2	5.8	12.6	3.6	2.4
Oral contraceptive use	—	—	—	—	—	4.4
Essential hypertension	89.0	72.6	87.3	79.3	94.0	89.4

led to changes in the initial evaluation process. A careful history, a physical examination, and a few selected laboratory procedures usually suffice. More complex and specific diagnostic procedures might be added if (1) the intial evaluation uncovers clues suggestive of underlying causes, or (2) treatment prescribed for essential hypertension does not alleviate the patient's problem.

CLUES FOUND IN THE PATIENT'S HISTORY

If the physician finds that the patient's blood pressure is elevated on several occasions, questions asked in taking the patient's history will emphasize certain areas discussed below. Certain symptoms, previous illnesses or chronic

TABLE 3.2
Clues from the Patient's History Suggesting Secondary Hypertension

Potentially Correctible Condition	Clue
Estrogen contained in pills	Oral contraceptive use
Renovascular hypertension	Fixed hypertension appearing before age 25 or after age 50; rapidly progressive course; severe and of recent onset
Pheochromocytoma	Episodic symptoms; paroxysmal headaches, palpitations, sweating; dizziness or fainting when standing up; others in family have disorder
Primary aldosteronism	Muscle weakness, intermittent paralysis
Cushing's syndrome	Weight gain centered in trunk, "moon face," buffalo humps, plethora, menstrual irregularities, recurrence of acne, hypertension, violet scars and stretch marks, muscle weakness

conditions, or the use of some medications may suggest secondary hypertension (Table 3.2). The history or the examination may indicate the involvement of target organs in long-standing or more advanced hypertension. In addition, the physician obtains an overall view of the patient's state of health.

Essential hypertension tends to occur in families, so the physician will ask about other family members. Although it may appear at any age, onset of fixed elevated blood pressure is in the thirties. It is insidious and painless. Some patients report having a pounding pain in the back of the head and the nape of the neck in the morning upon arising. The pain wears off as the day progresses. This condition is not common, however, and it is particularly unusual in mild and moderate hypertension. Several studies have shown the prevalence of headaches to be the same in both normotensives as in hypertensives. This finding also applied to other symptoms commonly attributed to high blood pressure: nose-bleeds, ringing in the ears (*tennitus*), dizziness, and fainting.

Target Organ Involvement

Decreased tolerance for exercise, shortness of breath (dyspnea) with exertion, and episodes of sudden shortness of breath during the night that awaken the patient from sleep suggest failure of the left ventricle of the heart. Discomfort just beneath the breastbone brought on by exercise and relieved by rest is consistent with coronary artery disease. Memory defects, unsteady gait, and intermittent deficiency of muscle power, sensation, coordination, or vision may indicate atherosclerotic obstructive disease of the arteries supplying blood to the brain.

Birth Control Pills

A small percentage of women taking estrogen-containing oral contraceptives develop substantial blood pressure elevation which usually returns to normal levels after the use of the pill is discontinued. Unless some other condition suggests urgency or blood pressure is dangerously high, the physician may postpone further tests or treatment for three to six months after discontinuing the drug. A return to normal blood pressure may lag for this length of time once the inciting agent has been discontinued.

Ischemic Renovascular Disease

Although secondary causes for blood pressure elevation are the exception rather than the rule, renal (kidney) disorders are the most commonly encountered. Hypertension due to lesions obstructing blood flow through the renal artery (ischemic renovascular disease) can be corrected by surgery. If fixed hypertension appears before age 25 or after age 50, if it is of short duration and severe, or it is rapidly progressive, the physician will suspect and test for a renovascular cause. In the younger group, especially in women, fibromuscular dysplasia (Chapter 4) of the renal artery is likely. In the older group, mainly in men, atherosclerotic occlusive disease of the renal artery is the usual cause. Not all patients present the classic symptoms, however. In a study of a large number of cases of proved renovascular hypertension, it was found that blood pressure ranged from mild to severe levels of elevation and that it occurred at any age in both sexes. A positive history certainly suggests renovascular hypertension, but in some instances there may be nothing in the history to differentiate the patient's disorder from essential hypertension.

Pheochromocytoma

Pheochromocytoma is a rarely occurring tumor of chromaffin cells (synthesizers of the catecholamines norepinephrine and epinephrine). It arises most frequently from the inner portion of the adrenal gland (the adrenal medulla). Excessive secretion of these catecholamines produces various clinical features. Elevated blood pressures may be episodic if secretion is intermittent, but sustained hypertension with superimposed fluctuations to even higher levels is found in over 50 percent of cases. In almost every instance, paroxysmal headaches, sweating, racing of the heart, and heart palpitations occur singly or in combinations. About two-thirds of patients with this disorder suffer lightheadedness or dizziness, and even fainting, when they first stand up from a sitting or lying position.

Hyperaldosteronism

Primary hyperaldosteronism is another rare cause of secondary hypertension. It results from hyperactivity of the adrenal cortex (the outer portion of the adrenal gland) or from a tumor of this structure. In this situation, excessive amounts of aldosterone are produced completely unrelated to the RAA axis (Chapter 2). The major symptoms that may appear are related to potassium deficiency: Potassium wasting (excessive excretion) by the kidneys is one of the physiologic responses produced by excessive aldosterone in the bloodstream. There may be frequent urination of large quantities, muscle cramps, muscle weakness, and/or intermittent paralysis of the larger muscle groups around the origin of the arms and legs from the body (proximal muscles of the limbs). It is possible, though, that none of these problems may be present in individuals suffering this disorder.

Cushing's Syndrome

In Cushing's syndrome there is either a tumor or hyperactivity of the adrenal cortex, as in hyperaldosteronism but affecting different cells. No specific historical facts may be elicited, though some patients may report weight gain; frequent urination of large quantities; swelling of hands, ankles, and face; menstrual irregularities; recurrence of acne; or muscular weakness.

CLUES FOUND IN THE PHYSICAL EXAMINATION

The physician will conduct the physical examination in the usual manner but will focus on some specific areas described below.

Funduscopic Examination

Examining the fundus (inner lining) of the eye yields valuable information about the status of the arteries (Table 3.3). A scope with a light source—an opthalmoscope—permits the physician to see this structure as well as the retina (which contains the perceptive structures of the eye—the rods and cones, the nerve fibers), the end of the optic nerve which is an extension of the brain itself, and the small arterioles and veins of the retina. In fixed essential hypertension the major hemodynamic change is increased total peripheral resistance, which reflects the widespread constriction of the arteriolar bed. Thus, the retinal arterioles are narrowed in patients with this condition.

The usual normal ratio of the diameter of the retinal arterioles to the diameter of the retinal veins is 3:4. In essential hypertension, it is frequently 1:2. As arteriosclerosis develops in the arterioles, a result of longstanding high blood pressure, an indentation or nicking of the retinal veins where the arterioles cross them appears (AV nicking). If the arterioles have been damaged by vasculitis (inflammation), due to very high pressures, retinal hemorrhages and exudation (seeping) of plasma are visible. Finally, if high blood pressure within the brain causes it to swell (cerebral edema), the process is reflected by the end of the optic nerve, which also swells and bulges forward in the eye globe (*papilledema*).

Additional observations that can be made include color changes of arterioles as arteriosclerosis progresses. Ordinarily, the veins have a deep red color and the arterioles are more pinkish. The latter tend to reflect some of the light of

TABLE 3.3
Funduscopic Changes in Hypertension

	Early Hypertension	Long-standing Hypertension	Accelerated Hypertension*	Malignant Hypertension*
A-V ratio	1:2	1:2	1:3	1:3
A-V nicking	0	+	+ +	+ +
Hemorrhages	0	0	+ +	+ +
Exudates (seepage of plasma)	0	0	0	+
Papilledema (swelling of the optic nerve)	0	0	0	+

*See Chapter 13.

the opthalmoscope back, and there is a narrow central glistening along the course of the normal arterioles. As arteriosclerosis progresses, the narrow central light reflex tends to widen and may occupy most of the vessel, giving the appearance of copper wiring. In far advanced sclerosis, the arterioles look like a silver wire. The more advanced the funduscopic changes in a patient with hypertension, the worse the prognosis.

Measurement of Blood Pressure

At the initial evaluation, blood pressure should be checked with the patient lying down (supine), sitting, and standing. In normal individuals and in most patients with untreated essential hypertension, the systolic pressure drops slightly and the diastolic pressure rises slightly after quiet standing for three minutes. If pressure drops 10 mm Hg or more when the patient assumes the upright posture, the physician must consider the possibility of either pheochromocytoma or primary hyperaldosteronism unless the patient is taking antihypertensive medication. Such a drop in pressure upon standing (*orthostatic hypotension*) may also occur in other disorders unrelated to hypertension, such as pooling of blood in the lower body because of severe varicose veins, depletion of plasma volume no matter what the cause, or diabetic neuropathy. In addition, blood pressure should be measured in both arms, at least at the initial evaluation. Normally, there may be 10 to 15 mm Hg difference between the arms, but a difference of more than 20 mm Hg suggests aortic arch disorders such as occlusive atherosclerotic disease where the major artery branches off to an arm from the aorta, a congenital constriction of the aorta (coarctation of the aorta) between the major artery takeoffs for the right and left arms, or a dissecting aneurysm of the aorta.

Coarctation of the aorta usually occurs after the takeoff of the artery supplying the left arm. In sequence, the arteries in the aortic arch supply the right arm, right brain, left brain, and left arm. Therefore, with the classic form of this aortic constriction, blood pressure is very high in both arms and the brain and very low in the lower part of the body. The diagnosis of this congenital disorder relies largely on the physical examination. In children, blood pressure is easily measured in the arms and in the legs. In adults, the physician may detect diminished strength of pulses of the femoral arteries, which supply the legs, compared to the carotid arteries in the neck, which supply the brain. In older adults with hypertension, femoral pulses weaker than those of the carotid arteries are more frequently due to atherosclerotic occlusive disease of the lower aorta or its major branches to the lower extremities. Nevertheless, the physician will order diagnostic steps to clarify the situation. (Aortography—injection of radiopaque contrast material into the aorta followed immediately by x-ray studies—is the usual procedure.)

Other Clues for Secondary Hypertension

The physical examination may provide additional clues leading to suspicion of other secondary causes (Table 3.4).

TABLE 3.4
Clues from the Physical Examination Suggesting Secondary Hypertension

Potentially Correctible Condition	Physical Findings
Coarctation of the aorta	Diminished femoral pulses compared to carotids
Renovascular hypertension	Abdominal bruits
Pheochromocytoma	Lean body habitus, nervousness, tremor, rapid heart rate, sweating, orthostatic hypotension
Cushing's syndrome	Moon face, weight gain centered in trunk, buffalo hump, plethora, muscle weakness, acne, hirsutism, violet scars and stretch marks
Primary aldosteronism	Muscle weakness, edema, orthostatic hypotension

Renovascular Hypertension. Considerable emphasis must be placed on auscultation (listening through the stethoscope) over the abdomen. The most significant finding in patients with renovascular hypertension is a sound reminiscent of water flowing under pressure through a tightened nozzle of a garden hose (a *bruit*), heard best over the *epigastrium*—the "pit of the stomach" below the breastbone. The bruit is produced by the turbulent flow of blood through the partially obstructed renal artery. This bruit or murmur is heard in 50 to 60 percent of patients with proved renovascular hypertension, more commonly in those with fibromuscular dysplasia (which will be described later) of the renal artery. The presence of factitious bruits which are of no clinical significance increases in frequency in individuals over 50 years of age, both normotensives and those with hypertension. Many bruits are due to turbulence and eddies of blood flow about atherosclerotic deposits within the abdominal aorta. Although an abdominal bruit synchronous with cardiac contraction (systolic bruit) is not as diagnostic in this age group, patients should be evaluated further for the possibility of renovascular stenosis if it is heard. If the bruit is both systolic and diastolic (during relaxation of the left ventricle) in timing, renal artery disease is very likely no matter what the age.

Pheochromocytoma. As with the clues obtained from the history, pheochromocytoma presents variable physical findings. These patients tend to be tremulous, and to have a rapid resting heart rate. They usually have lean bodies because the tumor greatly speeds their metabolism. Blood pressures may alternate from normal to paroxysms of drastic elevation, or they may be above normal continuously with exaggerated fluctuations upward. Orthostatic hypotension can be demonstrated frequently. About 10 percent of pheochromocytomas occur in a familial distribution. The disorder may be associated with tumors of the nerves (neurofibromatosis) which frequently include nerves of the lips and/or the tongue. Medullary carcinoma (cancer) of the thyroid gland may also accompany pheochromocytoma. Remember that this condition is rare, accounting for only 0.2 percent of cases of hypertension.

Cushing's Syndrome. Patients with Cushing's syndrome usually can be identified by their appearance. The body distribution of fat, particularly obvious on the face (moon face) and trunk but sparing of the limbs, is a very suggestive sign. Frequently, there are associated fat pads above the collar bones and a "buffalo hump" in the upper back. This central obesity plus a florid complexion (plethora), easy bruisability, and muscular weakness (inability to rise from a deep knee bend) are the best distinguishing features. Other commonly accompanying findings such as acne, hirsutism (hairiness), purplish scars and stretch marks, and swelling of ankles and hands are also suggestive but less discriminatory, since many individuals without Cushing's syndrome also have them.

CLUES FOUND IN LABORATORY STUDIES

As a rule, in the initial evaluation of a patient with hypertension, only simple and relatively inexpensive tests are needed. The minimal laboratory tests (Table 3.5) suggested by the Joint National Committee on Detection, Evaluation, and Treatment of High Blood Pressure[7] are quite sufficient. This author's approach, however, is somewhat more inclusive for the reasons given below. Needless to say, if the history and/or physical examination suggests the presence of anything beyond essential hypertension, additional specific procedures based on the physician's judgment are in order (Chapter 4).

A complete blood count (CBC) is part of any comprehensive medical evaluation. For the patient with hypertension, the CBC also provides a baseline for subsequent monitoring for bone marrow suppression or red blood cell destruction (*hemolysis*). These are uncommon but possible untoward effects of some of the antihypertensive drugs that might be utilized.

TABLE 3.5
Minimal Laboratory Tests in Initial Evaluation of the Patient with Hypertension*

Procedure	To Include
Urinalysis	Protein (albumin)
	Blood
	Glucose
Blood chemistry	Creatinine
	Potassium
	Glucose
	Cholesterol
	Uric acid
Electrocardiogram (EKG)	
Complete blood count (CBC)	Only if indicated by other findings

*As suggested by the Joint National Committee on Detection, Evaluation, and Treatment of High Blood Pressure.[7]

Urinalysis also is an integral facet of a medical examination. White blood cells (leukocytes), red blood cells (erythrocytes), casts, and protein (albumin) in the urine all suggest that kidney tissue disease may be the cause of the hypertension. In addition, protein in the urine is a late finding in the natural course of uncontrolled essential hypertension. It heralds the development of nephrosclerosis (sclerosis and obstruction of the renal arterioles due to high blood pressure).

Serum creatinine is an indicator of kidney excretory function and aids in the assessment of renal damage that may have occurred. Abnormal kidney function has both diagnostic and therapeutic implications.

Since many of the patients with hypertension will receive diuretics (agents that cause increased sodium and water excretion through the kidneys) as part of their therapeutic regimens, determination of serum electrolytes (sodium, potassium, carbonate, chloride) is a reasonable procedure. The findings serve as a baseline for serial comparison. They will be useful during therapy in helping detect trends toward electrolyte derangements, particularly hypokalemia (excessive loss of potassium). Furthermore, determining the serum potassium level helps exclude the possibility of primary hyperaldosteronism as a cause for the elevated blood pressure. Hyperaldosteronism involves potassium wasting by the kidney, and a finding of hypokalemia in a patient who is not taking diuretic drugs may indicate this disorder. Primary aldosteronism is most unlikely if serum potassium is within the normal range, (3.5 mEq/l to 5.0 mEq/l). Potassium wasting is indicated when the serum potassium is 3.0 mEq/l and the total 24-hour urine excretion of potassium is greater than 50 mEq/l.

Serum glucose determinations are useful for several reasons. High serum glucose levels (*hyperglycemia*) are a manifestation of diabetes. Complications of diabetes, such as kidney damage, and retinal abnormalities leading to blindness progress much more rapidly, if hypertension is present. Vigorous control of both the diabetes and the hypertension is in order.

In addition, abnormally elevated serum glucose levels are found frequently in patients with pheochromocytoma, Cushing's syndrome, and primary aldosteronism. If an elevated serum glucose level is found, the physician will give further consideration for these three disorders, which may be underlying the high blood pressure. Most often, however, hyperglycemia in a hypertensive patient will be due to diabetes and essential hypertension occurring in the same individual. Finally, some degree of hyperglycemia may result as a side effect of some of the antihypertensive drugs that may be used. A baseline determination before initiating such therapy is useful for monitoring for this eventuality.

A high level of serum cholesterol (*hypercholesterolemia*) is a major risk factor for the same degenerative and obstructive atherosclerotic changes as those produced by hypertension. The presence of both of these factors in one individual multiplies the risk of stroke and coronary heart disease. The physician must design a therapeutic program to manage both hypertension and hypercholesterolemia. It should be noted that use of some antihypertensive drugs may raise levels of low density lipoprotein (LDL) cholesterol, which is thought to be the culprit in atherosclerosis, while decreasing levels of high density lipoprotein (HDL) cholesterol, which may help prevent atherosclerosis. This area will be discussed more thoroughly in later chapters.

Serum uric acid levels rise with long-term diuretic therapy—a common form of treatment for essential hypertension. Elevated uric acid levels not only precipitate gout in those patients who are predisposed, but also may be related to an increased incidence of coronary heart disease.

The electrocardiogram (EKG) is valuable in the initial evaluation because it helps exclude the possibility of previously unrecognized myocardial infarction (heart attack). An unrecognized myocardial infarction is not an uncommon occurrence, particularly in older hypertensives. Electrocardiographic evidence of left ventricular hypertrophy indicates a poorer outlook, but successful therapy may improve it.

DEBATABLE PROCEDURES FOR THE INITIAL EVALUATION

Patients, physicians, and providers of insurance have become increasingly sensitive to rising health care costs. This awareness has led to more careful consideration of cost:benefit ratios for all medical procedures. In the case of diagnostic procedures, predictive value must be carefully weighed against cost, the risks inherent in the procedure, and the risk to the patient if a condition is not quickly diagnosed. There are some debatable procedures regarding the initial evaluation of a patient with high blood pressure. Two of the more controversial procedures are discussed below.

Intravenous Pyelogram (IVP)

Although correctable causes for secondary hypertension account for less than 6 percent of patients with hypertension, the most common of them (not including estrogen-containing oral contraceptives used by women) is renovascular ischemic disease (obstruction to flow of blood in the renal artery). Some physicians consider the rapid infusion IVP (excretory urogram) to be a relatively innocuous screening procedure for renovascular hypertension. A large dose of radiopaque contrast material, which will be excreted rapidly through the kidney, is given intravenously as fast as possible and then x-ray films are taken over the abdomen. If there is delay in filling or emptying of one of the kidneys, if one kidney is smaller than the other, or if there is hyperconcentration of the contrast material on one side, ischemic renal vascular disease is likely. However, false-positive and false-negative results vary widely. In a large cooperative study,[8] sensitivity of this test was 78 percent and specificity 89 percent. In other words, 22 percent of patients with true renovascular hypertension had normal IVP studies, and 11 percent of hypertensives with normal renal arteries had abnormal IVPs.

To a physician who really suspected renovascular hypertension, a negative IVP would not exclude the possibility. Renal artery angiography (radiopaque contrast material is injected directly into the renal artery and x-rays are then taken) would be needed. Furthermore, if the IVP had been abnormal and suggestive of renal artery obstructive disease, the physician would still obtain renal angiograms to identify the location and type of lesion. Many authorities do not recommend routine IVP as part of the initial evaluation of a patient with hypertension unless clues from the history, physical examination, or the basic laboratory studies described earlier indicate a need for more extensive renal evaluation.

A physician is likely to consider prescribing an IVP or

perhaps renal arteriography if a patient has sustained hypertension and if one or more of the following are present:
1. The patient is less than 25 years of age or shows first signs of hypertension after 50 years of age.
2. The patient has severe elevation of blood pressure—that is, sustained diastolic pressure of 130 mm Hg or greater.
3. The patient has had a sudden onset of fixed hypertension.
4. Chronic stable hypertension suddenly worsens.
5. Abdominal bruits are heard.
6. Other indications of renal or genitourinary disease have been found in the history or physical examination.
7. Therapy appropriate for essential hypertension is ineffective.

Plasma Renin Activity

Determination of plasma renin activity has gained attention since patients with essential hypertension have been shown to fall into three groups when categorized by their renin activity (Chapter 2). Approximately 55 percent have mid, 30 percent have low, and 15 percent have high renin activity. The test remains somewhat expensive and difficult for the ordinary clinical laboratory to perform accurately. Unless the patient's state of sodium balance is related to renin levels that are obtained, the results may be misleading. Generally, plasma renin activity is not considered a routine test in the initial evaluation of a patient with high blood pressure unless experienced and reliable laboratory support for the procedure is available at reasonable cost.

The vast majority of patients with high blood pressure are seen when they visit the physician's office, and will fall into a group in whom essential hypertension can be presumed to exist. A thorough history, physical examination, and relatively simple tests and procedures will tend to confirm the diagnosis and exclude the presence of causes of secondary elevation of blood pressure fairly adequately. The physician will have obtained a good determination of the patient's general health and the status of target organ involvement. Obviously, if suspicions are raised during such an evaluation, a more specific, in-depth diagnostic program will be required. There is no assurance that all patients with secondary hypertension will have been identified by the approach described in this chapter. A very small number of such individuals will slip through. If appropriate therapy for essential hypertension does not alleviate the condition, or if new suggestive signs or symptoms develop, reassessment is in order. Clues and specific diagnostic approaches for causes of secondary hypertension are discussed next in this text.

REFERENCES: CHAPTER 3

1. Gifford RW Jr: Evaluation of the hypertensive patient with emphasis on detecting curable causes. *Milbank Mem Fund Q* 1969; 47:170–186.
2. Kennedy AC, Luke RG, Briggs JD, et al.: Detection of renovascular hypertension. *Lancet* 1965; 2:963–968.
3. Iimura O: Actual incidence of secondary hypertension. *Jpn Circ J* 1973; 37:1040–1044.
4. Boch K, Hilden T: The frequency of secondary hypertension. *Acta Med Scand* 1975; 197:69.
5. Berglund G, Andersson O, Wilhelmsen L: Prevalance of primary and secondary hypertension: Studies in a random sample population. *Br Med J.* 1976; 2:554–556.
6. Ferguson RK: Cost and yield of the hypertension evaluation. *Ann Intern Med* 1975; 82:761–765.
7. The 1980 report of the Joint National Committee on Detection, Evaluation, and Treatment of High Blood Pressure. *Arch Intern Med* 1980; 140:1280–1285.
8. Bookstein JJ, Abrams HL, Brunger RE, et al.: Radiologic aspects of renovascular hypertension. Part 2. The role of urography in unilateral disease. *JAMA* 1972; 220:1225–1230.

CHAPTER 4

FINDING AND TREATING THE CAUSES OF SECONDARY HYPERTENSION

YOUR physician will consider further examination and testing if your initial evaluation suggests that a specific disorder may be causing secondary hypertension, if your hypertension is severe and rapidly progressive, or if treatment for essential fails to help you. He or she will choose diagnostic procedures appropriate for the suspected disorder, hoping to confirm the suspicion or to exclude the possibility. Only a very small portion of patients with hypertension will require such an approach, but the possibility should be kept in mind.

As already discussed, many causes for secondary elevation of blood pressure have been identified. These causes may be generally classified as those involving the endocrine (hormonal) system, those related to kidney disorders, coarctation of the aorta, and diseases of the central nervous system (brain and spinal cord) (Table 4.1).

TABLE 4.1
Potential Causes of Secondary Hypertension

Endocrine disorders:
Oral contraceptives
Adrenal cortical disorders
   Cushing's syndrome
   Primary aldosteronism
Adrenal medullary disorder
   Pheochromocytoma
Thyroid disorders
   Hyperthyroidism (excessive activity)
   Hypothyroidism (insufficient activity)
Hyperparathyroidism
Acromegaly

Renal (kidney) disorders
Renovascular hypertension
Obstructive uropathy disorder of the urinary tract
Renal parenchymal disease

Coarctation of the aorta

Central nervous system disorders
Brain tumor
Increased intracranial pressure from any cause
Cerebrovascular accident (stroke)
Guillain-Barré syndrome

PROBLEMS RELATED TO ENDOCRINE (HORMONAL) FUNCTION

Oral Contraceptive Use

In almost all women who use estrogen-containing oral contraceptive pills, there is an increase of 2 to 14 mm Hg in systolic pressure and 1 to 8 mm Hg diastolic pressure when compared to controls or nonusers. In the majority of women, blood pressure levels remain within the normal range despite this elevation. In about 5 percent, however, diagnosable hypertension does occur. High blood pressure occurs 2.6 times as often in pill users than in women not using the pill. The degree of elevation ranges from mild hypertension in most to malignant hypertension (see Chapter 13) in a few. Fortunately, the elevated blood pressure usually is reversible when the pill is discontinued. Although onset of oral contraceptive hypertension can occur within a few weeks of beginning use of the pill, in most instances it appears within ten weeks. Once the agent is discontinued, blood pressure elevation may persist for three and even six months.

It appears that the renin-angiotensin-aldosterone mechanism (Chapter 2) plays a major role in this kind of hypertension. Renin substrate (angiotensinogen) increases two-to fivefold when oral contraceptives are used. Estrogen has been shown to stimulate the liver to increase its synthesis of angiotensinogen. If the blood contains an overabundant quantity of angiotensinogen, renin activity increases and production of angiotensin II rises as well. Plasma volume, cardiac output, pheripheral resistance, and blood pressure rise. If this cause of secondary hypertension is a possibility in a female patient, the physician will generally advise her to discontinue the oral contraceptive and substitute some other form of birth control. If after three to six months, the patient continues to have high blood pressure, the causative mechanism probably is not related to the estrogen-containing pills. The physician will then order appropriate evaluation and will prescribe antihypertensive therapy.

Disorders of the Adrenal Cortex

Cushing's Syndrome. Although less than 0.5 percent of patients with high blood pressure suffer from Cushing's syndrome, approximately 85 to 90 percent of those who do have this disease are hypertensive. The hallmark of Cushing's syndrome is the chronic excessive quantity of the adrenal cortical hormone, cortisol, circulating in the bloodstream. Cortisol is vital to carbohydrate and protein metabolism. It also influences sodium and water balance within the body.

High concentrations of cortisol result in sodium and water retention, increased concentrations of plasma renin substrate (angiotensinogen), and potentiation of the pressor effects of catecholamines—all contributors to the development of hypertension. Cortisol production by the adrenal cortex normally is dependent upon stimulation by the pituitary gland hormone ACTH. Under normal circumstances, when cortisol levels in the blood rise, the pituitary decreases ACTH production.

The symptoms of Cushing's syndrome appear whenever cortisol levels are high for a long period, no matter what the reason. Basically, ACTH stimulation of the adrenal cortex must be excessive or the cortex may produce excessive cortisol without stimulation. In the first instance, both ACTH and cortisol levels will be increased; in the second instance, cortisol levels will be elevated but ACTH secretion will be inhibited and the level diminished (this is the normal response of the pituitary gland to high cortisol levels). Although any one of several disorders may produce Cushing's syndrome, they fall into one of three categories: (1) excessive secretion of ACTH by the pituitary gland, (2) production of ACTH at some other site (ectopic production—some nonpituitary tumors develop the ability to produce ACTH), and (3) autonomous excessive production of cortisol by the adrenal gland (Table 4.2).

In each of these instances, the clinical features reflect the metabolic effect of increased cortisol production. In addition to hypertension, one sees hyperglycemia (abnormally elevated blood sugar levels), purplish skin stretch marks and scars, swelling (edema) of the hands and feet, increased hair on the face and body, and recurrent acne. However, since these findings are so frequent in individuals without Cushing's syndrome, they are of little diagnostic value in themselves. On the other hand, obesity confined to the trunk of the body and sparing the limbs, "moon face" and florid complexion, menstrual irregularities, muscle weakness (inability ro rise from a deep knee bend), easy bruisability, and osteoporosis of the bones on x-ray film are more discriminatory from a diagnostic standpoint.

No matter what the underlying cause, the diagnosis of

TABLE 4.2
Common Mechanisms for Cushing's Syndrome

	ACTH level	Cortisol level
Pituitary-induced increased adrenal cortical activity 　Pituitary tumor 　(10% of all cases) 　Hyperactive pituitary 　gland (55% of all cases)	Normal to elevated	Elevated
Ectopic ACTH production (20% of all cases) 　Lung tumors (most common) 　Thymus gland tumors 　Cancer of the pancreas	Markedly elevated	Elevated
Autonomous adrenal cortical increased production of cortisol (5–15% of all cases) 　Benign tumors (adenomas) 　of adrenal cortex 　Autonomous hyperactivity 　of adrenal cortex	Diminished	Elevated

Cushing's syndrome depends first on confirming the fact that there is chronic excess production of cortisol. Normally, secretion of both ACTH and cortisol follows a diurnal pattern, high peaks occurring in the morning and the lowest levels by late afternoon or evening. Patients with Cushing's syndrome lack this normal diurnal rhythm and have high levels constantly. If plasma measurements are made in the morning, there is considerable overlapping between the levels of those with Cushing's syndrome and some normal persons. The separation of the two groups is much more apparent if testing is done later in the day.

Diagnostic accuracy is greatly enhanced by a finding that

administration of dexamethasone does not suppress cortisol secretion. Dexamethasone is a synthetic adrenocorticoid steroid very similar to cortisol. In normal individuals, it will suppress ACTH release from the pituitary gland, and consequently cortisol secretion from the adrenal cortex. However, in the various disorders producing Cushing's syndrome, this response is muted or does not occur at all.

Your physician can administer the simplest of these tests as an office procedure. You will be given a single dose of dexamethosone to take at midnight. The next morning a blood sample will be taken. Normally, serum cortisol the following morning at 8:00 A.M. should be less than 10 $\mu/g/dl$. A higher level is highly suspicious. A more definite suppression test can be done. It is more conveniently performed if the patient is hospitalized. Doses of dexamethasone are given orally every 6 hours for 48 hours. If the pituitary–adrenal cortical axis is functioning normally, plasma cortisol levels should drop to less than 5 $\mu g/dl$ and urinary hydrocorticosteroids, the major metabolites of cortisol excreted by the kidneys, should be less than 2.5 mg per gram of creatinine per 24 hours.

Unfortunately, there are false-negative and occasionally false-positive results in all these tests. The diagnosis requires that this battery of tests, some repeated several times, be correlated with the clinical findings, and that all put together they point to Cushing's syndrome.

The next order of business is to identify the specific underlying disorder (pituitary, ectopic ACTH, adrenal cortical), since the treatment will vary with each. At this point, most physicians consider it to be wise to consult with a specialist who is accustomed to dealing with the intricacies of hormonal function—most likely an endocrinologist.

Primary Hyperaldosteronism. Hypertension secondary to primary hyperaldosteronism is also an uncommon abnormality. In an unselected population, the prevalence is less than 1 percent. In this syndrome, the adrenal cortex autonomously overproduces aldoserone. This overproduction may occur because a tumor is secreting the hormone or because the glandular cells that produce this hormone are overactive (a condition known as *hyperplasia*). When circulating aldosterone is in excess, more is retained, and tissue fluid volume and plasma volume expand—all leading to hypertension. In addition, too much potassium is excreted in the urine. The serum level of potassium falls below normal (hypokalemia), which may lead to serious disruption of the heart's rhythm and perhaps to sudden death. Increased plasma volume and hypertension produce an increased perfusion pressure in the renal afferent glomerular arterioles and consequently suppress the renin-angiotensin-aldosterone system. Primary hyperaldosteronism, then, is characterized by hypertension, hypokalemia, low levels of plasma renin activity, and elevated aldosterone levels.

Usually there are no symptoms that specifically identify this disorder. On occasion, in far advanced cases, the symptoms of hypokalemia might appear: muscle weakness, muscle cramping, paralysis of the proximal muscles of the extremities, cardiac rhythm disturbances, increased frequency and quantity of urination (*polyuria*) and increase in blood glucose levels. Hypokalemia may also blunt the autonomic reflexes that constrict arterioles and veins when humans assume an upright position. These reflexes normally prevent pooling of large amounts of blood in the lower part of the body due to the effect of gravity. When the reflex is blunted, there may be an orthostatic (positional) drop in blood pressure. Less blood, and therefore less oxygen, reaches the brain. The patient becomes lightheaded and dizzy and may even faint.

If laboratory studies indicate low serum potassium levels during the initial evaluation of a patient with high blood pressure, the physician may prescribe more specific diagnostic tests to determine whether the patient has primary hyperaldosteronism. A three-step sequence is logical and easily performed.[1]

The patient is asked to collect all urine excreted over a 24-hour period (24-hour urine specimen). The urine is tested on the morning when the urine collection is completed to determine urinary potassium levels. Under normal circumstances the body tries to conserve potassium when levels are low, and little is excreted in the urine. Most patients with primary hyperaldosteronism, however, will excrete more than 50 mEq of potassium in 24 hours even if serum potassium is low. Therefore, if a patient has hypokalemia but less than 30 mEq/24 hours of potassium is excreted in the urine, the body is conserving potassium physiologically and there is no primary aldosteronism. Under this circumstance, the physician will try to determine whether potassium is being lost through the gastrointestinal tract (for example, if the patient is using laxatives) or whether the loss was incurred through use of diuretic drugs.

If 50 mEq or more potassium is excreted into the urine in 24 hours even though the patient is hypokalemic, the possibility that primary hyperaldosteronism exists remains viable. The next step is to measure plasma renin activity. If it is high, the patient cannot have aldosteronism. The physician will then consider such things as estrogen therapy, ischemic renovascular hypertension (which will be discussed later in this chapter), or other situations stimulating high plasma renin activity and a secondary increase in aldosterone as a consequence of the renin-angiotensin-aldosterone mechanism.

If potassium urinary excretion is high despite concomitant hypokalemia, and if plasma renin activity is low, primary hyperaldosteronism continues to be a possibility. The final step is to measure the plasma aldosterone level. If it is high, the diagnosis of primary hyperaldosteronism has been confirmed.

At this point, it is important to determine whether the overproduction of aldosterone is related to a secreting tumor or to hyperplasia of the adrenal cortex on both sides of the body. If a tumor exists, operative removal yields a high rate of cure. Surgery is much less successful in treating bilateral hyperplasia, but good control is often obtained by long-term administration of the drug spironolactone (an aldosterone inhibitor).

Once again, the physician is likely to consult specialists who treat many patients with the problem. Several techniques are available to distinguish a tumor, which is almost always unilateral (on one side), from hyperplasia, which is bilateral (affecting both glands). A CT scan may be used, or x-ray studies may be done after injection of contrast material in the veins of the adrenal gland. Other possibilities include radioactive isotope scanning of the adrenal glands and sampling of adrenal venous blood for hormone measurements. Since none of these techniques is infallible, wide experience in this area is needed for best interpretation.

Pheochromocytoma

It is estimated that 0.1 to 0.2 percent of patients with high blood pressure have a pheochromocytoma to which the hypertension is secondary. The prevalence is quite low, but a large proportion of these cases are potentially curable, so it is important to identify them.

Pheochromocytoma is a tumor of chromaffin cells (synthesizers of the catecholomines norepinephrine and epinephrine). It may appear anywhere that chromaffin tissue is present. About 90 percent originate in the vicinity of or within the inner part (medulla) of the adrenal gland. The remainder usually are found within the chest or abdomen arising from structures of the sympathetic nervous system. Most pheochromocytomas produce and secrete excesses of

TABLE 4.3
Physiologic Effects of Catecholamines

Norepinephrine (Noradrenoline)
- Peripheral arteriolar vasoconstriction resulting in increased peripheral vascular resistance and systolic and diastolic hypertension
- Some increase in heart rate

Epinephrine (Adrenoline)
- CNS stimulation
- Increase in metabolic rate
- Glycogenolysis (hyperglycemia)
- Increased sweating
- Constriction of vessels of skin (pallor), mucous membranes, and splanchnic bed
- Dilatation of vessels in muscles
- Increase in heart rate
- Increase in cardiac output
- Increase in systolic blood pressure

both norepinephrine and epinephrine; the former is usually in greater concentration and therefore its effects predominate. Catecholamine concentrations may be sufficient also to evoke physiologic responses, depending upon the plasma levels of each (Table 4.3). Some tumors secrete only norepinephrine and, rarely, some release only epinephrine.

More than a casual relationship has been shown between pheochromocytoma and neurofibromatosis of Von Recklinghausen (tumors affecting the nerves). This disease gained publicity from the film *The Elephant Man*. In 10 percent of pheochromocytomas there is an associated familial incidence of this disorder. Familial pheochromocytomas may be associated with pituitary gland, pancreatic, or parathyroid gland tumors (multiple endocrine adenomatosis). More commonly, an association exists with medullary carcinoma of the thyroid gland and tumors or hyperplasia of the parathyroid glands (Sipple's syndrome). Rarely, it occurs with neuromas (nerve tumors) in the mucous membranes of the body, medullary thyroid carcinoma, thickened corneal nerves, or a tall, thin, spindly body shape.

The clinical picture reflects the excessive concentration of circulating catecholamines (norepinephrine, epinephrine) and their stimulating effects on the alpha- and beta-adrenoreceptors in the body (Chapter 2). About 30 percent of the patients will have only intermittent acute paroxysms of hypertension and associated symptoms, another 30 percent will have persistent hypertension only, and the rest will have persistent hypertension with superimposed, intermittent paroxysms or spells. Paroxysms occur when the tumor suddenly releases excessive amounts of catecholamines into the circulation. Symptoms usually last 15 minutes to an hour. Although manifestations vary, the most commonly encountered are severe paroxysmal headaches, excessive sweating, and heart irregularities and palpitations. There is a marked increase in blood pressure during these episodes. Paroxysms may appear spontaneously with no apparent causes, or during abdominal palpation, induction of anesthesia, manipulation of the tumor during surgery, during childbirth, with emotional disturbances or changes in body posture, with exercise, and after drugs such as ACTH, glucagon, histamine, phenothiazines, propranolol, saralasin, tricyclic antidepressants, or tyramine. An unusual presenting picture is one of classical paroxysms appearing during the act of urination. Pheochromocytomas do occur in the urinary bladder.

Aside from paroxysms, patients with pheochromocytoma may have an increased resting pulse rate, may be tremulous, and may be lean in body shape. They may be hypermetabolic without thyroid gland abnormalities. Many suffer orthostatic hypotension when standing up, with lightheadedness, dizziness, or even fainting. The drop in blood pressure upon standing presumably is due to a "numbing" of the normal vasomotor reflexes that prevent pooling of blood in the lower body. It is thought that chronic exposure of receptors to excessive levels of catecholamines results in such an alteration of the reflex mechanism. Increased catecholamine levels also block insulin release, inhibit utilization of glucose by the tissues, and stimulate conversion of glycogen to glucose (glycogenolysis). Consequently, hyperglycemia (high blood sugar) is a common finding.

In the evaluation of a patient with high blood pressure, if any of the clinical features described above are detected, or if the patient does not benefit from antihypertensive treatment (or even gets worse), further testing for pheochromocytoma is in order. Radioenzymatic assays provide a method to measure levels of catecholamines in the circulation directly. Some patients with this tumor consistently have elevated plasma catecholamine concentrations. The test is difficult to perform, costly, and time consuming, however. The variability and range of plasma catecholamines in normal subjects, hypertensives without pheochromocytoma, and those definitely with the tumor overlap, so it is difficult to establish absolute levels to confirm the presence of pheochromocytoma. Finally, both false-positive and false-negative results are not uncommon. The assay, therefore, is best used as a confirmatory rather than a screening procedure.

The measurement of catecholamines and their metabolites (metanephrines, normetanephrines, and vanillylmandelic acid or VMA) in the urine will be abnormal in 95 percent of patients with this tumor. These tests have proved to be the prime screening procedures. Initially, the tests were performed on 24-hour urine collections and the findings were reported as micrograms per milligram (μg/mg) of creatinine in the urine (Table 4.4). Urinary catecholamines are technically

TABLE 4.4
Urinary Findings in Pheochromocytoma (Urinary excretion as micrograms per milligram (mg) of creatinine in 24-hour urine collection)

	Normal Levels	Levels in Pheochromocytoma	Patients with Positive Assay
Urinary catecholamines	less than 0.1	0.1 to 10.0	99%
Total metanephrines plus normetanephrines	less than 1.2	1.0 to 100	97%
Vanillylmandelic acid (VMA)	less than 6.5	5.0 to 600	90%

more difficult to measure than the metabolites. Most clinical laboratories usually perform the latter. It has been agreed generally that determination of total urinary metanephrines (using photometric methods) is the best screening test. More recently, a total metanephrine-normetanephrine measurement on a single-voiced urine specimen has proved to be a highly reliable screening procedure. Less than 1 μg/mg of creatinine is the normal level. This test is simple and inexpensive. It should be remembered that in patients who have intermittent paroxysms with normal blood pressures in between, the tests may be positive only during or immediately after an acute episode. Localization of the tumor is best accomplished with computed tomography (CT scan).

The preferred treatment is surgical removal of the pheochromocytoma. In inoperable situations or in patients with tumor that has spread to other sites in the body, alpha- and beta-receptor blocking medications may be of value. Recently available metyrosine (Demser), which inhibits both epinephrine and norepinephrine production by the tumor, shows promise for such cases as well.

Problems Related to Renal (Kidney) Function

The fundamental mechanism in renovascular hypertension is sufficient obstruction of the renal artery to one of the kidneys so that perfusion pressure of its glomerular afferent arterioles drops. Renin is released into the plasma, and the renin-angiotensin-aldosterone mechanism (Chapter 2) comes into play. The pressor action of angiotensin II (predominantly) and the plasma volume expansion of the aldosterone combine to cause hypertension. Because of the obstruction in the renal artery, the perfusion pressure in the glomerular afferent arterioles remains low despite this compensatory mechanism. Renin continues to be released and the hypertension continues unabated.

It is estimated that up to 5 percent of patients with hypertension have renovascular hypertension. Aside from the high blood pressure state that appears in women taking birth control pills, this entity is the most common form of potentially curable hypertension secondary to correctible causes. Renovascular hypertension occurs less frequently in blacks than in whites. Two groups of disease-producing conditions are responsible for the majority of cases: (1) atherosclerosis that obstructs the renal artery or its major branches, and (2) fibrodysplasia of the renal artery, a condition in which normal arterial muscle tissue is replaced by inelastic fibrous tissue (Table 4.5). The renal artery dysplasias occur in younger patients (average age of 35 years) and predominantly in women. Atherosclerotic renal artery obstructive disease occurs in older patients and in men more frequently.

Clinically, many patients with renovascular hypertension cannot be distinguished from those with essential hypertension. With both disorders, patients largely are asymptomatic (without symptoms). A family history of renovascular hypertension is less common than one of essential hyperten-

TABLE 4.5
Characteristics of Renal Arterial Dysplasia

	Type of Disease (% of Patients Affected)	Appearance of Lesion	Sexual Distribution
Intimal fibroplasia	5	Long, tubular stenosis	Equal in both sexes
Medial hyperplasia	1	Focal stenosis	Women primarily
Medial fibromuscular dysplasia	85	Multiple constrictions with intervening aneurysmal dilitations	95% in women
Perimedial dysplasia	9 to 10	Multiple stenoses without intervening aneurysms	Women primarily

sion. A few characteristics are more apt to occur in those with renovascular hypertension, however. Relatively severe hypertension in a young person, sudden onset of high blood pressure, or sudden worsening in established hypertension suggests underlying kidney disease. An abdominal bruit indicates renovascular hypertension (Chapter 3); it is the most specific clinical finding for this disorder.

Abdominal bruits occur in 50 to 60 percent of patients with renovascular hypertension and are more likely to be found in those with fibromuscular dysplasia. The characteristic murmur of renovascular hypertension is a high-pitched bruit heard over the upper abdomen ("pit of the stomach") during both systole (while the heart is contracting) and diastole (when the heart is relaxing and refilling). Murmurs or bruits occurring during systole only are not as diagnostic. They may be heard also in those with essential hypertension and normal renal arteries; insignificant systolic bruits become more common as patients pass 50 years of age.

Other than inspection at surgery, injecting radiopaque contrast material directly into the renal arteries and studying them with x-ray (renal arteriography, or renal angiography) is the only definitive method to confirm a suspicion of renovascular stenosis or obstruction. However, the procedure is expensive, may require hospitalization, and is not without risk. Arterial hemorrhage or thrombosis, dissection of the renal artery, and kidney failure can occur, although these complications are uncommon. The Cooperative Study of Renovascular Hypertension[2] showed that 0.11 percent of patients died from this procedure, and major complications occurred in 1.2 percent.

Even though these rates are not high, physicians would be unwilling to subject a patient to such an invasive procedure as part of a routine workup. They would prefer a more benign screening test that would identify patients in whom arteriography would be most likely to demonstrate renal artery stenosis. Some feel that the rapid sequence intravenous pyelogram (IVP) serves this purpose and even that it should be a part of the diagnostic evaluation of any patient with high blood pressure. Some feel that the IVP not only screens for renovascular hypertension but also may reveal other less common kidney abnormalities that can cause hypertension such as obstructive lesions of the ureter so urine cannot reach the bladder, kidney cysts or tumors, and unilateral underdeveloped (hypoplastic) kidney. The rapid sequence IVP consists of rapid intravenous injection of a dose of radiopaque contrast material. X-ray films over the abdomen are exposed sequentially at one, two, and three minutes. Subsequent films are obtained at 10 and 20 minutes, just as in an ordinary IVP. Criteria by which renovascular hypertension may be distinguished from essential hypertension by IVP are based mainly on how frequently a particular x-ray finding tends to occur in patients with each disease. Data in the table are based on the Cooperative Study of Renovascular Hypertension.[3]

In a number of studies, the rapid sequence IVP (sometimes called an excretory urogram) identified correctly 53 to 83 percent of patients whose renovascular hypertension was later proved (true-positive results). In other words, 17 to 47 percent of the x-rays were false negatives in those who actually had this disorder. Stanley and Fry[4] showed that sensitivity of the IVP in identifying patients with renovascular hypertension who would benefit from surgery varied according to the kind of underlying problem (Table 4.6). The least success occurred in children (pediatric cases) and most (73 to 78 percent) in atherosclerotic renal artery disease. There were 11.4 percent false positives in 771 cases of essential hypertension in the Cooperative Study on Renovascular Hypertension.[3]

TABLE 4.6
Abnormal IVP (Excretory Urogram) as a Predictor of Surgical Correction of Renovascular Hypertension

Group	Total No. of Patients	Patients with Abnormal Excretory Urogram
Pediatric	17	4 (24%)
Adult fibrodysplastic	105	52 (50%)
Focal arteriosclerotic	44	32 (73%)
Generalized arteriosclerosis	32	25 (71%)

These were hypertensive patients without renal artery stenotic lesions who nevertheless had abnormal IVP findings compatible with renovascular obstruction.

Although the risk with the IVP procedure is not so great as that of the arteriogram, serious allergic reactions and some deaths do occur. Because of the false negatives in patients subsequently shown to have renovascular hypertension and the false positives in individuals with ordinary essential hypertension, some physicians feel that the rapid sequence IVP is not a valid screening test. They recommend that patients who have the signs and symptoms shown in Table 4.7 and who would be candidates for surgery if the test were positive, be hospitalized to undergo renal artery angiography. This procedure also yields excellent excretory urograms in the process as a by-product.

TABLE 4.7
Clinical Indications Suggesting Renovascular Hypertension

- Abdominal bruits
- Significant hypertension in patients less than 25 years of age
- Sustained diastolic pressures of 130 mm Hg or more
- Sudden onset of fixed hypertension
- Rapid worsening of previously stable hypertension
- Ineffectiveness of appropriate therapy

If a patient shows none of the clinical features in Table 4.8 but does not respond to appropriate therapy for essential hypertension, the physician will consider an IVP or even renal artery angiography. For a sizable number of patients with renovascular hypertension, nonsurgical treatment does not control the blood pressure. Therefore, failure to achieve control may indicate renal origin.

A recent technique called digital subtraction angiography shows promise in diagnosing renovascular hypertension. It employs computer enhancement of x-ray images, requires only a peripheral venous injection of a small amount of contrast material, and has, in some cases, produced excellent visualization of the renal arteries. It appears to carry a negligible risk, and the procedure can be done on an outpatient basis. As the technique and equipment improve, and as experience is gained, digital subtraction angiography may become the preferred procedure.

Once an obstructive lesion in the renal artery has been demonstrated, its relationship to the hypertension must still be established. Not all obstructive lesions seen in renal artery angiograms are functionally significant in terms of producing hypertension. Some patients with essential hypertension may eventually develop a degree of renal artery narrowing which may not be contributing to the origin of high blood pressure. The obstructive lesion may be secondary to the essential hypertension, since hypertension stimulates atherosclerosis. Surgery is likely to be helpful only in true renovascular hypertension, in which the arterial lesion is instrumental in stimulating increased RAA axis activity. Demonstrating this relationship may be difficult.

Determination of plasma renin activity levels in blood obtained from a peripheral vein (the usual way of getting blood for tests) is disappointing from a diagnostic point of view. The renin levels in such samples are not always elevated in renovascular hypertension nor do they help distinguish between it and high-renin essential hypertension. In renovascular hypertension, the renin release produces marked elevation of activity in the blood of the affected kidney's veins. The effect of the RAA axis activity that follows—the increased blood pressure and expansion of plasma volume—suppresses renin release by the unaffected kidney (the perfusion pressure in its glomerular afferent arterioles is more than adequate and renin is not released). Therefore, plasma renin activity determined in separate samples of blood taken from the renal vein of each kidney would be expected to be more discriminating.

Such sampling is accomplished by inserting a polyethylene catheter into a femoral vein in the groin. The catheter is guided up into the major vein of the body (inferior vena cava) and then into the right and left renal veins under fluoroscopic visualization. Blood samples are drawn from the vein of each kidney. Surgical correction of the narrowed renal artery of the affected kidney, or surgical removal of that kidney, has produced distinct improvement in 80 to 90 percent of patients in whom renal vein renin activity on the affected side has been at least 1.5 times the level of the normal kidney on the other side. This means that the test will not identify 10 to 20 percent of patients who would benefit from surgery.

Another method for determining the significance of a renal arterial obstructive lesion as a factor in originating and maintaining high blood pressure is the *Saralasin test*. This drug inhibits the activity of angiotensin II, the main effector hormone of the RAA axis. When Saralasin is administered intravenously, from 63 to 76 percent of patients with renovascular hypertension have a drop in blood pressure that is diagnostic. In addition, however, 15 percent of patients with essential hypertension and no renal artery obstructive lesions also had positive (false-positive) results. False positives occurred mainly in patients with high-renin essential hypertension.

It should be obvious that no clinical finding, single test, or combination of tests and procedures will be consistently successful in detecting patients with renovascular hypertension. A physician must be knowledgeable in all these areas and must then proceed according to his or her best clinical judgment.

The recommended current therapy for renovascular hypertension in a young person with high blood pressure of less than five years' duration, with renal single-vessel occlusive disease demonstrated to be functionally significant, is surgical revascularization or removal of the affected kidney. Medical (nonsurgical treatment) is usually tried first if the patient is an older person who has generalized atherosclerosis (including known coronary artery disease) and/or involvement of the arteries supplying the brain (cerebrovascular disease), who has a long history of high blood pressure, and who also happens to have functionally significant renovascular hypertension. These two situations represent opposite ends of a spectrum. In cases lying between these two extremes, the physician is called upon to make individual decisions, once again interpreting the findings and then relying on experience and clinical judgment as well.

Most forms of fibromuscular dysplasia are progressive; that is, they continually worsen if untreated. These cases have a much more favorable outlook with surgery. The patients are younger and usually do not have additional problems such as coronary artery disease. Patients with atherosclerotic renovascular hypertension are older, have more extensive kidney damage, and have coronary artery and cerebrovascular atherosclerotic disease as well. They are more likely to die during surgery and less likely to be helped by surgery. Pinedo and his associates[5] followed a group of older patients with renovascular hypertension, 71 having been treated successfully with surgery and 42 on medical regimens. At the end of five years, longevity of those who responded to either course of treatment was essentially the same. It seems reasonable to treat all older patients medically first. If the response is not satisfactory in 30 to 90 days, then surgery might be considered more strongly.

Selected patients with occlusion of the coronary artery or peripheral artery have been treated successfully with a recent technique called *percutaneous transluminal dilatation* (passing a catheter through a narrowed area and inflating a balloon on its end). This procedure may offer another alternative for renovascular hypertension. The balloon widens the arterial channel by forcing some of the atherosclerotic material into the walls of the vessel. Attempts at treating renovascular hypertension similarly have been yielding promising results. The procedure is much less traumatic than surgery, a distinct advantage for elderly patients. As more experience is gained along this line, it is hoped that this technique may become a primary treatment alternative.

REFERENCES: CHAPTER 4

1. Kaplan NM: *Clinical Hypertension*. Baltimore, Williams and Wilkins Co, 1982, p 306.

2. Reiss MD, Bookstein JJ, Bleifer KH: Radiologic aspects of renovascular hypertension. 4. Arteriographic complications. *JAMA* 1972; 221:374–378.

3. Bookstein JJ, Abrams HL, Buenger RC, et al.: Radiologic aspects of renovascular hypertension. Part 2. The role of urography in unilateral renovascular hypertension. *JAMA* 1972; 220:1225–1230.

4. Stanley JC, Fry WJ: Surgical treatment of renovascular hypertension. *Arch Surg* 1977; 112:1291–1297.

5. Pinedo HM, deGraeff J, Struyvenberg A: Prognosis in arteriosclerotic renovascular hypertension. *Clin Sci Mol Med* 1973; 45:309S–310S.

CHAPTER 5

HOW EFFECTIVE IS TREATMENT?

IN the early 1900s, many physicians believed that an elevated blood pressure was considered a good thing—a compensatory mechanism to provide adequate perfusion of blood as the arteries supplying the brain, heart, and kidneys thickened and narrowed with age. They feared that lowering the blood pressure would result in inadequate blood supply to the kidneys, for example, causing the kidneys to fail. Then Janeway reported in 1913 that "hypertensive cardiovascular disease" was accompanied by a decreasing life span, the medical profession and the public paid little attention to his findings.

By the early 1930s, cardiologists (a small number of physicians in a fledgling specialty) suggested that high blood pressure might be harmful. In 1934, it was demonstrated that no significant change in the urea clearance test (an indicator of kidney function) occurred in patients with hypertension when blood pressure was lowered. Soon after, the sympathetic ganglion blocking agent hexamethonium became available. It lowered blood pressure indirectly by blocking activity of the sympathetic nerves of the arteriolar smooth muscles, thereby reducing total peripheral resistance. Physicians who used this drug soon found that reducing blood pressure in patients with severe, rapidly progressive hypertension allowed more patients to survive for longer periods, particularly if therapy was begun before severe kidney damage had occurred. Before hexamethonium came into use, survival for one year after onset of this type of hypertension had been practically zero. Successful lowering of blood pressure resulted in 70 to 80 percent survival at the end of one year and five-year survival of 60 percent.

Most physicians now agreed that it was beneficial to treat severe, rapidly progressive hypertension and also left ventricular failure, cerebral hemorrhage, or dissecting aortic aneurysm associated with high blood pressure. The value of lowering the blood pressure with antihypertensive drugs in patients with less severe conditions remained controversial. Remember that the agents available at that time all had significant undesirable side effects. Small wonder that there was little enthusiasm for lifelong therapy in patients with relatively no symptoms, since no one seemed sure that there was benefit to be derived. As late as 1965, Goldring and Chassis[1] wrote:

> "It is established that more advanced vascular disease is often associated with high levels of blood pressure, but there is no support for the contention that further increase in blood pressure levels precedes and induces advancing vascular disease. Acceptance of this lack of causal relationship, then, would destroy the thesis on which antihypertensive drug therapy is based.... After about 15 years of assorted data collecting, we believe that the alleged usefulness of antihypertensive drugs on conclusions drawn from notoriously uncertain statistical complications compounded by equally uncertain estimates of morbidity and mortality in the natural history of a disease of highly unpredictable course.... The primary purpose of this statement is to emphasize the need for more convincing proof of the clinical usefulness of antihypertensive drugs."

They were right! Medical literature was replete with clinical studies, some supporting the value of treatment and others showing no significant effect. These were generally retrospective studies; that is, patients were selected for study after diagnosis and treatment. Most studies had flaws in design that caused doubt about the validity of their conclusions. Many had no controls (untreated patients) for comparison and in others where attempts at control had been made, the treated and untreated groups were not identical in other respects.

The first sizable, controlled, randomized study regarding the effects of antihypertensive treatment in humans with high blood pressure was reported by Hamilton and his associates in 1964.[2] Sixty-one patients, men and women with sustained diastolic pressures of 110 mm Hg, were divided randomly into treated and untreated groups. None had evidence of atherosclerotic disease upon entry into the study. The followup period ranged from two to six years. Sixteen of the 31 untreated patients developed significant complications attributable to hypertension, while only 5 of the 30 on treatment did the same.

Wolff and Lindeman in 1966[3] reported a prospective, controlled, randomized series of 87 treated and untreated patients with hypertension followed for two years. Episodes of illness that could be attributed to high blood pressure were three times greater in the untreated group when compared to the treated group.

THE VETERANS ADMINISTRATION COOPERATIVE STUDY

In 1967 and in 1970, the results of a prospective, controlled, randomized study, the Veterans Administration Cooperative Study[4,5] (VA study) were reported. An additional facet in this experiment was that the study was of the double-blind type; that is neither the physician nor the patient knew whether the patient was receiving active medications or placebos (completely inert pills and capsules that were indistinguishable from the active drugs). This effort, under the direction of Dr. E. D. Freis, included 523 adult male patients. One group with diastolic pressures of 115 to 129 mm Hg included 143 subjects. A second group of 380 men had diastolic pressures of 90 mm Hg through 114 mm Hg. Initially, the researchers planned to observe and compare the course of these patients for five years.

After an average followup of only 20 months, however, the statisticians informed Dr. Freis and his collaborators that there was undeniable evidence that those in the first group (diastolic pressures of 115 to 129 mm Hg upon entry into the study) who were receiving a placebo were definitely in jeopardy (Table 5.1). There had been 4 cardiovascular deaths and 23 major nonfatal events in the placebo group compared to no cardiovascular deaths and only two major nonfatal events in the treated group. The investigators decided that it was wrong ethically and morally to continue the observation period in the first group, and all patients were offered antihypertensive therapy.

After an average followup of 40 months, similar trends were noted in the second group, those with diastolic pressures initially ranging from 90 to 114 mm Hg upon entry into the study (Table 5.2). There had been 19 cardiovascular deaths and 37 major nonfatal events in the placebo group compared to 8 cardiovascular deaths and 14 major nonfatal events in the treated group. Once again, the observation period was terminated, and all patients were offered active treatment. It should be noted that in the second group, the

TABLE 5.1
Episodes of Illness (Morbid Events) in Patients with Diastolic Pressures Averaging 115 to 129 mm Hg (VA Study)

	Placebo	Treatment
Deaths (all causes)	4	2
Cerebrovascular accident (stroke)	4	1
Coronary artery disease	2	0
Congestive heart failure	2	0
Accelerated hypertension	12	0
Other	3	1

TABLE 5.2
Episodes of Illness (Morbid Events) in Patients with Diastolic Pressures Averaging 90 to 114 mm Hg (VA Study)

	Placebo		Treatment	
	Nonfatal	Fatal	Nonfatal	Fatal
Cerebrovascular accident (stroke)	13	7	4	1
Coronary artery disease	2	11	5	6
Congestive heart failure	11	0	0	0
Accelerated hypertension	4	0	0	0
Other	7	1	5	1

major benefit occurred in those who had received active treatment and whose diastolic pressures initially ranged from 105 to 114 mm Hg. In the milder group (diastolics 90 to 104 mm Hg), there was a similar beneficial trend with active treatment, but the numbers were too small to be statistically significant (Table 5.3).

These studies confirmed the validity of the interpretations suggested by earlier reports: antihypertensive therapy reduced rates of mortality (death) and morbidity (illness). There was no question but that successful treatment had a distinct beneficial impact on the rates of stroke and congestive heart failure and that it helped prevent rapidly progressive hypertension. The effect on coronary artery disease was not

TABLE 5.3
Complications in Patients with Moderate Hypertension Compared to Patients with Mild Hypertension (VA Study)

	Treated		Untreated	
	No. of Subjects	Complications	No. of Subjects	Complications
Moderate (105–114 mm Hg)	100	8%	110	31.8%
Mild (90–104 mm Hg)	86	16.3%	84	25.0%

so clear, however. Although the treated group appeared to be more likely to *survive* myocardial infarction (heart attack), heart attacks occurred with essentially the same frequency in both treated and placebo groups.

Since the number of patients with mild hypertension upon entry into the study was too small for statistical validity, conclusions that antihypertensive therapy was beneficial could be applied only to those whose initial diastolic pressures had been 105 mm Hg or higher. Further analysis showed, however, that in any age group, no matter what the severity of the hypertension, there was definite benefit from active treatment if, upon entry into the program, the patient had any indication of accompanying coronary artery disease or congestive heart failure, or if there was electrocardiographic evidence of left ventricular hypertrophy. In addition, the researchers analyzed the records of patients 50 years of age or older who were in the group with initial diastolic pressures in the 90 to 104 mm Hg range. These patients were at greater risk and gained considerable benefit from treatment.

THE U.S. PUBLIC HEALTH SERVICE HOSPITALS COOPERATIVE STUDY

The U.S. Public Health Service sponsored a cooperative effort in which the effects of the antihypertensives chlorothiazide and rauwolfia were studied over 7 to 10 years. There were 389 subjects, men and women. Ages ranged from 21 to 55 years. None of the subjects had evidence of target-organ involvement upon entry into the study. Although diastolic pressures ranged from 90 to 115 mm Hg initially, more than 75 percent of the patients had mild hypertension (90 to 104 mm Hg). This was an active treatment (193 subjects) versus a placebo (196) program.

At the end of the study, there had been eight events attributable to hypertension (heart attack, stroke, sudden death) in the treated group and nine such events in the placebo group. Obviously, no statistically significant difference was detected between the two groups, but the number of all events was small, the subjects were young, and the hypertension was mild. The followup period may have been too short to allow for a clear end-point. The major contribution of the study was the finding that active drug treatment was almost 60 percent effective in preventing the progress of disease manifested by rising diastolic pressure and the appearance of left ventricular hypertrophy on the EKG. In the placebo group, 12.2 percent had a progressive rise of diastolic pressure into higher levels of severity, but none did so in the treatment group. So in relatively young patients with mild hypertension, treatment does prevent the hypertension from becoming worse in some, and therefore it probably protects from target-organ involvement in the long run.

THE AUSTRALIAN NATIONAL BLOOD PRESSURE STUDY

A total of 3,427 subjects, Australian men and women aged 30 to 69 years, participated in a prospective, controlled, placebo versus active treatment trial.[7] Initial blood pressures ranged from 95 to 110 mm Hg diastolic and less than 200 mm Hg systolic. None of the subjects had evidence of target-organ damage. The average followup was four years. The subjects were stratified by sex and age and then randomly allocated to a placebo group or an active group. The latter received chlorothiazide as the first-order drug. If blood pressure control was not achieved, a second-order drug (methyldopa, propranolol, or pindolol) was added. If necessary, a third-order drug (hydralazine or clonidine) was added later. Initially, the goal was to reduce diastolic pressure to 90 mm Hg or less. After two years, the target was lowered to 80 mm Hg or less.

During the period of observation, the subjects in the actively treated group experienced a lower rate of cardiovascular disease and death than those in the placebo group. It should be noted that the death rate was reduced primarily in patients 50 years of age or older. In addition, significant benefit was gained in the actively treated patients whose diastolic pressures had been 100 mm Hg or more initially. There was a favorable trend for treated patients whose diastolic pressures had been less than 100 mm Hg, but the sample size was inadequate for statistical validity. The lower death rate in the actively treated group resulted from a decrease in deaths due to myocardial infarction (heart attack) and stroke (Table 5.4).

This study suggests that antihypertensive therapy for those 50 years and older whose diastolic pressures are 100 mm Hg or more does decrease morbidity and mortality. As in the VA cooperative studies, treatment did not seem to protect against the occurrence of myocardial infarction so much; rather, it appeared to protect the patient from dying of the heart attack. There is no question but that the treated group had about half the incidence and half the mortality from cerebrovascular disease (stroke). Of those subjects in the placebo (untreated) group whose diastolic pressures had been at 100 mm Hg initially and remained so on repeated examinations, 126 progressed to diastolic pressures of 110 mm Hg or greater during the trial.

THE OSLO STUDY

In a prospective, controlled study conducted in Oslo, Norway,[8] 785 men, all below 50 years of age and with diastolic pressures of 90 to 110 mm Hg, were randomized into a no-treatment group and one placed on an active antihypertensive drug regimen. The treated patients received hydrochlorothiazide initially; subsequently methyldopa or propranolol was added if necessary. None had evidence of target-organ involvement. The mean followup period was 66 months.

In those with diastolic pressures of 100 mm Hg or less, there was no significant difference in mortality or cardiovascular morbidity between the two groups. In those with diastolic pressures of greater than 100 mm Hg, there was a reduction in the incidence of strokes in the treated group, but the results were nullified by a small increase of coronary artery disease in this group compared to the no-treatment group. Statistical validity in either direction was not achieved because of the small numbers involved. It is noteworthy, however, that in 17 percent of the untreated group whose

TABLE 5.4
Mortality and Morbidity in the Australian Blood Pressure Study

	No. of Trial End-Points	
	Treatment	Placebo
Fatal myocardial infarctions (heart attacks)	2	8
Nonfatal myocardial infarctions	18	17
Angina, ischemic EKG changes	50	63
Fatal cerebrovascular events (strokes)	2	4
Nonfatal cerebrovascular thrombosis or hemorrhage	7	13
Transient cerebral ischemic attacks (TIAs)	3	8

initial diastolic pressures were lower, diastolic levels rose to 110 mm Hg.

THE HYPERTENSION DETECTION AND FOLLOW-UP PROGRAM (HDFP)

In a large U.S. study, almost 11,000 patients in 14 communities were studied prospectively (that is, subjects were selected before treatment or placebo was initiated.[9,10] Their ages at the time of entry into the program ranged from 30 to 69 years (2,376 of the subjects were over 60 years old). About 70 percent of this entire group of all ages suffered mild essential hypertension (diastolic pressures 90 to 104 mm Hg). Men, women, blacks, and whites were included. The followup period was five years.

Unlike the previous studies that have been cited, this program was not a comparison between treated and untreated groups. The participants were divided randomly into two groups, but one was treated in special centers by a specific system of treatment (protocol) as advocated by the National Committee on Detection, Evaluation, and Treatment of High Blood Pressure (the special care—SC—group). The other was referred to the practicing medical community for customary treatment (referred care—RC—

group). In the SC program, strong positive steps were taken to keep the patients actively participating and to encourage them to comply with the prescribed treatment.

At the end of five years, 78 percent of the SC subjects still were participating actively and 65 percent had attained normalization of their blood pressures. In the RC group, however, only 58 percent still were actively participating and only 44 percent had achieved normalization.

At the end of five years, there was a 17 percent difference in the mortality rate between the two groups. The SC group, those who had achieved a higher success rate in reaching treatment goals, had a significantly lower overall death rate than the RC group. The SC group also had lower mortality from cardiovascular disease, cerebrovascular accidents (strokes), and myocardial infarction (Table 5.5). If only those with mild hypertension were compared, the SC group again had lower mortality than the RC group, particularly in death due to heart attack (Table 5.6).

The greatest benefits for those in the SC group were found in the total mortality of the older patients. There was a small decrease in mortality in the SC group compared to the RC group in those between 30 and 49 years of age. The greatest reduction occurred in the 50- to 59-year group, and

TABLE 5.5
Mortality After Five Years in the Hypertension Detection and Follow-up Program (HDFP)

	Referred-Care	Stepped-Care (SC)	Difference
	No. (%)	No. (%)	
All causes	419 (7.68)	349 (6.36)	(−17%)
Cardiovascular disease	240 (4.39)	195 (3.55)	(−19%)
Cerebrovascular accident (stroke)	52 (0.95)	29 (0.52)	(−45%)
Myocardial infarction (heart attack)	69 (1.26)	51.(0.92)	(−26%)

TABLE 5.6
Mortality from Mild Hypertension Compared to All Subjects in HDFP

	All Subjects			Mild Hypertension		
	RC	SC	Difference	RC	SC	Difference
All causes	419	349	(−17%)	291	231	(−20%)
Cardiovascular disease	240	195	(−19%)	165	122	(−20%)
Cerebrovascular accident (stroke)	52	29	(−45%)	31	17	(−45%)
Myocardial infarction (heart attack)	69	51	(−26%)	56	30	(−46%)

those aged 60 to 69 years also did well (Table 5.7). However, the greatest beneficial effect in decreasing both nonfatal and fatal coronary artery disease events (26 percent less) was found in those aged 30 to 49 years upon entry into the program who were assigned to the SC group.

Finally, the mortality rates were lower in the SC group when compared according to race and sex. In descending order, the greatest benefit was derived by black women, then by black men, and then by white men. No apparent differences were noted between the two groups when the data for white women was scrutinized (Table 5.8). It should be noted, however, that this last group had an almost equal percentage of subjects continuing into treatment after five years and the least difference on goal attainment between the SC and RC groups.

TABLE 5.7
Mortality Rates by Age Group in HDFP

Age Group (yr)	Referred-Care (RC)	Stepped Care (SC)	Difference
	No. (%)	No. (%)	
30 to 49	82 (3.5)	81 (3.3)	(− 5.7%)
50 to 59	159 (8.3)	115 (6.2)	(−25.3%)
60 to 69	178 (15.2)	153 (12.7)	(−16.4%)

TABLE 5.8
Mortality Rates by Race and Sex in HDFP

	Mortality RC(%)	Mortality SC(%)	Difference (%)
Black men	13.0	10.6	−18.5
Black women	7.2	5.2	−27.8
White men	6.8	5.8	−14.7
White women	4.8	4.9	+2.1

CONCLUSIONS

It is clear that antihypertensive therapy is beneficial for those whose diastolic pressures are consistently at the 100 mm Hg level or higher prior to the institution of drug therapy. Such patients stand to benefit whether or not end-organ damage has occurred. The potential advantages for those with milder hypertension will be considered in Chapter 12. The major benefits appear to be due to a decrease in those complications thought to be related primarily to the high intraarterial pressures—progression to more severe levels of hypertension, congestive heart failure, strokes, kidney failure. In coronary artery disease (and heart attack) the findings of the intervention trials are not as clear. The Hypertension Detection and Follow-up Program showed a distinct decrease in both fatal and nonfatal coronary artery events in the group treated more successfully. Other studies, however, show very little change with treatment in incidence and mortality from coronary artery disease.

Coronary atherosclerosis is a complex, multifaceted process. Although high blood pressure is a major risk factor, it may be unreasonable to expect that the modification of just this one element over the relatively short period of time of these intervention studies cited would yield clear-cut results. One should consider the long duration of development of atherosclerosis and eventual coronary artery occlusion. The process usually begins years before antihypertensive treatment is instituted. This particular consideration will be discussed further in the chapter dealing with management of mild hypertension.

REFERENCES: CHAPTER 5

1. Goldring W, Chassis H: Antihypertensive drug therapy: an appraisal. *Arch Intern Med* 1965; 115:523–525.
2. Hamilton M, Thompson EN, Wisniewski TKM: The role of blood pressure control in preventing complications of hypertension. *Lancet* 1964; 1:235–238.
3. Wolff FW, Lindeman RD: Effects of treatment on hypertension: results of a controlled study. *J Chronic Dis* 1966; 19:227–240.
4. Veterans Administration Cooperative Study Group on Antihypertensive Agents: Effects of treatment on morbidity in hypertension. Results in patients with diastolic blood pressures averaging 115 through 129 mm Hg. *JAMA* 1967; 202:1028–1034.
5. Veterans Administration Cooperative Study Group on Antihypertensive Agents: Effects of treatment on morbidity in hypertension. II Results in patients with diastolic blood pressure averaging 90 through 114 mm Hg. *JAMA* 1970; 213:1143–1152.
6. Smith W. Treatment of mild hypertension: results of a ten-year intervention trial. *Circ Res* 1977; 40(suppl 1):98–105.
7. Report by the Management Committee: The Australian therapeutic trial in mild hypertension. *Lancet* 1980; 1:1261–1267.
8. Helgeland A: Treatment of mild hypertension. A five-year controlled drug trial: The Oslo Study. *Am J Med* 1980; 69:725–732.
9. Hypertension Detection and Follow-up Program Cooperative Group: Five-year findings of the Hypertension Detection and Follow-up Program. I. Reduction in mortality of persons with high blood pressure, including mild hypertension. *JAMA* 1979; 242:2562–2571.
10. Hypertension Detection and Follow-up Program Cooperative Group: Five-year findings of the Hypertension Detection and Follow-up Program. II. Mortality by race, sex, and age. *JAMA* 1979; 242:2572–2577.

CHAPTER 6

USING NONDRUG TREATMENTS FOR ESSENTIAL HYPERTENSION

WHEN one thinks of treatment in hypertension, drug therapy usually comes to mind. There are, however, several approaches involving changes in diet and lifestyle that may prove to be effective in lowering blood pressure without resorting to drugs. Unfortunately, there are no good scientific studies to indicate whether such treatment prolongs life or prevents the complications of high blood pressure. Such studies simply have not been done. Nevertheless, studies *have* shown that these measures may normalize blood pressure in some people particularly if hypertension is early and mild. Even if they do not lower the pressure to normal, less medication may be required to achieve successful reduction when the two forms of treatment are combined. Since less medication for control may mean less drug side effects, and since treatment for hypertension is lifelong, such a combination is desirable in almost every patient.

LOW-SODIUM DIET

Dating back to 1850, repeated observations throughout the western world indicated that reducing the amount of salt consumed led to lowering of blood pressure in hypertensive individuals. Salt was and continues to be the greatest contributor to sodium in our diet. As early as 1922, it was shown that some patients benefited from a salt-restricted diet. In 1944, Kempner reported[1,2] that his markedly low-sodium rice-fruit diet brought about improvement in 66 percent of his patients with malignant hypertension and normalized the blood pressure in about 25 percent of patients with essential hypertension. This report kindled great interest in exploring the link between salt (sodium) and essential hypertension. A number of apparent studies followed.

It was found that populations whose diets were extremely low in salt intake had very little hypertension. In these populations, blood pressure did not rise with advancing age. Conversely, in Akita prefecture in Japan, the diet contained a great amount of sodium and the prevalence of high blood pressure and stroke was quite high. In Newfoundland, the inhabitants of coastal villages whose diet was high in sodium (salt fish is a major staple) were found to have a significantly higher prevalence of hypertension then those who lived inland and consumed much less sodium.

Although the vigorous restriction of dietary sodium (for example, by the Kempner rice-fruit diet) did lower blood pressure in some patients with hypertension, such a fare is unpalatable, lacks essential nutrients, and is not practical for lifelong treatment. More recently, prospective and controlled

Table 6.1
Converting Grams of Salt to mEq Sodium

1 milliequivalent (mEq) sodium	=	23 milligrams (mg) sodium
43 mEq sodium	=	1000 mg (1 gram) sodium
salt (Nacl)	=	40% sodium
1 gram salt	=	400 mg or 17 mEq sodium

studies have shown that more palatable diets with a relatively modest decrease in sodium to 60 to 80 milliequivalents per day (mEq/day) lower blood pressure by 8 to 10 mm Hg in some patients. Parenthetically, dietary sodium of Americans ranges from 170 to 225 mEq/day. Table 6.1 shows how grams of sodium may be converted to milliequivalents.

Only about 40 percent of patients with essential hypertension respond to salt (sodium) restriction.[3] It is also true that even among higher prevalence of hypertension related to dietary sodium intake, many people remain normotensive. When humans with hypertension are purposely given high dosages of salt (salt-loading),[3] only some respond with a significant rise in pressure. The responders, the "salt-sensitive" group, retain more sodium, gain more weight, and have increased cardiac output. The "salt-resistant" group shows only minor alterations. In some salt-resistant persons, hypertension is actually aggravated by sodium restriction.[4] Perhaps they respond with vigorous activity of the renin-angiotensin-aldosterone axis and/or of the sympathetic nervous system when plasma volume is reduced by sodium depletion.[5] (See Chapter 2.)

It is reasonable to suppose that genetically susceptible "salt-sensitive" humans become hypertensive if their intake of sodium (salt) is moderately high. If their lifelong consumption of sodium is low, they may remain normotensive despite their predetermined risk. On the other hand, genetically "salt-resistant" humans may continue high-salt diets for long periods without becoming hypertensive. Such is the course of events in salt-sensitive and salt-resistant rats in the laboratory.

A high percentage of people with hypertension are "salt sensitive." Even hypertensives who are not salt sensitive will require less medication to control their blood pressure if sodium intake is restricted. Moreover the vast majority of people in the United States eat much more sodium than they will ever need. For these reasons, it is reasonable to use a low-salt diet (Table 6.2) as part of the therapeutic strategy in treating essential hypertension. The use of salt substitutes for those who find it difficult to follow a low-salt regimen is discussed in Chapter 8 in relation to use of diuretics.

TABLE 6.2
Recommended Low-Salt Diet for Patients with Essential Hypertension

- Use no salt in cooking
- Add no salt at the table
- Avoid processed meats (ham, sausage, luncheon meats, etc.)
- Avoid processed (canned) vegetables and soups
- Avoid cheese
- Avoid salad dressings, catsup, mustard
- Avoid pickles, pretzels, potato chips, and other salted foods
- Use salt-free crackers or bread
- Keep total salt consumption to 4 grams of salt (70 mEq sodium) or less per day

WEIGHT REDUCTION

In the Framingham study where 5,127 men and women were followed longitudinally, relationships between obesity and level of blood pressure were noted and reported after 12 years.[6] During the initial evaluation, hypertension was found more commonly in the obese, and the greater the degree of overweight, the higher the prevalence. During the 12-year observation period, it was noted that those who had normal blood-pressure levels but who were obese at the beginning developed hypertension more frequently over the years. Those who had normal pressure and were not obese at the start showed a rising trend in average blood pressure during this time if they gained more weight than their cohorts of the same height. Since then, other studies have confirmed the conclusion: "The higher the weight beyond the standard, the more likely the blood pressure will be higher."

Studies addressing the effect of weight reduction on elevated blood pressure generally indicate that patients who lose weight show a significant decrease in pressure when compared to those who do not lose weight.[7] Note that weight loss all the way down to recommended levels is not necessary before significant drops in blood pressure occur. Moderate loss such as 5 to 6 percent of the initial body weight may be very effective.[8]

Some physicians have raised the question of whether it is a reduction in sodium intake or even a reduced-calorie diet that is really responsible for lowered blood pressure in patients who lose weight. In Israel, 81 hypertensive subjects were studied.[9] They were placed on a weight-reduction diet for four months. To rule out sodium effect, the diets were restricted in calories, but high sodium foods were included so that the subjects' sodium intake was not significantly decreased. The patients lost an average of 21 pounds in weight, and blood-pressure drop averaged 30 mm Hg systolic and 20 mm Hg diastolic. In another study,[10] a group of middle-aged men who were hypertensive and moderately obese were placed in one of three diet groups: a sodium-restricted diet, a weight-reduction diet, and a combination of the two. Each resulted in modest blood-pressure reduction, but the combination of the two was the most effective.

We do not yet understand the mechanism by which obesity may contribute to the development of hypertension. Basically, the physiologic changes that occur with excess body weight include cardiovascular, endocrine, and metabolic alterations, some of which may be implicated in the development of hypertension. Obesity is accompanied by increased sodium retention, increased blood volume, and increased cardiac output. Insulin production rises, but carbohydrate metabolism is disturbed because the cells become resistant to insulin. There is increased sympathetic activity, possibly due in part to the increased insulin. Nevertheless, not all obese individuals develop high blood pressure. Perhaps in those who are genetically predisposed, obesity serves as a triggering factor. With weight reduction, all of these physiologic changes revert toward normal, and in some, elevated blood pressure normalizes or improves.

EXERCISE

When blood-pressure responses to physical conditioning programs are evaluated in young active men with normal blood pressures, very minor changes are found. In one study,[11] however, 42 normotensive but sedentary men with a mean age of 40 years were placed on a two-month vigorous physical training program. At the end, diastolic pressure was reduced significantly. In another program,[12] 66 men with a mean age of 69.5 years, all of whom had normal blood pressures at the start, were evaluated after six weeks of a physical conditioning period. Resting systolic and diastolic pressures were both lowered. Boyer and Kasch[13] observed blood pressure responses of 45 middle-aged men to a walk-jog twice-weekly program. Twenty-two of the subjects had normal blood pressure levels at the start, and 23 suffered mild to moderate essential hypertension (mean diastolic pressure of 105 mm Hg). After six months, there was a 12 mm Hg drop in resting diastolic pressure of the hypertensive group and a mean drop of 6 mm Hg in the normal men. In Canada, 165 middle-aged men, 37 of whom had mild hypertension and the remainder of whom were normotensive, were placed in a physical training program consisting primarily of calisthenics, walk-jog, and volleyball.[14] After six months, there was a mean drop in resting systolic pressure of 15 mm Hg and diastolic pressure of 8 mm Hg in those with mild hypertension. Once again, in normotensives there was a lesser lowering of 4 and 2 mm Hg respectively.

These plus other similar studies in patients with mild hypertension indicate that physical conditioning in the sedentary hypertensive may achieve a modest reduction of blood pressure. These clinical experiments, however, consist of relatively small numbers of subjects. Followup observations have been of short duration. Nevertheless, unless the patient's condition contraindicates exercise, a carefully developed physical conditioning program is a rational part of a therapeutic regimen for individuals with mild hypertension. A word of caution, however. The exercise programs that have been described above are all *isotonic* (aerobic) exercises such as walking, jogging, bicycling, volleyball, or swimming. *Isometric* (nonaerobic) exercises such as weight-lifting or other forms of physical activity that require pushing or pulling against resistance may be harmful. During such activity, significant elevation of both systolic and diastolic pressure may occur. This response occurs in those with normal blood pressure levels, and it is particularly marked in those with hypertension.[15]

REDUCING OR ELIMINATING ALCOHOL CONSUMPTION

In 1967, the report of the Los Angeles Heart Study revealed significant differences in mean blood pressure levels between nondrinkers of alcohol, those who consumed alcoholic beverages less than three times weekly, and those who drank three or more times weekly. Since then, a number of studies from the United States, United Kingdom, Sweden, and Australia have all indicated a link between alcohol consumption and hypertension. These population studies indicate that the higher the range of long-term alcohol consumption, the higher the prevalence of hypertension.

In 922 workers who were "problem drinkers," the prevalence of hypertension was 2.3 times greater than that in controls.[16] In the Framingham studies,[17] the prevalence of hypertension was found to be twice as great in those who drank 60 ounces of ethyl alcohol per month when compared to those who consumed less than 30 ounces. Table 6.3 shows the alcohol content of beer, wine, and hard liquor (spirits). In Sweden, 70 pairs of male twins, in which one of the brothers drank substantially greater amounts of alcohol than the other, were studied.[18] The heavier drinkers were found to have substantially higher blood pressure than their siblings.

Finally, in studying 132 hypertensive patients who habitually drank more than 80 grams of alcohol daily,[19] a long-term sustained reduction in blood pressure following abstinence from alcohol was noted. Conventional antihypertensive drug

TABLE 6.3
Common Beverage Equivalents of 30 ml of Ethyl Alcohol

Beer (regular)	: 2½ 12 oz cans or bottles
Table wine	: 8 oz
Spirits (80 proof)	: 2½ oz
Ethyl alcohol	: 28 grams of ethyl alcohol

therapy in such patients while they continue to imbibe usually fails. Similar reversibility of hypertension has been reported by others after cessation of alcohol ingestion.[20]

REDUCING OR ELIMINATING TOBACCO SMOKING

Independent of hypertension, tobacco smoking (cigarettes in particular) is a major factor for prematurely developing atherosclerosis of the arteries supplying the heart and brain. Smoking ravages the arterial system much as high blood pressure does, and the combination of the two leads to a more rapid and more severe progression of this process.

Nicotine stimulates increased release of norepinephrine, and in one study, smoking two cigarettes caused a transient rise of blood pressure of 10/8 mm Hg for about 15 minutes. Research suggests that chronic cigarette smokers may develop a tolerance, however, so that any rise in blood pressure due to nicotine is minimal.

Although no cause-and-effect relationship between smoking and the development of essential hypertension has been established, it is important for patients with high blood pressure to abstain from smoking or drastically cut down their cigarette consumption. Since a major goal of controlling hypertension is to prevent target organ involvement (heart attack, stroke), it seems foolish not to eliminate other powerful factors leading to these undesired results.

DIETARY SUPPLEMENTS

There are recently emerging suggestions that dietary supplements of either potassium or calcium may each help reduce blood pressure in some patients with mild hypertension. Much more information and confirmation must be obtained before such approaches can be considered except as topics for research. However, studies in humans with hypertension are providing a growing body of work suggesting a modest decline in blood pressure brought on by potassium dietary supplementation.[21,22]

More recently, a role for dietary calcium deficiency in the development of hypertension in some humans has been suggested. During the past two decades, in both the United States and in the United Kingdom, observations have suggested a lower mortality rate from cardiovascular disorders of all causes (including hypertension) in areas where water was hard. Calcium is the major element in determining water hardness.

In a study of newly diagnosed untreated patients with hypertension, daily calcium intake was determined using a 24-hour dietary recall technique.[23] These patients were found to ingest 22 percent less calcium per day than individuals with normal pressure. Others[24] have found that supplementing the usual diet with 1 gram of elemental calcium daily produced a reduction in diastolic pressure in young, healthy normotensive subjects. Needless to say, intervention experiments with calcium supplementation in hypertensives is continuing.

REFERENCES: CHAPTER 6

1. Kempner W: Treatment of kidney disease and hypertensive vascular disease with rice diet. *N C Med J* 1944; 5:125–133.

2. Kempner W: Treatment of hypertensive vascular disease with rice diet. *Am J Med* 1948; 4:545–577.

3. Kawasaki T, Delea CS, Bartter FC, et al.: The effect of high-sodium and low-sodium intakes on blood pressure and other related variables in human subjects with idiopathic hypertension. *Am J Med* 1978; 64:193–198.

4. Longworth DK, Drayer JIM, Weber MA, et al.: Divergent blood pressure responses during short-term sodium restriction in hypertension. *Clin Pharmacol Ther* 1980; 27:544–546.

5. Luft FC, Rankin LI, Henry DP, et al.: Plasma and urinary norepinephrine values at extremes of sodium intake in normal man. *Hypertension* 1979; 1:261–266.

6. Kannel, WB, Brand N, Skinner JJ: The relation of adiposity to blood pressure and development of hypertension— the Framingham Study. *Ann Intern Med* 1967; 67:48–59.

7. Hovell MF: The experimental evidence for weight-loss treatment of essential hypertension: A critical review. *Am J Public Health* 1982; 72:359–368.

8. Stamler J, Farinaro E, Monjonnier LM, et al.: Prevention and control of hypertension by nutritional-hygienic means. Long-term experience of the Chicago Coronary Prevention Evaluation Program. *JAMA* 1980; 243:1819–1823.

9. Reisen E, Abel R, Modan M, et al.: Effect of weight loss without salt restriction on the reduction of blood pressure in overweight hypertensive patients. *N Engl J Med* 1978; 298:1–6.

10. Gillum R, Prineas R, Elmer P, et al.: Independent effects of modest sodium restriction and weight reduction on blood pressure, abstracted. *Circulation* 1981; 64(suppl 4):322.

11. Kilbom A, Hartley LH, Saltin B, et al.: Physical training in sedentary middle-aged and older men. I. Medical Evaluation. *Scand J Clin Lab Invest* 1969; 24:315–322.

12. DeVries HA: Physiological effects of an exercise training regimen upon men aged 52 to 88. *J Gerontol* 1970; 25:325–336.

13. Boyer JL, Kasch FW: Exercise therapy in hypertensive men. *JAMA* 1970; 211:1668–1671.

14. Choquette G, Ferguson RJ: Blood pressure reduction in "borderline" hypertensives following physical training. *Can Med Assoc J* 1973; 108:699–703.

15. Ewing DJ, Irving JB, Kerr F, et al.: Static exercise in untreated systemic hypertension. *Br Heart J* 1973; 35:413–421.

16. D'Alonzo CA, Pell S: Cardiovascular disease among problem drinkers. *J Occup Med* 1968; 10:344–350.

17. Kannel WB, Sorlie P: Hypertension in Framingham, in Paul, O (ed): *Epidemiology and Control of Hypertension*. New York, Stratton Intercontinental Medical Book Corp, 1974, pp 553–592.

18. Myrhed M: Alcohol consumption in relation to factors associated with ischemic heart disease. *Acta Med Scand* 1974; 567 (suppl):40–46.

19. Saunders JB, Beevers DG, Paton A, et al.: Alcohol intake and hypertension. *Lancet* 1981; 2:653–656.

20. Peterson LD: Letter to the editor. *N Engl J Med* 1977; 297:451.

21. Parfrey PS, Wright P, Goodwin FJ, et al.: Blood pressure and hormonal changes following alteration in dietary sodium and potassium in mild essential hypertension. *Lancet* 1981; 1:59–63.

22. MacGregor GA, Smith SJ, Markander MD, et al.: Moderate potassium supplementation in essential hypertension. *Lancet* 1982; 2:567–570.

23. McCarron DA, Morris CD, Cole C: Dietary calcium in human hypertension. *Science* 1982; 217:267–269.

24. Belizan JM, Villar J, Pineda O, et al.: Reduction of blood pressure with calcium supplementation in young adults. *JAMA* 1983; 249:1161–1165.

CHAPTER 7

PLANNING A DRUG-TREATMENT REGIMEN

BEFORE beginning any form of therapy for essential hypertension, your physician will help you understand the damage the disease can do even though you have no symptoms, the need for lifelong treatment, and the desirability of reducing blood pressure gradually rather than abruptly. The physician will emphasize the fact that you must be an active participant in any treatment that is planned for you. A considerable part of the responsibility for a successful outcome will be yours.

The initial goal of the therapeutic program is to achieve and maintain diastolic pressure at a level less than 90 mm Hg, provided this level can be reached safely, and without significant side effects. If hypertension is severe, this degree of control may not attainable. Remember that lowering blood pressure even partially, to diastolic levels of 90 to 100 mm Hg, will be beneficial to you. This chapter provides an overall survey of the pharmacologic (drug) treatment options available. Each of these alternatives is then discussed in detail in the following chapters.

Treatment does not always imply antihypertensive drug

therapy in all instances, particularly in mild hypertension. Your physician may begin with nonpharmacologic measures as described in Chapter 6. If blood pressure drops to normal levels and is maintained there, these measures will be continued while the physician carefully monitors your progress. Remember, however, that such desirable results are relatively rare, except with the milder degrees of essential hypertension. In more severe cases, nondrug therapy is an effective supplement to the use of antihypertensive drugs. The desired effects can be achieved with lower doses of these agents, and therefore fewer undesirable side effects will appear.

When drugs are required in the treatment of hypertension, logic would guide us to use those agents that would correct whatever hemodynamic abnormality has produced the elevated blood pressure. As you have learned, the hemodynamic profile in the majority of patients with established, sustained essential hypertension is one of a normal cardiac output and an abnormally elevated total peripheral resistance (Chapter 2). The mechanisms that bring this state about vary in individuals, but there are vasodilator drugs that relax arteriolar smooth muscle and reduce its resistance, no matter what the underlying mechanism. Unfortunately, these agents alone are relatively ineffective in long-term treatment, although they do produce an initial drop in peripheral resistance. This drop in pressure stimulates body compensatory mechanisms that tend to counteract some of the pharmacologic effect of the vasodilator (Table 7.1).

Among the first responses to lowering of the arterial blood pressure below its "setpoint" is the *baroreceptor reflex*. It is the best understood of the body's compensatory mechanisms, and ordinarily it functions to control transient changes, up or down, in blood pressure. Sensory pressor receptors exist in the walls of the internal carotid arteries which supply blood to the brain and also in the arch of the aorta. With a rise in pressure and arterial distention beyond the body's "setpoint" (which is at a higher than normal level in hypertensives), these stretch receptors are activated to send impulses to pressure centers in the brain. They, in turn, inhibit sympathetic activity to the peripheral autonom-

TABLE 7.1
Normal Compensatory Mechanisms That Maintain Blood Pressure at Setpoint Level

Baroreceptor reflexes:
- Increase cardiac output by:
    Raising heart rate
    Increasing force of myocardial contraction
- Increase peripheral resistance by means of sympathetic vasopressor effect

Direct intrarenal mechanism: Sodium and water retention

RAA axis:
- Increases peripheral resistance due to angiotensin vasopressor effect
- Increases sodium and water retention due to aldosterone effect

---

ic nervous sytem so that the heart rate slows, the ventricles of the heart contract less forcibly, and the peripheral arteriolar and venous beds dilate. As a consequence of the decreased cardiac output and a drop in preload and in peripheral resistance (afterload), blood pressure is reduced.

On the other hand, if blood pressure should fall below the "setpoint" for a given individual, whether he be normotensive or hypertensive, even if the drop is purposely achieved by therapeutic vasodilator drugs, the converse sequence of events follows. Impulses from the stretch receptors diminish. Sympathetic activity increases. Heart rate, cardiac contraction, and cardiac output increase, the arterioles constrict, and peripheral resistance rises. This chain of events can diminish the blood pressure–lowering the effect of the vasodilating agent by as much as 75 percent.

The lowering of blood pressure, even with a therapeutic intent, may result in a decline of the glomerular filtration rate of the kidneys. Consequently, tubular reabsorption of sodium increases and, therefore, water retention as well. Many patients with essential hypertension excrete sodium "normally" only if the blood pressure is elevated (Chapter 2). When a vasodilating drug lowers blood pressure in such a patient, the kidneys retain sodium and water until the pressure returns to its previous level. This mechanism also blocks the effectiveness of the drug. It should be noted that these events, up to this point, do not involve the activation of the renin-angiotensin-aldosterone (RAA) axis.

Finally, if the blood pressure is lowered to a point where there is a drop in perfusion pressure to the glomerular afferent arterioles, the RAA axis constricts the blood vessels, causes the kidneys to retain more sodium and water, and expands the volume of tissue fluid and plasma. These compensatory mechanisms also act to render vasodilator therapy ineffective eventually.

It is obvious, then, that if the therapeutic programs are aimed at dilating the arterioles and lowering total peripheral resistance, the normal compensatory mechanism of the body must be held in check. If a diuretic is used to enhance sodium and water excretion, and a sympathetic inhibitor is added to dampen the baroreceptor reflex, then the vasodilator is free to perform its desirable pharmacologic function at relatively low dosages which are less likely to be accompanied by adverse effects. The combination of a diuretic, a sympathetic inhibitor, and a vasodilator can correct all degrees of hypertension that result from an elevated peripheral resistance. The two agents that are called upon to "run interference" for the vasodilator have antihypertensive capabilities of their own. If just one or the combination of the first two agents is effective, why add the vasodilator? The sequence may be tailored at one, two, or three steps, depending upon the patient's response.

THE STEPPED-CARE APPROACH

Up to 40 percent of patients with essential hypertension benefit significantly from diuretic therapy, and diuretic administration combined with any of the nondiuretic antihypertensive drugs prevents sodium retention and "pseudoresistance." Therefore, diuretics are widely used as initial treatment (step 1). Patients most likely to respond to diuretics alone include those with low-renin essential hypertension, older patients, and blacks.

If a desirable response is not attained in 8 to 12 weeks, a sympathetic inhibiting drug may be added to the diuretic (step 2). The starting dosage should be a low, safe one with gradual, incremental upward increasing of dosages until the desired blood pressure response has been obtained or adverse side effects appear. For most of these agents, there is a maximum dosage beyond which little additional antihypertensive benefit may be expected. Administering higher dosages merely increases the frequency and severity of side effects. The sympathetic inhibitor group is made up of various drugs (Table 7.2), many of which have different mechanisms of action, different side effects and toxic manifestations, and varying costs. In deciding which sympathetic

TABLE 7.2
Sympathetic Inhibitor Drugs
(Proprietary names in parentheses)

Central and peripheral catecholamine-depleting agents
- Reserpine
- Other rauwolfia alkaloids

Central alpha-adrenergic agonists
- Methyldopa (Aldomet)
- Clonidine (Catapres)
- Guanabenz (Mytensin)

Beta-adrenergic receptor blockers
- Propranolol (Inderal)
- Nadolol (Corgard)
- Metoprolol (Lopressor)
- Atenolol (Tenormin)
- Timolol (Blocadren)
- Pindolol (Visken)
- Acebutolol (Sectral)

Postsynaptic alpha-adrenergic blocker
- Prazosin (Minipres)

Combined alpha- and beta-receptor blockers
- Labetalol (Normodyne, Trandate)

Postganglionic sympathetic inhibitors (peripheral catecholamine depletors)
- Guanethidine (Ismelin)
- Guanadrel (Hylorel)

inhibitor to use, the physician considers all these factors.

In addition, the physician must consider the patient's state of health, the presence of other unrelated disorders, the patient's age and tolerance of the drug, and the physician's experience with and understanding of the agent. The physician may switch from one agent to another, if necessary, to tailor the specific regimen to the individual patient. Approximately 80 to 88 percent of those with mild to moderate essential hypertension may respond satisfactorily to a diuretic or to a combined diuretic–sympathetic inhibitor program. Finally, if an inadequate response to such a combination persists, the next step is the addition of a vasodilator (step 3). This stepped-care approach has been the strategy used in most of the clinical intervention trials to help determine the effectiveness of antihypertensive treatment.

SINGLE-DRUG THERAPY (MONOTHERAPY)

The need for multiple drugs in a therapeutic program undeniably tends to discourage compliance even though the patient's intentions and motivation are good. In addition, the more medications an individual takes, particularly at the higher dosage levels, the more likelihood of drug interactions or adverse effects. The administration of a diuretic as the first step in the stepped-care approach does normalize blood pressure in 20 to 40 percent of patients. Therefore, diuretic therapy provides a program of *monotherapy* (single-drug therapy) for a sizable portion of the hypertensive population. This group primarily includes patients with mild to moderate essential hypertension who are salt sensitive, are more likely to be black, tend to be older, and to a great extent are in the low-renin essential hypertension group.

Use of the sympathetic inhibitors reserpine, methyldopa, and guanethidine (step-2 drugs) for initial treatment was disappointing because of "psuedotolerance" to the drugs produced by the compensatory fluid retention. More recently, however, some of the newer sympathetic inhibitors have been successful as alternative drugs for monotherapy in some instances.

Beta-Blockers as Initial Therapy

When beta-adrenergic receptor blockers became available, physicians observed that when this type of sympathetic inhibitor was used alone in the treatment of essential hypertension, little or no sodium and water were retained, and only slight plasma-volume expansion occurred. These agents have the capability of blocking the baroreceptor reflex and also of inhibiting renin release. Studies indicate that some fluid retention may occur when these drugs are given for long periods. Often the amount of fluid retained is not sufficient to significantly alter the beta-blocker's mild antihypertensive effectiveness, particularly if the patient has mild hypertension. Usually, however, a lesser dose of the beta-blocker is needed for control if a diuretic is included in the regimen as well.

Beta-adrenergic blockers lower blood pressure most effectively in patients with high cardiac output. Such a state occurs most frequently in young adults with borderline or early hypertension. These patients also tend to have increased resting heart rates and high plasma renin activity. In those with established hypertension, the younger (less than 50 years of age), nonblack hypertensives also respond well to initial therapy with beta-adrenergic blockers. If so, such undesirable side effects of diuretic therapy as hypokalemia (potassium insufficiency) are avoided. If a patient's blood pressure is not sufficiently lowered or if the patient begins to develop apparent resistance to the beta-blocker after initially good results, a diuretic should be added. For the first time, in the 1984 report of the Joint National Committee on Detection, Evaluation, and Treatment of High Blood Pressure, the statement is made: "Beta-blockers may be favored as initial therapy in younger patients (less than 50 years), especially those with a rapid resting pulse rate and wide pulse pressure, and in patients with ischemic heart disease."[1]

Postsynaptic Alpha-Receptor Blockers as Initial Therapy

As described earlier (Chapter 2), sympathetic impulses proceeding from the brain to the responsive receptors throughout the body are transmitted through the autonomic nervous system by way of the sympathetic nerves. These nerves nearly touch the adrenoreceptors in various cells in the tissues and organs of the body. At this junction of nerve ending and receptor (the *synapse*) the impulse reaches the receptor by means of a chemical called a *neurotransmitter*. The nerve ending releases the neurotransmitter (the catecholamine norepinephrine), which occupies the adrenoreceptors and stimulates them to bring about the response of the individual cells. There are two types of alpha-adrenoreceptors: (1) *alpha-1 receptors* located after the synapse (postsynaptically) in smooth muscle cells (fibers) of blood vessels which stimulate contraction of the fibers and constriction of the vessels; and (2) *alpha-2 receptors* which are located before the synapse (presynaptically) in the sympathetic nerve endings. When they are stimulated by norepinephrine, they bring about inhibition of further norepinephrine release from the sympathetic nerve endings.

Prazosin (Minipres) The drug prazosin is a postsynaptic alpha-1 adrenoreceptor blocking agent. It acts by interfering with stimulation for arteriolar vasoconstriction, bringing about a decrease in total peripheral resistance and a drop in blood pressure. The presynaptic alpha-2 receptors are not blocked, further release of norepinephrine is impeded, and the baroreceptor reflex as well as release of renin, which are dependent on beta-receptors being stimulated by norepinephrine, are minimized despite the drop in blood pressure.

Although the renin-angiotensin-aldosterone mechanism may not be brought into play fully, the lowering of blood pressure, particularly if it is more than a modest drop, still initiates a mechanism for sodium and water renention. If the blood pressure is lowered to a point where there is a drop in glomerular filtration rate, there is increased sodium reabsorption in the proximal kidney tubule completely independently of the RAA axis. In the long run, a degree of plasma volume expansion may occur solely as the result of this compensatory mechanism. Since not all patients will develop sufficient plasma volume expansion to counteract the antihypertensive effect of the drug, however, it may be used as initial therapy and, depending upon the patient's response, it may be adequate for monotherapy.

In a long-term clinical trial, Bradley[2] initiated therapy with prazosin alone in 26 patients with mild to moderate essential hypertension. In 12 of these patients the drug was inadequately effective from the beginning. A diuretic was added, and distinct improvement resulted. At the end of 42 months, on the combination of prazosin and the diuretic, 10 of the 12 patients still had diastolic pressures of less than 90 mm Hg. In the 14 remaining subjects, prazosin alone brought about normalization of blood pressure; for these patients, monotherapy was continued. At the end of 42 months, 7 of the 14 continued to have diastolic pressures of less than 90 mm Hg.

Centrally Acting Alpha-Receptor Agonists (Stimulators)

Experiments have shown that stimulation of several areas in the brain raises or lowers blood pressure (Chapter 2). Blood pressure–raising impulses from the central nervous system (CNS) are transmitted through the autonomic nervous system network and affect the heart and the blood vessels through release of norepinephrine. Drugs that stimulate alpha-2 adrenoreceptors found within the brain reduce sympathetic outflow to the peripheral autonomic system and diminish stimulation of this system. A reduction in blood pressure follows. There is considerable experience with these agents as step-2 drugs, but some success has also been obtained when they are chosen for initial therapy in patients with mild to moderate essential hypertension.

Clonidine (Catapres) One of the central alpha-receptor agonists available in the United States is clonidine. As an inhibitor of sympathetic outflow to the periphery, it lowers peripheral resistance and blood pressure, but also it suppresses renin release to a degree and blunts the baroreceptor reflex. As with the other sympathetic inhibitors, if the drop in blood pressure is sufficient to lower the glomerular filtration rate, the proximal kidney tubules reabsorb a greater amount of sodium than usual. Consequently, some degree of water retention, plasma volume expansion, and increase in cardiac output reduce the drug's antihypertensive effect. This action is dependent on the magnitude of blood pressure lowering.

For one year, Onesti[3] followed 115 patients who had responded well to clonidine initially. At the end of the observation period, good response persisted in 16 percent and modest response in 36 percent, but in 58 percent, little or no response remained even though clonidine had been continued as monotherapy.

Guanabenz (Wytensin). Another centrally acting alpha-receptor agonist guanabenz, has become available in the United States more recently than clonidine. In several studies it appeared to be effective as a sole antihypertensive agent with little blunting of its effect in a larger proportion of patients. In patients with moderate to severe hypertension, however, diuretics often had to be added to the regimen to gain satisfactory control of the blood pressure level. There is a suggestion, therefore, that this drug may be superior to the other centrally acting alpha-receptor agonists for monotherapy. More experience and comparisons are needed.

Angiotensin-Converting Enzyme Inhibitors

Another class of drugs acts by inhibiting the action of certain enzymes in the RAA cycle. Captopril (Capoten) has been used with some success as an initial agent in the treatment of essential hypertension. It has been effective as a monotherapeutic agent in patients with high plasma renin activity whose blood pressure elevation was in the mild and moderate ranges. If it fails to maintain control in the long run, the addition of a diuretic enhances its effectiveness considerably.

As you can see, the choice of a drug-therapy regimen to control hypertension in any given person is a complex one. The physician must consider many factors before prescribing any drug initially and must then monitor the patient's response carefully over time. A single drug may be used at the start—in combination with the non drug measures discussed in the previous chapter. The drug may be changed, or others may be added as a single drug is found to be inadequate or if its effect becomes blunted by natural body responses. In the chapters that follow, various kinds of drug therapy regimens are described in more detail.

REFERENCES: CHAPTER 7

1. The 1984 Report of the Joint National Committee on Detection, Evaluation, and Treatment of High Blood Pressure. *Arch Intern Med* 1984; 144: 1045–1057.
2. Bradley WF: A long-term clinical trial of prazosin. *Postgrad Med* 1974; 56(suppl Nov):95–101.
3. Onesti G, Bock KD, Heimsoth V, et al.: Clonidine, a new antihypertensive agent. *Am J Cardiol* 1971; 28:74–83.

CHAPTER 8

DIURETICS

AS already mentioned (Chapter 6), physicians have long been aware of a relationship between blood pressure level and the amount of salt (sodium) in the diet. They also learned that about 40 percent of patients with essential hypertension would tend to normalize their pressures if they adopted a diet severely restricted in sodium. Not all patients with essential hypertension respond this way, however. Nearly *two-thirds* do not. It now appears that only people with genetically predisposed salt sensitivity benefit from sodium restriction. Nevertheless, salt-sensitive individuals are a considerable proportion of hypertensive patients, so management of sodium intake is potentially a major therapeutic approach. Most Americans, accustomed to a high level of salt in their food, find it very difficult to tolerate a diet that is sufficiently low in salt to be effective in lowering blood pressure. No matter how well motivated and cooperative they may be, drastic lifelong salt restriction is not a practical option for most patients. The challenge, then, is to find a therapeutic agent that counteracts the effects of sodium consumption by promoting excretion of sodium and water by the kidneys: in other words, a diuretic.

To be practical for long-term treatment, the drug had to be available in a form that could be taken orally (by mouth) over long periods without dangerous side effects.

In 1956 the diuretic chlorothiazide became available. Earlier therapeutic experiences with restricted-sodium diets led investigators to use this agent in hypertensive patients. It lowered blood pressure in about 40 percent of patients with essential hypertension. Even in those who did not respond to diuretic therapy alone, chlorothiazide enhanced the effectiveness of other antihypertensive drugs so that lower dosages were needed to produce the desired results. Diuretics and low-sodium diets produce similar responses through the same mechanisms.

When diuretic therapy is initiated, more sodium and water are excreted in the urine. As a consequence, total body sodium and total body water are reduced. Water is lost from both the intravascular compartment (blood plasma) and the extravascular compartment (water in the tissues). As plasma volume drops, cardiac output falls. Recall that blood pressure is the product of cardiac output and total peripheral resistance (TPR); thus, a reduction in cardiac output leads to prompt lowering of blood pressure. Although the baroreceptor reflex comes into play, it usually is not able to cancel the effect of the decreased plasma volume and decreased cardiac output. Maximum excretion (diuresis) occurs on the first day of therapy, and then the amount of urine excreted daily gradually returns to pretreatment levels by the third or fourth day despite daily diuretic administration. During diuresis approximately one to two liters of accumulated body fluid are lost, and the patient loses several pounds of body weight ("water weight"). This loss in weight is maintained but not increased if diuretic therapy continues. If diuretics are discontinued, the lost weight is immediately regained.

At the end of the first week of continuous therapy, fluid gradually moves from the tissues to the plasma. Plasma volume and cardiac output tend to return to normal. The patients who continue to show a lower blood pressure even though cardiac output has been restored (40 percent), do so because a significant drop in total peripheral resistance has occurred.

Why should this reduction in peripheral resistance occur? The complete explanation is still not clear. One possibility relates to sodium: calcium balance. It is known that long-term diuretic therapy does diminish vasoconstrictor response to norepinephrine in laboratory animals. There is evidence also to suggest that as body stores of sodium increase, the sympathetic nerve endings release more norepinephrine; conversely, as sodium stores diminish, less norepinephrine is released. Researchers have found that the red and white blood cells of some patients with essential hypertension contain abnormally high levels of sodium (increased intracellular sodium concentrations). There are indications that a defect in cellular transport of sodium may be involved. If sodium levels in the smooth muscles of the arterioles are increased, intracellular calcium levels also increase. Higher levels of calcium induce increased smooth muscle contractility, increased arteriolar tone, arteriolar constriction, elevation of TPR, and increased levels of blood pressure. It is possible that by causing sodium to be excreted from the body, diuretic therapy leads to a gradual decline in intracellular sodium (and therefore in intracellular calcium) within the smooth muscles of the arteriolar walls. Relaxation of these muscles would follow. Peripheral resistance and blood pressure would drop.

DIURETIC AGENTS

Any number of effective oral diuretic agents are currently available (Table 8.1). Most are derivatives of or related to sulfonamide, one of the first antibacterial drugs. In appropriate doses, each has been successful in lowering blood pressure. Minor side effects are common, but major problems are rare. Nevertheless, the physician will be alert for signs of toxicity or for unusual reactions such as skin eruptions, depression of bone marrow function, and inflammatory reactions of blood vessels. Metabolic effects are far more common. These include elevation of serum uric acid, blood urea nitrogen, serum creatinine, serum calcium, and serum glucose, plus the lowering of serum potassium. Recently,

TABLE 8.1
Sulfonamide-Derivative Diuretics

Benzothiadiazine compounds—the thiazides
- Chlorothiazide (Diuril)
- Hydrochlorothiazide (Hydrodiuril, Esidrex, Oretic)
- Bendroflumethiazide (Naturetin)
- Methyclothiazide (Enduron, Diutensen)
- Hydroflumethiazide (Saluron, Diucardin)
- Benzthiazide (Exna, Aquatag, Hydrex)
- Polythiazide (Renese)
- Cyclothiazide (Anhydron)
- Trichlormethiazide (Naqua, Metahydrin)

Phthalimidine compound
- Chlorthalidone (Hygroton)

Quinazoline compounds
- Quinethazone (Hydromox)
- Metolazone (Zaroxolyn)

Indoline compound
- Indapamide (Lozol)

(Proprietary names in parentheses)

increasing attention is being focused on the effects of these diuretics on the levels and proportions of lipids (fats) circulating in the blood. These effects require further study.

Sulfonamide Derivatives

Thiazides. The greatest experience with diuretics in the treatment of essential hypertension has been with the thiazides (see Table 8.1). They have a relatively narrow effective dosage range. Once the dosage exceeds the upper limits of the recommended range, there is very little additional diuresis, but the incidence of toxicity and side effects rises.

Chlorthalidone (Hydroton). The drug chlorthalidone induces prolonged diuresis (24 to 36 hours) and provides smooth antihypertensive control on a once-daily dosage regimen. Tweedle and his colleagues,[1] using various daily doses in patients with mild to moderate essential hypertension, found it to have a broader dose response curve than the thiazides. Each dose was given in random order for eight weeks. All patients received all four dosage levels by the end of the study. The blood pressure–lowering effect was maximal in most patients at relatively low daily dosages. In the remaining patients, larger doses were required to show maximal antihypertensive effect. Higher water losses and alterations in levels of serum potassium and uric acid were clearly related to the higher doses. For this reason, low dosages are generally prescribed when treatment is begun. If response is inadequate in eight to twelve weeks, dosages may be increased somewhat. If the effect is still inadequate, diuresis and antihypertensive effect can be attained at still higher dosages, but at the cost of increasing hypokalemia (potassium defect). For this reason, the physician may add a second drug instead of increasing the dosage of chlorathalidone.

Even thiazides with their relatively narrow effective dosage range have been found to lower blood pressure in smaller than usual dosages in many individuals with hypertension. In the VA Cooperative Study,[2] it was noted that of the patients whose blood pressure was lowered to normal levels by hydrochlorothiazide alone, half the usual dosage was sufficient for 50 percent, the usual dosage was sufficient for 30 percent, and 20 percent required twice the usual dosage. It appears now that with all diuretics, blood pressure often drops before full diuresis is achieved, although some diuresis must occur before blood pressure is lowered. It seems prudent, then, to begin diuretic therapy with low doses and to increase the dosage slowly in small increments. Once good control is reached, the lowest effective dosage should be maintained.

Metolazone (Zarorolyn). Although metolazone may function as a diuretic at the proximal tubule (sites of action will be discussed more thoroughly later), its primary site of action is at the ascending distal portion of the renal nephron, like the thiazides. It is a long-acting agent, a single daily dose provides diuretic action for 24 hours. An advantage of this drug for some patients is that unlike the thiazides progressively increasing doses eventually may produce diuresis even if the patient's kidneys are beginning to fail (early renal insufficiency).

Indapamide (Lozol). Another long-acting oral diuretic requiring only once daily dosage, indapamide, has become available in the United States recently. Initial studies show it to be an effective antihypertensive agent associated with minimal blood chemistry alterations and side effects. A small dosage produces mild diuresis, but its ability to lower peripheral resistance greatly exceeds that of the diuretics customarily used. It appears to have an arteriolar vasodilating effect in addition to a modest diuretic effect. Since it is becoming apparent that vigorous diuresis is not necessary for lowering blood pressure in many hypertensives, and since this agent has considerable peripheral resistance–lowering characteristics, it may well be that it will prove to be one of the more suitable diuretics for initial treatment of patients with essential hypertension.

Loop Diuretics

The so-called loop diuretics are among the most potent. Their greater pharmacologic effect is a reflection of their site of action in the loop of Henle of the renal nephron. They prevent reabsorption of 20 to 30 percent of the sodium that passes into the tubules in the glomerular filtrate (Chapter 2), resulting in a marked increase of sodium and water excreted by the kidneys. This category includes furosemide, ethacrynic acid, and bumetanide. Furosemide has enjoyed the wider use in the United States.

Furosemide (Lasix). Although furosemide is a sulfonamide derivative also, it is classified as a loop diuretic because its site of action is distinctly different from that of the thiazides and the thiazide-like agents discussed up to this point. Unlike the thiazides, and more like metolazone, furosemide does not have a flat dosage response curve. Desired pharmacologic effect occurs within a narrow dosage range.

Exceeding this level with higher dosages does not add any additional desired pharmacologic effect. If the patient has resistant hypertension, the physician can prescribe higher dosages in excrements until diuresis is obtained (even in patients with poor kidney function). Because of this characteristic, furosemide is the preferred diuretic for treating hypertensive patients with renal insufficiency. It is a comparatively short-acting drug (four to six hours) and is administered at least twice a day.

In patients with normal kidney function, twice-daily doses of furosemide are less effective than equivalent doses of hydrochlorothiazide given twice daily. This difference is thought to be related to the short duration of action of furosemide, which permits sodium to be replenished from the ordinary American diet while the action of the drug has diminished.

Some patients have normal renal function but have hypertension sufficiently resistant to a diuretic, a sympathetic inhibitor, *and* a vasodilator for control. The sodium-retaining ability of the latter two drugs may overwhelm the action of many diuretics. Fluid retention and false tolerance to the drug therapy may follow, and blood pressure will rise to high levels again. Substituting furosemide for the thiazide in this instance may restore the effectiveness of the previously successful therapeutic regimen.

SODIUM AND WATER EXCRETION AND OTHER METABOLIC EFFECTS

In the previous discussion, we alluded to the fact that not all diuretic drugs affect sodium retention and excretion at the same site or in quite the same way. The site and mode of action relate both to the effectiveness of therapy and its effects on the body.

Sites of Diuretic Action

The primary immediate objective of diuretic therapy is to induce the kidneys to excrete more sodium and water.

Normally, approximately 100 milliliters (ml) of filtrate per minute pass from the glomeruli into the renal tubules (Chapter 2). The concentration of sodium and other electrolytes in the filtrate is the same as that in the blood plasma. In the upper part (cortical part) of the proximal tubule, about 50 to 70 percent of the filtered plasma water and sodium normally are reabsorbed back into the bloodstream. The quinazoline compounds may interfere with some sodium reabsorption at this site.

About 20 to 30 percent of the sodium that came through in the glomerular filtrate is reabsorbed at the thicker ascending part of the loop of Henle. The loop diuretics interfere with this process at this location. The remaining filtrate continues on through the upper part of the ascending distal tubule (cortical diluting segment and distal tubule) where about an additional 10 percent of the original sodium load is reabsorbed. The thiazide and thiazide-like diuretics exert their major inhibitory influence here. Finally, the remaining filtrate passes into the distal convoluted tubule and into the collecting tubule. At this last site of sodium reabsorption only 5 percent of the original sodium in the filtrate remains. Almost all of it, 4 percent, is reabsorbed, and therefore only 1 percent of the amount originally filtered through the glomeruli into the tubules is excreted into the urine.

At this point, sodium reabsorption is at least partially under the influence of aldosterone. This hormone is essential for the cellular transport of sodium into the bloodstream in exchange for potassium and hydrogen ion, which are transported from within the capillaries into the tubule and out with the urine. This exchange will gain considerable importance when low serum potassium levels (hypokalemia) as a result of diuretic therapy are discussed.

The amount of sodium and water that will be excreted finally into the urine obviously will be the amount that remains after reabsorption by all portions of the nephrons: the proximal tubule, loop of Henle, cortical diluting segment and distal tubule, and the distal convoluted and collecting tubule. These quantities and the diuretics that affect them are summarized in Table 8.2. Continual alteration of excretion and reabsorption by diuretic therapy has various

TABLE 8.2
Areas of the Renal Tubules Where Diuretics Act

	Sodium Reabsorbed (%)	Diuretic Inhibition
Cortical proximal tubule	50–70	Quinazoline compounds (modest effect)
Thick ascending limb of loop of Henle	20–30	Loop diuretics
Cortical diluting segment and distal tubule	10	Benzothiadiazines, phthalimidines, quinazolines, and indoline
Distal convoluted and collecting tubule	4	Potassium-sparing agents

effects on metabolism (the body's production and use of energy and excretion of wastes). The more significant of these effects are discussed below.

Hyperuricemia

Long-term diuresis somewhat diminishes effective plasma volume, reduces renal blood flow, and decreases the glomerular filtration rate. An important function of the kidneys is to excrete the toxic waste uric acid, a product of protein metabolism carried in the blood. When glomerular filtration diminishes, less uric acid passes into the tubules to be excreted. In addition, as blood flow in the tubules slows, more time is available for uric acid to be reabsorbed and returned to the bloodstream. Consequently, abnormally high levels of uric acid circulate in the serum (*hyperuricemia*). In itself, hyperuricemia requires no treatment unless symptoms occur. Gout, a painful form of arthritis that is characterized by high uric acid levels is not likely to occur in diuretic-treated hypertensives unless the patient has some hereditary predisposition for gout itself. Should it appear, the treatment is the same as for anyone else with gout, and diuretic therapy is continued.

Hyperglycemia

The sulfonamide derivative diuretics tend to produce an elevation of blood sugar levels (impaired carbohydrate tolerance). It appears that this effect is mediated through a combination of mechanisms: release of insulin by the pancreas is suppressed, and the cells' normal utilization of glucose is inhibited. The changes are minimal in most individuals who are not diabetic. Even in some patients with diabetes, altering the diet or slightly increasing the dosage of the agent used to control the blood sugar levels suffices to cover this effect. Occasionally, however, long-term diuretic therapy in patients with diabetes has been associated with diabetic coma. In such patients, or those in whom diuretics have considerably increased the insulin required for control the physician may prescribe spironolactone or ethacrynic acid. These agents are nonsulfonamides and are unlikely to cause carbohydrate intolerance.

There is some indication that potassium depletion, which may result from diuretic therapy, might cause increased carbohydrate intolerance. One study has shown that thiazide-induced glucose intolerance and hypokalemia both can be reversed by replenishing potassium.

Hypokalemia

When thiazides, related compounds, or loop diuretics are used, sodium reabsorption at the cortical diluting segment or at the thick ascending limb of the loop of Henle is blocked. Such an effect allows a higher than usual concentration of sodium to reach the distal convoluted tubule where, in the presence of aldosterone, sodium is reabsorbed into the blood and potassium plus hydrogen ion are excreted into the urine. When a greater than usual concentration of sodium reaches this site, activity is increased. More than the usual amount of sodium is reabsorbed and more than the usual amount of potassium is excreted. The increased sodium reabsorption falls short of the amount blocked upstream by the diuretics, however. The end result is an increase in sodium and water excretion by the kidney (the goal of diuretic therapy), and increased potassium excretion (an undesired byproduct).

The usually cited normal range for serum potassium is 3.5 to 5.0 milliequivalents per liter (mEq/l). Levels lower than 3.5 mEq/l represent a potassium deficiency in the blood (*hypokalemia*). Serum potassium levels between 3.0 and 3.5 mEq/l occur in up to 30 percent of hypertensive patients treated with diuretics. In almost all patients on long-term diuretic therapy, serum potassium will drop an average of 0.66 mEq/l.

Experienced clinicians have tended not to supplement potassium unless the serum concentration drops to 3.0 mEq/l or below or the patient becomes symptomatic (muscle cramps, weakness, heart palpitations and irregularities). All agree, however, that potassium supplementation should accompany diuretic therapy from the beginning in patients who are taking digitalis preparations. In such patients, even a modest degree of potassium deficiency may lead to increasing myocardial irritability, abnormal heart rhythms (ventricular ectopy), and even sudden death. (This fact emphasizes the importance of telling any health professional who treats you what medications you are taking.)

More recently, physicians have become aware that some hypertensive patients on long-term diuretic therapy develop increased myocardial irritability and ectopic rhythms during rest and during exercise. This activity may appear even though the serum potassium levels are in the low normal range. Supplementation of potassium results in the diminution or disappearance of the myocardial irritability.

It has been recognized for some time that thickened heart muscle (hypertrophied *myocardium*) tends to be more irritable (easily stimulated) than normal heart tissue. In addition, even heart muscle that is not hypertrophied becomes more irritable if it is not receiving enough blood for its metabolic needs. This condition, known as *ischemia*, occurs in patients with coronary artery disease, among others. In many patients with essential hypertension, the myocardium is both hypertrophied and ischemic. Considering that the irritability promoted by these conditions may be compounded by hypokalemia due to diuretic therapy, serum potassium levels assume new importance. To counteract these effects, the physician should consider monitoring serum potassium levels, using the smallest effective dose of diuretics, advising the patient of dietary sources of potassium, replacing lost potassium with supplements, and even using potassium-retaining drugs.

Serum Potassium Monitoring. The physician will obtain baseline serum potassium levels before beginning diuretic therapy. The reduction of serum potassium begins to appear within a few days after diuretic therapy is initiated. It usually reaches the lowest level in about one month and then stabilizes. Periodic determinations once or twice a year after that are in order.

Smallest Effective Dosage. As discussed earlier, the antihypertensive effect of a diuretic may appear at a smaller dosage than the full diuretic effect. Although some diuresis must occur for blood pressure to be lowered, the primary reason for the antihypertensive effect is the lowering of total peripheral resistance and not maximum reduction of plasma volume. One begins at the lowest dose and slowly adjusts the dosage upward in increments (titrates upward) until pressure drops or the maximum recommended diuretic dosage is approached. A step-2 drug may be added if the hypertension is not alleviated at this level.

In selecting a diuretic for essential hypertension, the physician may consider indapamide (Lozol). This diuretic, which is a powerful vasodilator in small dosages, is relatively new. On the basis of body function, it would seem to be the ideal diuretic for essential hypertension. Perhaps because of its modest diuretic effect, three months' treatment of 4,600 patients showed a mean serum potassium fall of only 0.17 mEq/l.

Dietary Considerations. A diet high in potassium, low in sodium (and low in calories if weight reduction is needed) is helpful. Many physicians advise their patients to eat citrus fruit or drink citrus juices daily while on diuretic therapy. Other foods rich in potassium include tomatoes, white potatoes, green peppers, bananas, and nuts. These measures are likely to prove inadequate, however, for reasons discussed in the next section. It is particularly important to maintain low levels of sodium in the diet even though the patient is on a diuretic regimen. Recall that the more sodium reaches the distal convoluted tubule, the more potassium will be excreted in the urine through the action of aldosterone. Obviously, a low-sodium diet would minimize this activity. Ram and his coworkers[3] have demonstrated that diuretic-induced potassium loss was only half as great with a 72 mEq/day sodium diet as with a 195 mEq/day sodium intake.

Potassium Replacement. If there is significant lowering of the serum potassium level despite using the lowest effective dose of diuretic and following a low-sodium diet, active potassium replacement may be attempted. Potassium must be administered as a chloride salt (KCl) to correct the concentration within cells as well as in the plasma. The traditional use of 20 percent potassium chloride solution in fruit juice is not conducive to long-term compliance by many patients. The unpleasant taste cannot be disguised easily, and this form of therapy may cause irritation of the stomach and even diarrhea.

Suggesting that the patient eat oranges or bananas is not a practical way to solve the problem. To replace only 30 mEq of potassium, a patient must drink a quantity of orange juice that will supply 800 calories. Bananas would provide even a higher caloric value. If a patient is hypokalemic, at least 100 mEq of potassium must be administered daily until the deficiency is eliminated. To prevent a diuretic-treated hypertensive patient from developing hypokalemia, 40 mEq/day in addition to that received in the diet is needed. Some patients require up to 10 mEq/day.

It should be clearly understood that all potassium supple-

mentation or, as will be discussed later, potassium-sparing drugs, should be administered with great caution if the patient has impaired kidney function. In some instances of renal insufficiency, potassium excretion is diminished. Death due to too high serum potassium levels (hyperkalemia) is just as final as death due to low serum levels (hypokalemia).

In the 1950s, enteric-coated tablets of potassium chloride (KCl) were widely used. The intent was to avoid the unpleasant taste and the irritation of the stomach that were so disturbing. However, when the coating dissolved in the intestines, concentrated potassium chloride was able to attack localized areas of the lining of these structures. Ulcerations, scarring, constriction, and even perforations developed in many patients, and the enteric-coated pills were withdrawn from the market in the United States. Commercially, various liquid preparations of supplemental potassium are available now (Table 8.3). These compounds may be more palatable than the standard 20 percent solution. If the patient continues to find these intolerable, several other forms of oral potassium chloride have been developed. These preparations are also listed in Table 8.3.

TABLE 8.3
Potassium Chloride Preparations

Liquid Preparations	mEq KCl/15 ml (tbsp)
• Kaochlor 10% liquid	20
• Kaon-Cl 20%	40
• Kay Ciel	20
• Klorvess 10% liquid	20
• K-Lyte/Cl (powder to be liquefied)	25

Slow-Release Preparations	mEq KCl/Tablet or Capsule
• Wax matrix	
Kaon-Cl	6.67
Slow-K	8.0
Klotrix	10.0
• Microencapsulated crystals	
Micro-K Extencaps	8.0

The slow-release, wax-imbedded potassium chloride tablet has become quite popular. The wax slowly melts, gradually and diffusely releasing potassium as the tablet traverses the intestinal tract. This method has been effective and relatively safe except in instances where the tablet might be trapped (hiatus hernia, diverticulum, partial intestinal obstruction or other causes of impaired motility) and concentrated release might occur. A more recent variation is to provide a film-coated tablet containing potassium chloride in a wax matrix in an attempt to further minimize highly localized concentrations within the gastrointestinal tract.

Another development is that of microencapsulated potassium chloride in which single crystals are coated with a water-permeable polymer to produce microcapsules. These are then encased in a hard gelatin capsule similar to that used for many over-the-counter cold medications. As the capsule disintegrates in the intestinal tract, the tiny microcapsules are widely dispersed, and the potassium and chloride ions slowly diffuse through the polymer membrane over eight to ten hours. This approach may provide additional protection against irritation and ulceration.

Since patients with hypertension may be on a low-sodium diet as well as on diuretics, salt substitutes that contain up to 90 percent potassium chloride by weight are available, ostensibly to make the diet more palatable. Taste prefer-

TABLE 8.4
Commercially Available Salt Substitutes Containing Potassium

Product	Manufacturer
Adolph's Salt Substitute	Adolph's Ltd.
Co-Salt	USV Pharmaceutical Corp.
Diasal	E. Fougera and Co., Inc.
Featherweight "K" Salt	Chicago Dietetic Supply
Neocurtasal	Winthrop Laboratories (Sterling Drug, Inc.)
Sweet 'N Low Brand Nu-Salt	Cumberland Packing Corp.
Morton Salt Substitute	Morton Salt Division, Morton-Norwich Products

ences for each of these products vary among individuals. Their value as potassium supplements may exceed their value as flavorings (Table 8.4). Your physician will caution you not to use more than one-half level teaspoonful daily (about 65 mEq potassium). Probably you should limit use to one meal per day. Obviously, using these preparations as a form of potassium supplementation would obviate the need for other supplements or for potassium-sparing drugs. A word of caution: There is a tendency to think of salt substitutes as food items and not as drugs. Dangerously high potassium levels (hyperkalemia) may ensue if salt substitutes and supplement preparations are used simultaneously. Once again, salt substitutes should be administered with caution in patients with renal insufficiency. Also, note that not all salt substitutes contain potassium chloride; a number of herbal combinations (Ms. Dash, for example) are also available commercially.

Most patients find the salt substitutes to be somewhat bitter or to have a metallic taste. Many prefer a preparation called Lite-Salt (Morton Salt Company). This product is approximately 50 percent sodium chloride and 50 percent potassium chloride. One level teaspoonful daily provides approximately 48 mEq of sodium and 40 mEq of potassium. A possible source of error is the fact that the same company that produces Lite-Salt also produces a salt substitute. Be sure not to confuse the two and take inappropriate amounts.

Potassium-Sparing Drugs. Another way to combat diuretic-induced hypokalemia is to include a potassium-sparing diuretic with the primary diuretic. Potassium-sparing compounds have mild or minimal diuretic action of their own but are able to prevent potassium loss with the diuresis. If these agents are to be used, supplemental potassium in any form should be omitted in most cases.

Spironolactone. The drug spironolactone is an antagonist of aldosterone. The receptors in the cells of the distal convoluted and collecting tubules cannot distinguish between spironolactone and aldosterone. If they accept spironolactone to occupy them, the process of exchanging sodium from the renal tubule with potassium and hydrogen ion from the bloodstream is impeded. The net effect of sprionolactone, when given with a primary diuretic, is to increase sodium and water excretion while preventing potassium loss. It may cause tender breast nipples in men and menstrual irregularities and excessive facial hair (hirsutism) in women. Serum potassium levels should be monitored more closely since even when combined with thiazides, and even in the presence of normal renal function, all potassium-sparing agents can produce hyperkalemia.

Triamterene. The drug triamterene affects the luminal surface of the cells in the distal convoluted and collecting tubules to prevent sodium reabsorption and potassium excretion. It is a weak diuretic in itself but augments the effects of primary diuretics. The possibility of triamterene-initiated stones exists, especially in persons who have had kidney stones before. It is estimated that this complication occurs annually in 1 per 1,500 persons taking this drug. Finally, serum potassium levels should be monitored since, even when combined with thiazides, triamterene can produce hyperkalemia.

Amiloride. The drug amiloride is an $Na^+K^+ATPase$ inhibitor (Chapter 2). It prevents sodium reabsorption and potassium excretion by the distal convoluted and collecting tubules. It has mild antihypertensive effects of its own but is most effective in combination with a primary diuretic. Serum potassium levels should be monitored for hyperkalemia as with other potassium-conserving drugs.

LIPID CHANGES ASSOCIATED WITH DIURETIC THERAPY

Any number of studies agree that long-term diuretic therapy may raise the overall level of serum cholesterol and especially the level of low density lipoprotein (LDL) cholesterol. LDL cholesterol has been recognized as a factor leading to progression of the atherosclerotic process. Furosemide (Lasix) used does not elevate LDL levels when used in long-term therapy, but it may diminish high density lipoprotein (HDL) levels. High-density lipoproteins represent cholesterol being moved to the liver for excretion rather than being deposited into the atherosclerotic plaque and thus are thought to be beneficial. It may be noteworthy that one group of subjects treated with long-term diuretics (chlorthalidone) plus a cholesterol-lowering diet showed no significant changes in LDL and HDL cholesterol levels.

Finally, indapamide has been associated with minimal biochemical alterations in long-term studies. In one situation where 12 patients were treated with this agent for one to three years, there was no significant change in either LDL or HDL cholesterol. Obviously this number of subjects is not sufficient to be certain that this characteristic will continue to be identified as much larger numbers of patients are followed. It is worthwhile, however, to be alert for additional reports.

REFERENCES: CHAPTER 8

1. Tweedle MG, Oglivie RI, Ruedy J: Antihypertensive and biochemical effects of chlorthalidone. *Clin Pharmacol Ther* 1977; 22:519–527

2. Veterans Cooperative Study Group on Antihypertensive Agents: Comparison of propranolol and hydrochlorothiazide for the initial treatment of hypertension. I. Results of short term titration with emphasis on racial differences in response. *JAMA* 1982; 248:1996–2003.

3. Ram CVS, Garrett BN, Kaplan NM: Moderate sodium restriction and various diuretics in the treatment of hypertension. *Arch Intern Med* 1981; 141:1015–1019.

CHAPTER 9

SYMPATHETIC INHIBITORS

IN the stepped-care approach for the treatment of essential hypertension another drug is added as step 2 if diuretics do not satisfactorily reduce blood pressure. This second drug is a sympathetic inhibitor—an agent that interferes with sympathetic-nerve stimulation of the smooth muscle fibers of the arterioles. A number of different drug groups that have this characteristic have been developed. Their mechanisms of action vary, but the expected end result is decreased stimulation of smooth muscle contraction, reduction of total peripheral resistance, and lowering of blood pressure. Although they may be unrelated compounds, each is considered to be a sympathetic inhibitor. As discussed in Chapter 7, each of them may bring about compensatory mechanisms of the body resulting in varying degrees of sodium and water retention, expansion of plasma volume, and pseudotolerance with diminishing antihypertensive effectiveness. With some of these drugs, this response is less of a problem, and they may be used initially as sole agents for treatment. Some even may be successful in long-term monotherapy. More often, however, they are most effective and at lower doses when used to augment diuretics.

RESERPINE

Reserpine is an alkaloid of a medical herb from India, the powdered root of *Rauwolfia serpentina*. This drug had been used for many years to treat and tranquilize the mentally disturbed before it was found to be effective also in the treatment of essential hypertension. *R. serpentina*, particularly in the form of reserpine, became widely used clinically.

Rauwolfia alkaloids lower blood pressure by several mechanisms. They deplete the myocardium, the adrenal medulla, the brain, and the presynaptic nerve endings of bionic amines (catecholamines and serotonin). They prevent the normal uptake and storage of the catecholamine norepinephrine by the sympathetic nerve endings. The free norepinephrine that remains is destroyed by monamine oxidase. When a sympathetic nerve is stimulated, less norepinephrine than usual is available for release into the synapse to stimulate the adrenoreceptors. Therefore, the responses of the effector cells such as the arteriolar smooth muscle fibers or the myocardial (heart muscle) fibers are diminished. Total peripheral resistance decreases, the heart rate slows, and blood pressure drops. In addition, there is a direct influence on the brain (CNS) to inhibit sympathetic outflow to the autonomic nervous system and, therefore, to the tissues of the body via the sympathetic nerves. Although this central mechanism serves to decrease vascular (blood-vessel) sympathetic tone, the major antihypertensive effect of *R. serpentina* is related more to its peripheral (sympathetic nerve endings) effect discussed earlier than to its CNS mechanism.

Reserpine is usually taken once daily in a fairly small dose. Higher quantities are tolerated poorly by most patients when administered over a prolonged period. There is no additional antihypertensive effect, and undesirable side effects increase progressively with increasing doses. It may take two to six weeks for the full effect of reserpine to become apparent. Similarly, accumulation of the drug within the body is prolonged. Evidence of catecholamine depletion may persist for one to two weeks after the drug has been discontinued.

For the best result, reserpine is administered with a diuretic. It is primarily a step-2 drug. Since it needs to be taken only once daily, its combination with a long-acting diuretic such as chlorthalidone provides a convenient and inexpensive method for effective treatment. Such a combination will result in satisfactory control in up to 70 percent of patients with mild or moderate essential hypertension. However, about one-third of those responding satisfactorily from the standpoint of blood pressure lowering may develop significant side effects, particularly severe persistent nasal stuffiness, that will necessitate a change to another sympathetic inhibitor. It has been found that half the usual dose achieves 90 percent of the blood pressure–lowering effect of the standard dosage. Even one-fifth of the usual dosage achieves 82 percent of the reduction. Since side effects are largely dose related, and since lower dosages than those presently recommended may be effective, the physician may begin by adding a minimal dose of reserpine to a diuretic when a step-2 drug is indicated. If needed, small increments of reserpine can be gradually added as necessary.

Because reserpine inhibits only the sympathetic nervous system, the balance between sympathetic and parasympathetic influences may be upset. The parasympathetic system is a partially parallel involuntary nerve network that is antagonistic to the influences of the sympathetic system. Ordinarily, each keeps the other in balance. However, reserpine inhibits the sympathetic system sufficiently to cause the uninhibited parasympathetic network to predominate. Blood vessels in the lining of the nose dilate, the nasal lining swells, and the patient experiences watery running of the nose and nasal stuffiness. This reaction is the most common undesirable side effect of reserpine. The symptoms are particularly troublesome at night and may reach a severity that many patients cannot endure. Other manifestations of an overriding parasympathetic nervous system include increased stomach acid secretion, peptic ulcer, increased "hunger" contractions, diarrhea, and further slowing of the heart rate.

The most important side effect of the *R. serpentina* alkaloids is mental depression. Central nervous system depletion of catecholamines and serotonin leads to drowsiness, behavioral changes, nightmares, and depression. The depression can be truly a serious reaction because it may lead to suicide before it is recognized. Quetsh and his colleagues[1] found that 26 percent of patients on reserpine developed some manifestations of depression compared to only 5 percent of hypertensive individuals receiving no antihypertensive therapy. There may be gradual appearance of melancholia, loss of self-confidence, reduced appetite, and awakening in the early hours of the morning. The incidence of such depression, however, is dose-related. The frequency of this complication when reserpine is used in the presently recommended doses is quite small—no greater than when methyldopa or propranolol (agents to be discussed later) are used in standard recommended doses.

In 1974, several reports appeared associating long-term reserpine therapy with a possible increased incidence of breast cancer in women. This possibility does not seem to hold up, however, when one compares these observations to

TABLE 9.1
Characteristics of Reserpine (Rauwolfia alkaloid)

Mechanism of action:
- Prevents uptake and storage of catecholamines by sympathetic nerve endings
- Depletes myocardium, adrenal medulla, and brain of bionic amines

Best antihypertensive activity: When added to diuretic

Common side effects:
- Drowsiness, lassitude
- Nasal stuffiness
- Bradycardia (slow heartbeat)
- Gastric hyperacidity
- Diarrhea
- Nightmares
- Depression

the previously published studies showing increased breast cancer incidence in postmenopausal hypertensive women who had never received this drug. The 1974 studies did not select controls for comparison from hypertensive populations. Subsequently, after careful analysis, no evidence was found for an association between either reserpine or thiazide diuretics and the occurrence of breast cancer.

It should be noted that reserpine was the selected sympathetic inhibitor in practically every one of the key intervention studies that showed the effectiveness of treatment for hypertension (Chapter 5). It has served well. It is inexpensive, and having to take a drug only once a day makes it much easier for patients to follow their regimens. The properties of reserpine are summarized in Table 9.1.

METHYLDOPA (Aldomet)

Another sympathetic inhibitor that may be added to a diuretic if the latter alone does not result in a satisfactory reduction of blood pressure is methyldopa (Aldomet). This agent was introduced in 1960, and its clinical effectiveness was established shortly thereafter.

The principle underlying the use of methyldopa in controlling hypertension is to "deceive" the alpha-adrenoreceptors in the lower brain stem into accepting its metabolite, methylnorepinephrine, instead of norepinephrine. Stimulation of the receptors by this metabolite reduces sympathetic outflow to the peripheral sympathetic nervous system. (That is, the substance serves as an agonist.) This action leads to relaxation of the arteriolar smooth muscle, a drop in peripheral resistance, and lowering of the blood pressure. Its effect within the brain (CNS effect) is the major pathway by which methyldopa lowers blood pressure.

In addition, uptake of methylnorepinephrine instead of norepinephrine by some of the alpha-adrenergic receptors in the arteriolar smooth muscle fibers reduces their constrictive response, since methylnorepinephrine does not produce so great a vasoconstrictor response as norepinephrine. When arteriolar constriction is less than usual, the peripheral resistance drops, and blood pressure is lowered. This mechanism of action (the "false transmitter" action) is a secondary one and not so important as the CNS effect.

By reducing sympathetic outflow from the brain, methyldopa tends to inhibit the baroreceptor reflexes and to diminish release of renin as the blood pressure comes down. With long-term therapy, however, compensatory sodium and water retention occurs, expansion of plasma volume follows, and an apparent resistance to the drug's antihypertensive effect develops. Therefore, mythyldopa is best utilized as a step-2 agent added to a diuretic.

Initially, the drug is usually taken twice a day (b.i.d.) or four times a day (q.i.d.). The original dosage increases considerably in gradual increments. If the desired effect has not been reached by the time 2000 mg (2 grams) are being taken, additional quantities of the drug will yield very little if any further antihypertensive effect. If control is obtained, the total daily dosage required may be divided into two equal amounts each day.

Although methyldopa has been used widely with good success for more than two decades, there are side effects of which you should be aware. Drowsiness, a frequent problem, and depression, an infrequent one, are both related to methyldopa's effect on the brain. Unexplained episodes of high fever may be another undesired effect. Symptoms similar to those of flu appear 9 to 19 days after the drug has been initiated. Temperature may reach 104 degrees F. There may be associated chills, tiredness, and diarrhea. In about one-third of the cases, liver function tests become abnormal. The acute illness clears rapidly when methyldopa is discontinued. If, after recovery, the patient is given another dose of methyldopa, fever usually reappears within six to twelve hours. It is dangerous to use such a "challenge" to test for drug fever, however, since an episode of fatal liver necrosis thought to be secondary to methyldopa rechallenge has been reported. If the physician suspects that the patient is suffering a bout of drug fever, switching to another sympathetic inhibitor for controlling hypertension is advised.

Hepatitis (inflammation of the liver) is another uncommon complication of methyldopa administration. It may or may not be related to the flulike syndrome. It usually is not severe, but some fatalities have been reported. Characteristically, a low-grade fever appears during the first six weeks of treatment. Liver function tests become abnormal, but jaundice (yellowing of the skin) is not usual. The drug should be stopped in these instances also, and another sympathetic inhibitor selected.

About 20 percent of patients taking methyldopa for more than six to twelve months develop a positive direct Coomb's test (an indicator of immune changes in the red blood cells that may lead to their lysis or dissolution). Only a very small number of such patients go on to develop hemolytic anemia.

Although these side effects do occur, it must be emphasized that they are not common. Successful antihypertensive therapy in complete safety with millions of patient-years experience exists. There is no question but that possible side effects must be considered in developing a therapeutic program for a specific patient. If methyldopa suits that patient best, it may be prescribed with confidence while the patient's course is monitored carefully. Its properties are summarized in Table 9.2.

TABLE 9.2
Characteristics of Methyldopa (Aldomet)

Mechanisms of action:
- CNS alpha-receptor agonist (decreases sympathetic outflow)
- "False transmitter" to arteriolar smooth muscle
- Inhibits release of renin

Best antihypertensive activity: When added to diuretic

Side effects:
- Drowsiness
- Depression
- Febrile reaction
- Hepatitis
- Positive direct Coombs' test, rheumatoid factor, lupus factor
- Myocarditis

CLONIDINE (CATAPRES)

Like methylnorepinephrine, clonodine (Catapres) is a central nervous system alpha-adrenergic receptor agonist. It stimulates cells in various centers within the brain, resulting in decreased sympathetic outflow through the autonomic nervous system. In addition, it increases activity of the vagal nerves (antagonists of the sympathetic nerves), resulting in even more diminution of sympathetic influence in the peripheral tissues. As a consequence, the heart rate slows, cardiac output declines slightly, total peripheral resistance is reduced and blood pressure levels consequently fall. Clonidine also brings about a decrease in the release of renin in patients with high-renin essential hypertension. The decreased central sympathetic outflow combined with the increase in vagal effect slows down the heart rate and also blunts the effectiveness of the baroreceptor reflex that might be initiated by a drop in blood pressure.

As with other nondiuretic blood pressure–lowering drugs, fluid and sodium retention occurs in long-term therapy if clonidine is used alone. Such a response may lead to pseudotolerance with return of high blood pressure levels. Under such circumstances, administering a diuretic can significantly enhance the hypertensive effect and prevent sodium retention.

Since sodium retention that occurs when clonidine is administered alone is proportional to the magnitude of blood pressure reduction the drug brings about, some mild hypertensives may respond to it as the initial therapeutic agent, and control may persist with monotherapy. If not, a diuretic may be added. In 115 patients treated with clonidine alone for one year or more, good response persisted in 16 percent, and moderate response in 36 percent. In 58 percent, however, little or no antihypertensive effect remained. Diuretics, as one would expect, potentiated the reappearance of good control when they were added. Except for some instances of mild hypertension where monotherapy might be attempted, clonidine is best added to an established baseline regimen of diuretic therapy when additional antihypertensive response is needed.

Clonidine is most effective if administered twice daily (except in the elderly where once-daily dosage may suffice). Therapy usually is begun with a low dosage taken at bedtime daily to minimize the discomfort of such side effects as sedation and dryness of the mouth during the waking hours. These side effects are related to the magnitude of the dose and gradually diminish with time. As they diminish, dosage may be increased to twice daily (b.i.d.). The physician then continues to increase the dose by increments every several weeks until the desired blood pressure level is attained. The maximum effective dose is 2.4 mg per day in divided doses, but such high levels are not usually needed. Beyond the maximum effective dose, very little if any additional antihypertensive change is gained by more drug, but the side effects become more severe.

The most common side effects are drowsiness and dryness of the mouth. CNS alpha-adrenergic agonists inhibit the action of the brain centers that control the secretion of saliva. Unless large doses are required, however, these symptoms ordinarily diminish in two to four weeks and may even subside altogether. There may be some reduction in gastrointestinal motility and secretion to the point where constipation may develop. Like reserpine and methyldopa, clonidine may cause depression. Perhaps the most publicized side effect has been the so-called rebound effect that may occur if clonidine is stopped abruptly. The patient may experience nausea, vomiting, a rapid and severe rise in blood pressure, insomnia, restlessness, tremor, and headache. The syndrome can be controlled by reinstituting the clonidine therapy. If blood pressure continues to climb, propranolol and an alpha-adrenergic blocker may be used. In controlled studies in which clonidine was discontinued abruptly, this rebound phenomenon occurred only rarely when the patients were taking medication at the presently recommended doses. It should be noted that similar acute withdrawal syndromes have been reported with methyldopa and propranolol.

Clonidine is a useful antihypertensive agent in modern

TABLE 9.3
Characteristics of Clonidine (Catapres)

Mechanism of action: CNS alpha-receptor agonist
- Decreases sympathetic outflow
- Increases vagal effects on cardiovascular system

Best antihypertensive activity: When added to diuretic

Side effects:
- Drowsiness
- Dry mouth
- Depression
- Constipation
- Drug interaction with tricyclic antidepressants
- Withdrawal syndrome (not common; dose related)

---

therapy. As with all drugs, selection must be made after careful consideration of each patient's specific needs and the comparative advantages and disadvantages of the other available agents. The characteristics of clonidine are summarized in Table 9.3.

GUANABENZ (WYTENSIN)

Guanabenz is another CNS alpha-receptor agonist. It is like methyldopa and clonidine in that its antihypertensive action is based on stimulation of cerebral (brain) alpha-adrenoreceptors to reduce sympathetic outflow. Just as in the use of clonidine, some patients with mild and even moderate essential hypertension respond to treatment with guanabenz alone. In some, this benefit may persist without apparent significant sodium retention, fluid volume expansion, or pseudotolerance. In two studies guanabenz as the sole treatment has been shown to be successful for six months to two years in a number of patients. Such studies suggest that this drug may be superior to other centrally acting alpha-receptor agonists for monotherapy, but more experience and comparisons are needed. The concomitant administration of a diuretic with guanabenz is required to control and maintain benefit in patients with moderately severe to severe hypertension. Side effects reported up to this time include drowsiness, dry mouth, weakness, and dizziness. Guanabenz appears to be another worthy addition to the physician's tools for developing individual treatment plans (Table 9.4).

TABLE 9.4
Characteristics of Guanabenz (Wytensin)

Mechanism of action: CNS alpha-receptor agonist
- Decreases sympathetic outflow

Add to diuretic for moderately severe and severe hypertension

Side effects
- Drowsiness
- Dry mouth
- Weakness
- Dizziness

BETA-ADRENORECEPTOR BLOCKERS

In Chapter 2, we discussed the neural concept as a mechanism leading to hypertension. This theory is based on the known fact that stimulation of several areas within the brain raises or lowers blood pressure. Once its blood pressure–raising sectors are stimulated, the brain transmits impulses to the autonomic nervous system, which extends throughout the body through a network of sympathetic nerve branches. The endings of these nerves are close to special adrenoreceptors in the smooth muscle fibers in arteries, arterioles, and veins as well as the myocardial (muscle) fibers of the heart. At the *synapse,* where the nerve endings and receptors meet, the stimulus is transmitted to the receptor by means of a chemical (a *neurotransmitter*). To regulate blood pressure, the nerve ending transmits the neurotransmitter norepinephrine, which occupies the receptors an stimulates them to bring about the response of the individual cells (muscle fibers). There are two types of adrenoreceptors, alpha and beta. The latter are composed of two subgroups, beta-1 and beta-2 (refer to Figure 2.1).

When alpha receptors in the smooth muscle fibers of the vascular system are stimulated, the arteries and veins constrict. When beta-2 receptors of the blood vessels are stimulated, the vessels dilate (open up) slightly. Stimulation of beta-1 receptors, which are found mostly in the heart muscle fibers, causes the heart to beat faster. The interval for blood to be ejected from the ventricle shortens, and the force of myocardial contraction increases. Stimulation of beta-1 receptors in the kidneys leads to release of renin.

Beta-2 receptors are not limited to the vascular system. In the smooth muscle fibers of the bronchi (bronchial tubes), they bring about relaxation and bronchial dilatation. Beta-2 stimulation also results in release of insulin from the pancreas. Release of glucose by the metabolism of glycogen stores in muscles is beta-2–mediated.

The use of beta-adrenoreceptor blocking agents (*beta-blockers*) in blood pressure control is based on the fact that the adrenoreceptors cannot distinguish these chemicals from norepinephrine. If the receptor accepts the beta-blocker, this chemical occupies the space that otherwise would be occupied by norepinephrine. That effector cell is not stimulated to perform its usual action.

In 1964, while studying beta-blockers as therapeutic agents for angina pectoris (the chest discomfort brought on by exercise in those with coronary artery atherosclerotic disease), researchers learned that these agents also had a blood pressure–lowering effect in those patients who were also hypertensive. This result is somewhat surprising. Recall that the autonomic nervous system controls blood pressure and other vital functions by a system of "checks and balances." Beta-blockers impede the dilating (expanding) action that beta-receptors exert on the arteries and arterioles. This leaves the constricting (narrowing) action of the alpha-receptors unopposed. And, indeed, beta-blockers used in treating hypertension do allow arteriolar constriction that elevates total peripheral resistance to varying degrees. Yet, blood pressure does drop in many patients with essential hypertension when beta-blockers are administered.

Why blood pressure drops despite increased peripheral resistance is not understood completely. It is true that blocking the beta-1 receptors slows the heart rate, reduces the force of heart-muscle contraction, and reduces cardiac output. These effects could contribute to the lowering of blood pressure. Also, the beta-blockers interfere with the release of renin. In patients with high-renin essential hypertension these compounds may reduce blood pressure by diminishing the influence of the RAA axis. These are but two possible ways by which beta-adrenergic blockade might produce an antihypertensive action. There are probably others that remain to be clarified.

In the United States, seven beta-blockers are available currently for the treatment of hypertension. All of them are equally effective for controlling high blood pressure when administered in equipotent doses. They do, however, have other properties that the physician will consider in selecting

TABLE 9.5
Characteristics of Beta-Blockers

	Cardio-selective	Water-Soluble	Lipid-Soluble	ISA
Acebutolol (Sectral)	+	+	+	+
Atenolol (Tenormin)	+	+	0	0
Metoprolol (Lopressor)	+	0	+	0
Nadolol (Corgard)	0	+	0	0
Pindolol (Viskin)	0	+	+	+
Propranolol (Inderal)	0	0	+	0
Timolol (Blocardren)	0	0	+	0

the proper agent for a given patient (Table 9.5). The seven drugs may be classified according to their cardioselectivity, their water solubility, and their intrinsic sympathomimetic activity (ISA).

Cardioselectivity

Beta-blockers may be either *noncardioselective*, diminishing the activity of both kinds of receptors, or *cardioselective*, diminishing the activity of beta-1 receptors primarily and beta-2 receptors slightly. Presently available agents are either nonselective or beta-1 selective. Beta-1 blockade promotes alterations that contribute to the lowering of blood pressure and also to the control of angina pectoris: decreased heart rate, decreased force of myocardial contraction, decreased cardiac output, and reduction in the release of renin. Beta-2 blockade provides no pharmacologic advantage to lowering blood pressure but instead may result in undesired side effects. (Table 9.6). Beta-1 blockers would appear to have the advantage. It should be remembered,

---

TABLE 9.6
Effects of Beta-Adrenoreceptor Blockade

Beta-1 Receptors
- Decreased heart rate
- Slowing of atrioventricular (AV) conduction
  —*Caution in presence of AV block*
- Decreased force of myocardial contraction
  —*Caution in borderline cardiac compensation*
- Decreased renin release

Beta-2 Receptors
- Increased tendency for bronchoconstriction
  —*Caution in bronchospastic disease*
- Increased tendency for arterial constriction
  —*Caution in intermittent claudication*
- Decreased glycogenolysis and gluconeogenesis response
  —*Caution in brittle insulin-dependent diabetes*

however, that although cardioselectives exert their *major* influence on the beta-1 receptors, they also act on beta-2 receptors, though to a much lesser degree. As the dosage is raised, beta-2 blocking activity intensifies. At high dosages these agents may function as noncardioselective blockers for all intents and purposes.

Beta-Blockers and Bronchospastic Disease. If a noncardioselective agent such as propranolol is administered to a patient with bronchospastic disease—asthma, for example—the beta-2 receptor influence in the bronchi is inhibited, and stimulation for maintaining bronchial dilatation is reduced. Just a small dose of propranolol can precipitate bronchial spasm and an asthmatic attack even if there have been no symptoms for many years before. Even if obvious asthma does not appear, there may be a significant measurable decrease in the amount of air that the individual can force out in one second (the one-second forced expiratory volume–FEV_1).

Benson and his associates[2] studied five patients with a history of asthma. Two hours after the administration of a beta-blocker, FEV_1 determinations were obtained. There was a considerable decrease with propranolol and pindolol, both noncardioselective drugs. There was less reduction with metoprolol and the least with atenolol, both cardioselective agents. When isoproterenol, a beta-receptor agonist (stimulator), was administered 15 minutes later, FEV_1 increased to greater than baseline levels with atenolol and returned to baseline with metoprolol. With the noncardioselective agents, FEV_1 remained reduced. Although a beta-blocker is not a preferred drug for patients with a history of asthma, if it must be administered for any reason, acebutolol, atenolol, or metoprolol are the better choices.

Beta-Blockers and Peripheral Arterial Disease. Since the stimulus for the dilatation of the arteries depends on beta-2 receptor action, noncardioselective blockade impedes the dilating stimulus and so permits the influence of alpha-receptor stimulation to proceed without any opposition.

Some degree of vasoconstriction is to be expected. In older patients with atherosclerotic plaques partially occluding the major arteries, superimposed constriction (usually in the legs) leads to increasing muscle cramping with exercise (*intermittent claudication*). Other arterial spastic disorders such as Raynaud's phenomenon may appear in some individuals. These problems may be less likely if cardioselective beta-blockers are used.

Beta-Blockers in Patients with Diabetes. Insulin release normally is mediated by a beta-adrenergic mechanism. Propranolol and other noncardioselective beta-blockers depress the release of insulin by the pancreas in response to carbohydrate intake. As a consequence, blood sugar levels may rise to higher than normal values (*hyperglycemia*). Patients with diabetes develop increased difficulty in controlling this disorder.

Low blood sugar (*hypoglycemia,*) on the other end of the spectrum, also presents a problem to diabetic patients requiring insulin therapy for control. Some suffer occasional low blood sugar reactions ("insulin shock") from it. Insulin-induced hypoglycemia stimulates increased secretion of catecholamines. The resulting fast heart rate, heart palpitations, and tremulousness that follow frequently warn the individual of the problem in time for corrective action to be taken. All of these are warning signs beta-1 receptor–mediated and are suppressed by all beta-adrenergic blocking drugs, both cardioselective and noncardioselective. In other words, these drugs deprive the diabetic of the "early warning signs" of impending hypoglycemic shock.

Additionally, the restoration of blood sugar (glucose) levels after insulin hypoglycemia is highly dependent on sympathetic activity. Beta-adrenergic stimulation helps break down glycogen stored in muscle fibers to form lactate. The latter serves as a substrate for glucose production by the liver. Propranolol inhibits lactate production and prolongs the period of time required for the blood glucose level to return to normal. The prolongation of hypoglycemia is much shorter when beta-blockade is provided by cardioselective beta-adrenergic blockers.

Water Solubility

Beta-blockers may also be classified according to their solubility in lipids (fats) as compared to their solubility in water. Solubility characteristics vary among these drugs (scc Table 9.5). Those that are soluble in lipids are metabolized rapidly by the liver. Atenolol and nadalol are highly water soluble and are excreted by the kidneys. Acebutalol is more water than lipid soluble and is classified as a relatively water-soluble agent. If the patient has liver disease, water-soluble agents are preferable. Conversely, if the patient has renal insufficiency, lipid-soluble drugs are more desirable.

An advantage of water-soluble beta-adrenergic blockers is that they do not enter brain cells as readily as the lipid-soluble types. Those that are lipid soluble not only enter more easily but also tend to accumulate within brain cells. Beta-blockers can produce significant central nervous system side effects such as nightmares, insomnia, altered sleep patterns, fatigue, hallucinations, and depression. These effects are more likely to occur with lipid-soluble agents such as propranolol and are less likely with the water-soluble drugs.

Intrinsic Sympathomimetic Activity

Some beta-adrenoreceptor blocking agents have the ability to stimulate the sympathetic nervous system to some degree (*intrinsic sympathomimetic activity* or ISA). Recall that once the receptor accepts a beta-blocker, norepinephrine cannot enter to stimulate the normal response of the effector cell. However, a beta-blocker with ISA stimulates the effector cell slightly as it occupies its receptors. Sympathomemetic agents are just as effective in reducing blood pressure as the other beta-blockers, but with the important difference that they cause less reduction of heart rate and cardiac output when the patient is at rest. During exercise, however, generalized sympathetic activity is high. Blunting of increases in heart rate and in blood pressure is desirable for persons with angina pectoris or hypertension. The INA agents have the same blunting action during exercise as the other beta-blockers, but unlike the others, however, the ISA agents cause no increase, and perhaps even a decrease in total peripheral resistance. Conceivably, this desirable effect results from the partial agonistic effect of these drugs on beta-2 receptors. The absence of decrease in resting heart rate and cardiac output probably reflects partial agonist effect in beta-1 receptors.

Beta-blockers with ISA appear to be advantageous if beta-blocker therapy is desired in a patient with a slow resting heart rate or in one near myocardial failure before treatment is begun. The possibility that they might create less risk in patients with bronchial asthma, intermittent claudication, Raynaud's phenomenon, and in insulin-dependent diabetes warrants further study.

Beta-Adrenoreceptor Blockers After Acute Myocardial Infarction (Heart Attack)

The Norwegian Multicenter Study[3] has had considerable impact in medical practice. This was randomized double-blind study in which either inert placebo or 10 mg of timolol twice daily was administered, starting 7 to 28 days after acute myocardial infarction (heart attack). A total of 1,884 patients were followed for 12 to 33 months. A definite decrease in sudden death, in total mortality, and in reinfarction rates was demonstrated in the timolol-treated group compared to the placebo group (Table 9.7). Benefits were unrelated to the patients' ages.

TABLE 9.7
Outcome of Norwegian Multicenter Study (1,884 Patients)

	Mortality (No. of Patients)	Sudden Death	Second Heart Attack
Placebo	152	13.9%	20.1%
Timolol	98	7.7%	14.4%

Finally, in the United States, a beta-blocker heart attack trial (BHAT) was completed.[4] Both men and women between the ages of 30 and 69 years were included. A total of 3,837 subjects, 5 to 21 days after myocardial infarction, were randomized into placebo and propranolol groups. After an average of 25 months followup, the study was stopped because the findings had reached a level of statistical significance. Cardiac mortality and sudden death reduction in the propranolol group (Table 9.8) corroborated the findings of the Norwegian study. Once again, age did not have bearing. The beneficial effect of propranolol was most evident in the first 12 to 18 months after acute myocardial infarction. Some benefits continued, however, for the full 25 months of the study. The investigators concluded: "Based on the BHAT results, in conjunction with those of studies reported previously, the investigators recommend the use of propranolol for at least three years in patients with no contraindications to beta-blockade who have had a recent MI." If the postinfarction patient is hypertensive also, a beta-blocker would seem to be a logical ingredient for treating the high blood pressure as well.

Beta-Blocker Withdrawal Syndrome

Abrupt discontinuation of propranolol in individuals with either overt or latent coronary heart disease occasionally brings about a syndrome characterized by the appearance of rapidly progressive angina, abnormal heart rhythms, myocardial infarction, and sudden death. After this syndrome

TABLE 9.8
Outcome of Beta-Blocker Heart Attack Trial

	Total Mortality	Cardiac Mortality	Sudden Death
Placebo	9.8%	8.5%	4.6%
Propranolol	7.2%	6.2%	3.3%

had been recognized, similar withdrawal events were noted with some of the other beta-blockers.

In patients with hypertension, another type of withdrawal may occur if beta-blockers are discontinued abruptly. These episodes are very similar to those described earlier in this chapter for clonidine. Patients suffer significant elevations of blood pressure, rapid heart rate, tremulousness, anxiety, profuse sweating, and palpitations.

For both types, withdrawal symptoms usually begin 12 to 72 hours after cessation of the drug and may persist for several days. The mechanism of these syndromes is not understood completely. It is suspected that an increased number of beta receptors develop on cells during beta blockade. Such is certainly the case in human white blood cells (where receptors can be counted easily) after propranolol administration. Therefore, when the drug is discontinued abruptly, a greater than normal density of beta-receptors are available to respond to norepinephrine. There is a greater than normal response to its stimulation.

As in the withdrawal syndromes seen after sudden cessation of clonidine or methyldopa treatment, the beta-blocker events are not common. This possibility should not dissuade the physician from prescribing these drugs or the patient from taking them if they are indicated. Being forewarned of the syndrome, the physician may take steps to prevent it by tapering the dosage gradually over a two-week period before discontinuing the drug. Should withdrawal syndrome occur, reinstituting the agent usually reverses the acute situation.

Selection of a Beta-Blocker for a Given Patient

Once again, drug selection is dependent upon the total clinical picture presented by the patient. The physician tailors the selection according to the characteristics of the drug and to the needs, other concurrent disorders, and tolerances of the patient. He or she begins at the lowest dosage that may be of benefit and, if necessary, titrates upward in small increments until the desired effect is obtained, the patient develops significant side effects, or the maximal effective dose is reached.

PRAZOSIN (MINIPRES)

Prazosin is a postsynaptic alpha-adrenoreceptor blocker (Table 9.9). Just as there are beta-1 and beta-2 adrenoreceptors, there are also alpha-1 and alpha-2 receptors (Chapter 7). The alpha-1 receptors are located within the vascular smooth muscle fibers after the synapse (postsynaptic). When these receptors are occupied by catecholamines, constriction of the blood vessels occurs. The alpha-2 receptors are found at the sympathetic nerve endings just before the synapse (presynaptic). When catecholamines occupy them, they cause inhibition of further norepinephrine release from the storage vesicles of the nerve fibers.

TABLE 9.9
Characteristics of Prazosin (Minipres)

Mechanism of action:
Postsynaptic alpha-receptor blocker
- Arteriolar dilitation
- Venous dilitation

Does not trigger baroreceptor reflexes or renin release

Prazosin, having marked selectivity for postsynaptic alpha-1 receptors, blocks the constrictive stimulus. Vascular muscle relaxes, arterioles dilate, peripheral resistance drops, and blood pressure levels come down. This drug has no significant effect on the presynaptic alpha-2 receptors, and so the norepinephrine in the synaptic cleft is free to occupy and stimulate them. Further norepinephrine release ceases, so sympathetic activity is minimized. This decreased catecholamine release also tends to dampen the response of baroreceptor reflex and the release of renin by the juxtoglomerular (kidney) cells. Prazosin, then, lowers peripheral resistance, the major hemodynamic factor in fixed essential hypertension, without triggering two of the body's three compensatory mechanisms for reestablishing the original level of blood pressure.

Prazosin may be effective as a single agent in the treatment of essential hypertension in some patients. When it is used for long-term monotherapy, however, sodium and fluid retention with resulting increase in plasma volume may occur eventually and limit its antihypertensive effect (Chapter 7). When administered in conjunction with a diuretic, however, it is particularly effective. The blood-pressure-lowering effect of prazosin plus a diuretic is greater than that of either drug alone. The combination of the two drugs frequently produces equal blood pressure control with a lower dose of prazosin than would be required if it were used as the only antihypertensive agent. Prazosin alone may be effective as initial therapy in mild and perhaps in some instances of moderate hypertension. If needed, a diuretic could be added later. However, in patients with moderately severe and severe hypertension, it is best utilized as a step-2 drug added to a diuretic. It may be effective as a step-3 agent, augmenting the action of a diuretic plus a beta-blocker.

Prazosin is metabolized in large part by the liver, and most of it is excreted through the feces. It is a safe and effective drug in the management of severely hypertensive patients who have kidney disease or damage. Its antihypertensive effect is predominantly through peripheral action by blocking the postsynaptic alpha receptors, but prazosin does cross the blood-brain barrier. Lassitude, vivid dreams, hallucinations, and depression may appear as side effects, but not as frequently as with the other sympathetic inhibitors discussed.

The "first-dose phenomenon," although not common, has been well publicized. It is the major side effect concerning most physicians. This response is characterized by transient dizziness or faintness, heart palpitations, and occasionally even loss of consciousness when the patient stands up. The symptoms appear within three hours after the first dose or at subsequent times associated with increases in the dosage. These episodes are accompanied by drops of standing blood pressure (orthostatic hypotension). Postsynaptic alpha-blockade causes both arteriolar and venous dilatation. It is probably the pooling of blood in the lower body leading to decreased cardiac output and inadequate brain perfusion that causes these symptoms.

The first-dose phenomenon is dose related, and it is more likely to occur if there has been sodium depletion by preexisting diuretic therapy or marked dietary sodium restriction. The initial first few doses should be particularly low to help minimize this undesired reaction.

LABETALOL (NORMODYNE, TRANDATE)

A unique adrenoreceptor blocker, labetalol, recently has become available in the United States. It is a noncardioselective beta-blocker like propranolol but also a selective postsynaptic alpha-1 receptor blocker like prazosin. Its versatility is extended further by the fact that is has beta-2 intrinsic sympathomimetic activity. There is very little if any beta-1 agonist activity. It is primarily lipid soluble, and it passes the blood-brain barrier. Consequently, CNS side effects such as fatigue, sleep disorders, and depression do occur, but apparently less so than with other purely beta-receptor blockers.

Labetalol, then, blocks the beta-adrenoreceptors as part of its antihypertensive effect, but it also blocks postsynaptic alpha-1 receptors so that there is arteriolar relaxation and a drop in total peripheral resistance as well. Its beta-2 intrinsic sympathomimetic activity may enhance arteriolar dilatation. This agent is obviously another valuable tool in the antihypertensive armamentarium. It is being scrutinized and tested vigorously. Fuller understanding of its advantages should become apparent soon. One very evident desirable characteristic is its quick action. Labetalol can be given intravenously and it has proved to be an effective method for lowering blood pressure rapidly.

GUANADREL (HYLOREL)

Guanadrel impairs the ability of vesicles in the sympathetic nerve endings to store norepinephrine. In addition, it blocks the release of whatever norepinephrine is available when the nerve is stimulated. As a consequence, there is decreased stimulation of the arteriolar smooth muscle fibers, vasoconstriction is prevented, vascular resistance drops, and blood pressure is lowered. In addition, there is venous dilatation, pooling of blood in the lower body, and a decrease in cardiac output.

Unlike its predecessor guanethidine, its duration of action is about nine hours, and twice-daily dosing does not result in accumulation of the drug in the body. It provides smooth antihypertensive control with less side effects. It is a good step-2 agent when used with a diuretic. A major advantage is that guanadrel has no action within the central nervous system. Therefore, there is no drowsiness, sedation, sleep and dream disturbances, hallucinations, or psychic depression. Although experience is somewhat limited at this time, it may prove to be a useful agent in those patients with a tendency toward CNS side effects with other agents. A profile of the drug is given in Table 9.10.

TABLE 9.10
Characteristics of Guanadrel (Hylorel)

Mechanism of action:
Postganglionic neurone inhibitor
- Blocks release of norepinephrine from sympathetic nerve ending
- Impairs storage of norepinephrine in nerve vesicles

Does not trigger baroreceptor reflexes

Best effect: When administered with diuretic

Side effects (not common and less severe than with guanethidine)
- Orthostatic hypotension
- Diarrhea
- Sexual dysfunction

REFERENCES: CHAPTER 9

1. Quetsh RM, Achor RWP, Litin EM, et al.: Depressive reactions in hypertensive patients: a comparison of those treated with rauwolfia and those receiving no specific antihypertensive therapy. *Circulation* 1959; 19:366–375.
2. Benson MK, Berrill WT, Sterling GM, et al.: Cardioselective and non-cardioselective beta blockers in reversible obstructive airways disease. *Postgrad Med J* 1977; 53(suppl 3):143–148.
3. The Norwegian Multicenter Study Group: Timolol-induced reduction in mortality and reinfarction in patients surviving acute myocardial infarction. *N Engl J Med* 1981; 304:801–807.
4. Beta-Blocker Heart Attack Trial Research Group: A randomized trial of propranolol in patients with acute myocardial infarction. I. Mortality results. *JAMA* 1982; 247: 1707–1714.

CHAPTER 10

VASODILATORS, CONVERTING-ENZYME INHIBITORS AND CALCIUM-CHANNEL BLOCKERS

IF ongoing diuretic therapy and the addition of a sympathetic inhibitor have not provided the desired antihypertensive response, a vasodilator is added to the therapeutic regimen. This move is the third stage in the stepped-care approach. In this category two drugs, hydralazine (Apresoline) and minoxidil (Loniten) are currently available. Both can be administered orally over a long period.

VASODILATORS

The antihypertensive effect of hydralazine and minoxidil is related to their ability to relax arteriolar smooth muscle directly, perhaps by interfering with calcium activity within the cells themselves. The smooth muscle relaxation is limited largely to the arterial vessels, and the veins are not effected significantly. The arterioles dilate, peripheral vascular resistance drops, and blood pressure is lowered.[1] If the vasodilators were to be used as sole therapy, the drop in pressure would activate the compensatory mechanisms of the body that were explained in Chapter 7. The baroreceptor reflex would increase the heart rate, the force of myocardial contractility, cardiac output, and total peripheral resistance. In addition, the drop in perfusion pressure in the afferent glomerular arterioles of the kidney would lead to the release of renin and to activation of the renin-angiotensin-aldosterone (RAA) axis. This second compensatory mechanism would lead to further arteriolar constriction and increase in total peripheral resistance, sodium and water retention, and expansion of extracellular fluid (plasma) volume. These actions would all definitely limit the full antihypertensive effectiveness of the vasodilator during long-term use.

Since most patients with moderate or severe sustained hypertension have a normal cardiac output but an elevated total peripheral resistance, and since the latter is the major cause of the elevation in blood pressure, it seems logical that direct vasodilators should be the drugs of choice for them. However, as described above, the effect of vasodilators is greatly curtailed by the body's compensatory mechanisms, which attempt to maintain the pressure at its setpoint even though that setpoint may be elevated to abnormal heights. The baroreceptor reflexes and the release of renin in response to the drop in pressure can be prevented by concomitant administration of a sympathetic inhibitor—step 2 of the stepped-care approach. The most effective agent for this purpose is a beta-adrenoreceptor blocker. Propranolol has been used by most physicians the longest, and it has proved to be satisfactory. It prevents the rapid heart rate, increased cardiac output, and increase in renin release. The other beta-blockers perform equally well when administered in equipotent doses. Diuretic agents given daily—step 1 of the stepped-care approach—prevent sodium retention and expansion of extracellular fluid and plasma volumes.

Hydralazine (Apresoline)

The first vasodilator that could be taken orally for its antihypertensive effect was hydralazine. It appeared before the sympathetic inhibitor reserpine and the diuretic chlorothiazide. Since the normal compensatory mechanisms to lowering of the blood pressure were not fully appreciated at that time, and since diuretics and sympathetic inhibitors were being studied individually and independently, hydralazine was used as monotherapy. The baroreceptor reflexes induced angina pectoris, abnormal heart rhythms, and sudden death in patients with underlying coronary artery disease. The increased cardiac output, sodium retention, and expanded fluid volume all diminished the initial blood pressure–lowering response. Progressively higher doses, even beyond one gram per day, were prescribed. Eventually, it was noted that long-term administration of hydralazine in large doses led to a syndrome that simulated a disease called disseminated lupus erythematosus. As a consequence, the drug was considered of limited value until the stepped-care approach was introduced. The concomitant use of diuretics and beta-adrenoreceptor blockers with hydralazine has revived its use as an effective, valuable agent, since the combination approach allows it to be kept at safe dosage levels.

Hydralazine is absorbed best and is more effective if it is taken with meals. The antihypertensive action lasts for at least 12 hours with each dose. A small initial dosage taken twice daily (with meals) may be titrated upward until the desired effect is obtained or a total of 300 mg per day is reached. The physician watches for such nonspecific reactions as skin rashes or gastrointestinal disorders, although these side effects are not common. Even less commonly, drug fever and the signs and symptoms of serum sickness may appear after about one to two weeks of therapy with hydralazine. It also may precipitate vascular headaches.

The most notorious effect is, of course, the appearance of a disseminated lupus erythematosus syndrome in long-term hydralazine therapy. This complication has been shown to be dose related, and it eventually appears in up to 3 percent of patients who have been taking 400 mg per day or more. Fortunately, the syndrome is reversible after the drug is discontinued, but it may persist for up to several years.

Hydralazine is an excellent drug to add to the regimen of those patients with essential hypertension for whom the combination of a diuretic and a sympathetic inhibitor provides inadequate antihypertensive effects. Its properties are summarized in Table 10.1.

**TABLE 10.1
Characteristics of Hydralazine (Apresoline)**

Mechanism of action: Direct dilator of arteriolar tree

Administered by adding to therapeutic regimen after diuretic and sympathetic inhibitor therapy has been established and treatment goals are not being reached

Side effects:
- Dermatitis
- Nonspecific gastrointestinal symptoms
- Drug fever; serum sickness
- Peripheral neuropathy
- Vascular headaches
- Systemic lupus erythematosus-like syndrome (usually in those taking 400 mg/d or more)

Minoxidil (Loniten)

Minoxidil, another orally administered vasodilator, became available more recently than hydralazine. It, too, works directly on arteriolar smooth muscle to produce relaxation and consequent reduction in peripheral resistance. The mechanism of action may be related to interference with calcium activity within the muscle cells. It is more potent and more effective in lowering the blood pressure than hydralazine, and its use in a wide dosage range has not been accompanied by the lupus erythematosus–like syndrome. Like hydralazine, it has minimal if any influence on veins, and therefore pooling of blood in the lower extremities and orthostatic hypotension are not significant problems.

As would be expected, vasodilatation and the drop in blood pressure produced if minoxidil were to be administered alone would lead to the classic compensatory effects already mentioned so often; increased heart rate, increased cardiac output, increased plasma renin activity, and sodium retention. These compensatory measures would blunt the maximal attainable antihypertensive effect. The concomitant administration of beta-adrenergic blockers such as propranolol has proved to be successful in preventing the baroreceptor reflexes in most instances. In those situations where beta-blockers have been contraindicated (see Chapter 9), clonidine has been substituted with good results.

Retention of sodium and fluid is a significant, troublesome problem with minoxidil therapy in many patients, particularly in those with some degree of renal insufficiency. Weight gain and soft tissue swelling (*edema*) may begin early in the course of treatment in some individuals despite the concomitant administration of diuretics. Although the mechanism of sodium retention is extraordinary during treatment with minoxidil (there is additional sodium reabsorption in the proximal tubule not dependent upon aldosterone), it is felt that yet another superimposed factor produces excessive tissue edema. Possibly the magnitude of edema may be the result of marked arteriolar dilatation that permits transmission of a higher pressure into the capillary bed. This increased intracapillary hydrostatic pressure may result in a shift of fluid through the capillary wall into the adjacent soft tissue structures. If edema occurs despite diuretic therapy with thiazides or thiazide-like drugs, the diuretic of choice becomes furosemide. A total dose of up to 400 mg daily may be required to control fluid retention.

Minoxidil is an effective vasodilator when administered orally (Table 10.2). Its potency enables it to normalize vascular resistance even in severely vasospastic forms of hypertension. Used in combination with furosemide and beta-adrenergic blockers, it has proved to be successful in

TABLE 10.2
Characteristics of Minoxidil (Loniten)

Mechanism of action: Directly relaxes arteriolar smooth muscle resulting in decreased vascular resistance

Administer in conjunction with diuretic and beta-adrenoreceptor blocking agent

Effective treatment for hypertension refractory to other triple-drug therapy, with or without some degree of renal insufficiency

Side effects:
- Sodium and water retention; edema despite coadministered diuretic therapy
- Hypertrichosis
- Pericardial effusion
- Nonspecific T wave changes on EKG

---

the long-term control of hypertension in patients with impaired kidney function or in any others with severe hypertension. Many such patients are not helped by other triple-drug programs.

Increased hair growth (*hypertrichosis*) is an important adverse effect for some of those taking minoxidil. Elongation, thickening, and increased pigmentation of fine body hair is seen in approximately 80 percent of patients taking the drug. Most frequently, it becomes apparent on the face, forehead, temples, arms, back, and chest. Hair growth begins two to sixteen weeks after initiation of therapy and will cease with discontinuation of the drug. There are no endocrine gland changes to explain hair growth. It is thought to be related to increased blood circulation in the skin.

Although the patient may have no symptoms, nonspecific electrocardiographic (EKG) changes may appear after the institution of minoxidil therapy. These changes clear rapidly when the drug is discontinued. Occasional instances of pericarditis (inflammation of the sac surrounding the heart) and pericardial effusion (fluid within the pericardium) have been reported.

Minoxidil is a valuable addition to our antihypertensive tools, particularly for difficult-to-control cases. It is effective when used with a beta-blocker and a diuretic in even the severe forms of the disease.

CONVERTING-ENZYME INHIBITORS

As discussed in Chapter 2, a converting enzyme found primarily in the circulation through the lungs is required to convert physiologically inactive angiotensin I to potent angiotensin II. The latter is the key effector hormone of the renin-angiotensin-aldosterone (RAA) axis, and it brings about both peripheral vascular constriction and increased release of aldosterone by the adrenal cortex. Both of these actions lead to elevation of blood pressure. If the action of converting enzyme could be inhibited, the RAA axis could be "defused" as a factor in the production of hypertension in those instances where it plays a causative role.

Captopril (Capoten)

The first orally administered converting-enzyme inhibitor to become available in the United States is captopril. It is an effective antihypertensive agent when used alone at times, but even more effective when given with a diuretic.[2] Patients with malignant or renovascular hypertension, whose blood pressure elevation usually is associated with high plasma renin activity, respond very well to captopril therapy. So do patients with high-renin essential hypertension.

Surprisingly, some mid-renin and even some low-renin hypertensives respond with distinct reduction in blood pressure when treated with this drug. At first glance, it seems paradoxical that low-renin essential hypertension would be influenced in any way by an agent that inhibits production of angiotensin II, since it does not depend upon angiotensin II activity. It so happens that the angiotensin-converting enzyme is the same enzyme that serves to inactivate vasodilating bradykinin (Chapter 2). Since captopril inhibits this action also, bradykinin would accumulate and its blood pressure–lowering action would be enhanced.

The drug has been used as an initial agent in treatment of hypertension and has enjoyed some success as a monotherapeutic agent in patients with mild to moderate high-renin essential hypertension. Captopril's effectiveness is more pronounced when administered with a diuretic. Finally, captopril appears to be equal to or more potent than hydralazine when combined with propranolol and a diuretic in patients with apparently refractory hypertension.

This drug should be taken during a fasting state, one hour before or two hours after a meal. If taken with food in the stomach or upper intestinal tract, absorption into the bloodstream is reduced by 30 to 40 percent. A good portion of captopril in the blood is eventually excreted into the urine by the kidneys within 24 hours; therefore the usual dose must be reduced for patients with renal insufficiency to prevent accumulation and increasing blood levels of the drug.

In about 0.3 percent of patients initially treated with captopril, bone marrow depression, with decreased production of white blood cells predominantly, was encountered within the first three to twelve weeks of treatment. In many of these patients, there were preexisting disorders such as advanced kidney failure, malignant tumors that had spread throughout the body, and disorders of the immune system. Some were receiving other drugs that had the potential of causing bone marrow depression themselves. Increased loss of protein, usually an indicator of kidney damage, occurred in another 1 percent. As stated above, many of these first subjects had advanced kidney disease as a preexisting problem. However, it should be noted that acute kidney failure has been reported when captopril has been used in hypertensives who had renal artery obstruction of one or both kidneys. Another side effect is a temporary loss of taste or a metallic/salty taste sensation (*ageusia*) that may occur in a small number of patients. Frequently it is merely a transient occurrence and may disappear even though the medication is continued.

The adverse effects described are not common. They usually occur in patients with far-advanced diseases as well as severe hypertension where higher doses are needed. More recent studies are showing that lower doses of captopril are effective in patients with mild to moderate hypertension with a low incidence of adverse effects, provided the patients do not have coexisting disorders, such as diabetes, that damage the kidneys.

Enalapril (Vasotec)

The converting enzyme inhibitor enalapril, is a more recently available agent in this category. The converting enzyme inhibitors, offer another entirely different pharmacologic category of antihypertensive medication which might be considered suitable for step 1, step 2, and step 3 within the stepped-care scheme of therapeutic strategy in selected individuals.

CALCIUM-CHANNEL BLOCKERS

As discussed in Chapter 2, one of the possible mechanisms for the development of essential hypertension is increased intracellular sodium concentration within the arteriolar smooth muscle cells due to a defect in cellular sodium efflux. Sodium efflux rates have been found to be diminished primarily in patients with low-renin essential hypertension. Elevated intracellular sodium concentrations are accompanied by a rise in free intracellular calcium concentrations. The latter lead to increased tone, reactivity to stimulation, and contractility of the arteriolar smooth muscle, leading in turn to arteriolar constriction, increased total peripheral resistance, and hypertension. In this group of patients, a drug that would block the influx of calcium into the cell might blunt or inhibit the mechanism that leads to elevated blood pressure. Calcium-channel blocking agents do decrease the influx of extracellular calcium into the cell, inhibit smooth muscle contraction, and lower vascular resistance. In effect, they counteract the basic hemodynamic abnormality in essential hypertension.[3]

The various calcium-channel blockers available today differ considerably from one another in molecular structure and do not belong "in the same family." They do have the common property, however, of being able to inhibit the flux of extracellular calcium ions across the cell membrane. They all produce relaxation of smooth muscle, vasodilatation, and a decrease in total peripheral resistance. Calcium-channel blockers have proved to be most effective for the treatment of angina pectoris in those situations where coronary artery spasm has been a factor. They are more effective as antihypertensive agents in those with low plasma renin activity such as older patients and blacks. Currently there are three calcium-channel blockers available in the United States: nifedipine, verapamil, and diltiazem.

Nifedipine (Procardia)

Nifedipine, a calcium-channel blocker that has proved to be a valuable therapeutic agent for vasospastic angina, was demonstrated also to have a blood pressure–lowering action in 1977. The hypotensive effect appears within 15 minutes after placing nifedipine under the tongue or within 30 minutes if it is swallowed. Significant reduction of blood pressure is usually maintained for six to eight hours after a single dose. The rapidity of effective action and the ease of administration make it a useful agent for lowering blood pressure quickly.

Although current reports of long-term studies are limited to weeks or a few months, it appears that administration of nifedipine alone every eight hours will maintain good antihypertensive control in mild to moderate hypertension (step 1). In more severe hypertension, good responses have been noted when nifedipine is added to a diuretic or to a beta-adrenergic blocker (step 2). Similarly, it has functioned well as a step-3 agent in some situations.

Initially, when nifedipine is used as monotherapy for hypertension, the rapid vasodilatation it produces may bring about flushing, headaches, and stimulation of the baroreceptors resulting in rapid heart rate and palpitations. Investigators differ in their findings in studies lasting 3 to 16 weeks. Some do not find persistence of these signs when nifedipine is administered for longer periods, whereas others record persistent rapid heart rates for the full period of observation. There has been no evidence of sodium or water retention and no weight gain, although the addition of a diuretic frequently enhances the antihypertensive effect of nifedipine. The flushing, headaches, palpitations, and rapid heart rate are readily controlled by the addition of a beta-adrenergic blocker.

There is no change in serum levels of potassium, glucose, cholesterol (total, LDL, or HDL) when nifedipine is the sole antihypertensive drug used. If a form that will provide sustained action so that only one or two doses per day provide good control is produced, if present encouraging observations hold up in long-term studies, and if the Federal Food and Drug Administration approves it for use as an antihypertensive, nifedipine and the other calcium channel blockers will provide us with still another new category of pharmacologic agents to treat essential hypertension.

Verapamil (Calan; Isoptin) and Diltiazem (Cardiazem)

Verapamil and diltiazem are also calcium channel blocking drugs. They share the beneficial effects in coronary artery disease and appear to have equal but less prompt antihypertensive actions as nifedipine. Unlike nifedipine, however, there is no reflex rapid heart rate as the blood pressure drops. There has been no evidence of sodium or water retention after several months of continuous treatment. These two have a beta-adrenergic–like effect on the myocardium in that they slow the heart rate and decrease myocardial contractility. Unlike most beta-blockers, however, they lower total peripheral resistance. As with nifedipine, these agents may become increasingly more important antihypertensive drugs in the future as more knowledge is gained.

REFERENCES: CHAPTER 10

1. Koch-Weser J: Vasodilatation for vasospastic hypertension. *N Engl J Med* 1973; 289:213–214.

2. Johns DW, Baker KM, Ayers CR, et al.: Acute and chronic effect of captopril in hypertensive patients. *Hypertension* 1980; 2:567–575.

3. Guazzi MD, Polese A, Fiorentini C, et al.: Treatment of hypertension with calcium antagonists, *Hypertension* 1983; 5(suppl 2):85–90.

CHAPTER 11

HYPERTENSION IN ELDERLY PATIENTS

FOR many years, the medical profession as a whole generally believed that older individuals tolerated mild to moderate hypertension well. In the absence of overt target-organ involvement, elevation of blood pressure at these levels was regarded as a relatively benign condition. After all, since the arterial tree would not be subject to those elevated pressures for much longer, little damage could result. This view, coupled with the experience that using the usual dosages in severely hypertensive elderly patients frequently led to frightening and even tragic consequences, seemed to justify the decision to leave well enough alone. Gradually, however, it has become obvious that the risk from high blood pressure, even mild hypertension, becomes greater with age. The elderly tolerate hypertension less well than younger people. In both sexes, and in black and nonblack racial groups, mortality rates rise sharply in those with higher blood pressure levels.

In a discussion of hypertension in the elderly, one must consider three categories: (1) essential hypertension, usually a continuation from a younger age; (2) hypertension first appearing in older age—hypertension *de novo;* and (3) pure, isolated systolic hypertension.

ESSENTIAL HYPERTENSION

Epidemiologic surveys reveal that the prevalence of hypertension, using the World Health Organization definition (160/95 mm Hg or higher), in the U.S. general adult population is about 16 percent (9 percent in whites and 22 percent in blacks). The prevalence of this disorder in those over 65 years of age is still greater, remaining higher in blacks than in whites.

Cross-sectional studies of adult populations (concurrently evaluating different subjects in distinct age groups such as 20 to 30 years, 31 to 40 years, 41 to 50 years, etc.) in the Western nations reveal a tendency for both systolic and diastolic pressures to rise gradually with age so that "normal levels" of 160–180/90–100 mm Hg are reached between 60 and 80 years. Closer to the truth, however, are longitudinal studies (blood pressure determinations obtained repeatedly in the same individuals over a long period) which show that elevations in blood pressure are not related directly to aging but rather to the presence of mildly elevated blood pressure earlier in life. If an individual's blood pressure is in the upper 10 percent of "normal" initially, chances are good that it will continue to rise in subsequent years. Blood pressure does not increase from normal to abnormal levels during adult life in most other individuals. The classic form of essential hypertension in the elderly, then, is a continuation of essential hypertension, albeit mild, in earlier life.

Since the risk of cardiovascular events (heart attack or stroke) increases with the level of the blood pressure for each decade of age, and the difference in risk between hypertensives and normotensives increases with age, it was important to determine whether treatment exerted a beneficial effect. As described in earlier chapters, the Veterans Administration Cooperative Study on Antihypertensive Agents[1] revealed that therapy was highly effective in reducing illness and death for both middle-aged and older males whose diastolic pressures initially ranged between 115 and 120 mm Hg. In those with diastolic pressures in the mild to moderate category (90 to 114 mm Hg), there was similar benefit from treatment. In 81 subjects aged 60 to 69 years in the latter group, there was a marked reduction in the incidence of strokes (7.9 percent in the treated group versus 23.3 percent in the placebo group) and of congestive heart failure (0 percent versus 20.9 percent).

Priddle and his associates[2] studied 183 patients with blood pressure levels at 180/100 mm Hg or higher in metropolitan Toronto homes for the aged. Half received no therapy for hypertension while the other half received a thiazide diuretic daily. After four years, the mortality rate for the treated group was only half that for the untreated group. Beevers and his colleagues[3] treated 162 hypertensive patients who had suffered strokes. After four years, the lower the diastolic pressure range that was achieved, the lower the stroke recurrence rate (Table 11.1)

TABLE 11.1
Stroke Recurrence Rate Related to Level of Diastolic Pressure Attained by Antihypertensive Treatment (From Beevers, et al.[3])

Diastolic Pressure Range Achieved	Stroke Recurrence Rate (%)
Less than 100 mm Hg	16
100 to 109 mm Hg	32
110 mm Hg or more	55

In the Hypertension Detection and Follow-up Program (Chapter 5), almost 11,000 hypertensives in 14 communities were treated under strict stepped-care protocol (SC) or by doctors in the community to whom the subjects were referred for customary care (RC). Of these subjects, 2,376 were over 60 years of age upon entry into the study. About 70 percent of all subjects suffered mild hypertension (diastolic range 90 to 104 mm Hg). At the end of the five-year study period, it was readily apparent that in those in whom there was greater success in reaching the therapeutic goal of blood pressure normalization (the SC group), there was a greater decrease in overall mortality. Specifically, mortality due to stroke and to myocardial infarction (heart attack) was reduced considerably in this group. It should be noted that the benefits in overall mortality were not as obvious among the younger subjects but were distinctly and significantly present in the patient group that had been 50 to 69 years of age upon entry into the study. It is justifiable to conclude that treatment of hypertension, even mild hypertension, in older patients (at least up to the age of 74) is effective and likely to be of benefit. Unfortunately, there is little information about the risk:benefit ratio of drug therapy programs for patients over 75. Perhaps it would be wise to treat these patients with nondrug measures until blood pressure levels are consistently 160/100 mm Hg or higher, or if overt target organ damage is evident. Then drugs might be initiated cautiously.

There is no question but that drug treatment of all older patients requires greater care, closer observation, and versatility of the physician. An abrupt sizable reduction in blood pressure in this age group may lead to dire results. A drop in arterial pressure sufficient to compromise blood perfusion of vital organs such as the brain and the heart must be avoided. On the other hand, in the intervention studies described in Chapter 5, it is obvious that gradual lowering of blood pressure with antihypertensive agents is achievable without major ill effects in older patients. Certainly, no treatment at all may place them at risk.

One precaution must be emphasized. There is a tendency for blood pressure in older people to fall initially when they stand up (*orthostatic hypotension*) even if they are not taking antihypertensive drugs. Caird[4] showed that this phenomenon occurs in those with normal blood pressure levels as well as in those with hypertension (Table 11.2). The prudent physician, then, will base the decision to initiate drug therapy or adjust dosage on blood pressure measurements taken after one minute of quiet standing. Otherwise, one might overshoot the dosage needed and bring about profound hypotension when patients stand up.

TABLE 11.2
Drop in Systolic Pressure after One Minute Quiet Standing in 494 Subjects 65 Years or Older (From Coird[4])

Drop (mm Hg)	Subjects (%)
20	24
30	9
40	5

The standard stepped-care approach for hypertension treatment is a rational program for elderly patients as well as younger ones. The physician must be aware that the aging body adapts less readily than a younger one to environmental changes. Patience is needed. Rapid and drastic alterations should be avoided. Most physicians begin with a diuretic (Chapter 8). For a large percentage of older people, this agent alone is effective. Even when it is not, it enhances the action of other antihypertensive drugs that might be added. The desired effects of the second-step drugs will be reached at a lower dose, thus minimizing their side effects.

Hemodynamically, a large proportion of older individuals with sustained essential hypertension have low plasma volume, low cardiac output, and high total peripheral resistance. Diuretics initially cause a further decrease in plasma volume and cardiac output. To prevent inadequate perfusion of vital organs, the physician must begin with smaller than usual doses. As the drug is continued daily, diuresis diminishes; both plasma volume and cardiac output tend to move toward pretreatment levels (Chapter 8), but in those hypertensives who respond, peripheral resistance drops. If adequate lowering of blood pressure has not occurred in eight to twelve weeks and if the patient has not suffered any ill effects, the physician might increase the dosage for another six to eight weeks.

Indapamide (Lozol), a more recently available diuretic, offers an alternative to the more usually prescribed hydrochlorothiazide or chlorthalidone. As described in Chapter 8, indapamide is a weak diuretic, but a small dose that produces only about one-third the diuresis as the other two lowers peripheral resistance (and therefore blood pressure) equally as well as the more commonly used diuretics in standard dosage. Excellent antihypertensive results with few untoward effects are being reported with a once-daily dosage regimen in older people with essential hypertension. If elevated blood pressure levels persist despite a course of diuretics, the physician may proceed to the second stage and add a sympathetic inhibitor (Chapter 9).

It is important for both physician and patient to remember that liver and kidney function are diminished with aging, even though no disease of these organs is present. This means that most medications are excreted from the body more slowly and consequently remain in the blood and tissues longer. Obviously, the doses and dosage intervals specified for adults are likely to be inappropriate for elderly persons. Extended drug activity and accumulation of the drug in the body may be dangerous. The commonly held notion that "if a little is good for me, twice as much is twice as good" may pose lethal hazards for older people. In addition, certain drugs potentiate (increase) the effects of others when given in combination. This potential effect makes it especially important to keep your physician informed about *all* drugs you are taking, including vitamins and over-the-counter preparations like aspirin and cold remedies.

Reserpine

In both the VA Cooperative Study and the Hypertension Detection and Follow-up Program, the sympathetic inhibitor used was reserpine. If the dosage is maintained at no more than 0.1 mg per day in older patients, adequate pharmacologic action will be obtained and side effects such as nasal congestion, increased stomach acid secretion, drowsiness, lethargy, and depression are moderated. Nevertheless, since slowing of the thinking process and subtle depression are common in the elderly even without any medication, many physicians are reluctant to use reserpine for fear of compounding the problem. Conversely, the expectation of impaired thinking or depression as "part of getting old" may cause the patient or physician to overlook symptoms that are actually side effects of medication. Such symptoms should always be reported and investigated.

Beta-Adrenergic Blockers

Propranolol (Inderal) and other beta-adrenergic blocking agents are sympathetic inhibitors commonly used in the treatment of essential hypertension. They do not work as well in the elderly, however, for lowering blood pressure. The number of beta receptors in cells apparently decreases with age. The physician may try beta-adrenergic blockers, however, if the patient has not only hypertension but also angina pectoris. The drug provides considerable benefit to those afflicted with chest pain. Also, in the treatment of hypertension in those who have suffered a heart attack, a beta-blocker should be considered in view of its influence in reducing the death rate and the rate of recurrence. If a beta-blocker is to be used, it would seem reasonable to select a cardioselective agent to avoid the undesirable effects of beta-2 blockade. Also, using a water-soluble agent will minimize central nervous system symptoms (see Table 9.5). The beta-adrenergic blockers are just as effective in the elderly as in younger patients in the treatment of coronary heart disease.

Prazosin (Minipres)

The postsynaptic alpha-blocker prazosin (Minipres) has a primarily peripheral antihypertensive effect. It is effective and well tolerated in those less than 65 years of age. By blocking stimulation of the alpha-receptors in blood-vessel smooth muscle it causes both the arteriolar bed and the veins to dilate. Peripheral resistance drops, and blood pressure is lowered. The physician will be wary of the tendency for orthostatic hypotension in older people. A simple faint, fall, and fracture may be devastating to an aging person. Although not common, a first-dose phenomenon (orthostatic reduction in blood pressure which may result in lightheadedness or a faint) has been reported even in younger individuals. In older people, the danger continues beyond the first dose. This undesirable effect is more likely to occur if the patient is fluid volume–depleted by diuretic therapy.

Prazosin, however, is less likely to cause drowsiness, languor, slowing of the thinking process, nightmares, hallucinations, and depression than most of the other sympathetic inhibitors. It remains a valuable drug in the treatment of hypertension in older people when used judiciously. The possibility of orthostatic hypotension may be minimized by warning the patient against standing up too quickly and by beginning with smaller than usual doses and then proceeding with small, gradual incremental upward titration.

Central Alpha-Receptor Agonists

The central nervous system alpha-receptor agonists, methyldopa (Aldomet) clonidine (Catapres), and guanabenz (Wytensin) diminish the outflow of sympathetic impulses to the peripheral autonomic nervous system; consequently, the arterioles relax and blood pressure falls. Orthostatic hypotension is unusual with these agents.

Methyldopa (Aldomet). For many years, methyldopa has been used to treat hypertension in elderly patients. It is effective and is usually tolerated satisfactorily. Small doses may suffice initially. If necessary, gradual incremental increases are usually effective. Side effects include drowsiness, inability to perform complex mental tasks, fatigue, and depression. On occasion, these are sufficient to require discontinuing the drug. Rarely, methyldopa is related to drug fever which may or may not be associated with hepatitis. It is probably unwise to administer this agent to patients with evidence of liver disease.

Clonidine (Catapres). Also a CNS alpha-receptor agonist, clonidine is an effective antihypertensive drug in the elderly. It is well tolerated, and its duration of pharmacologic activity in older patients is such that once-daily dosing provides smooth 24-hour antihypertensive effect in most individuals. If necessary, careful, slow titration upward may be employed to attain the desired response. Clonidine frequently is effective in small doses. The major side effects, drowsiness and dry mouth, can be minimized by taking the once-daily at bedtime. By morning, these effects have worn off for the most part, while the antihypertensive effect continues during the day. Although any of the sympathetic inhibitors may be used in elders with proper dosage and caution, clonidine would seem to be one of the top choices.

Guanabenz (Wytensin). The most recent central alpha-receptor agonist to become available is also efficacious. Experience is too limited for this author to be able to comment further.

Hydralazine (Apresoline)

In that relatively small proportion of patients for whom a diuretic is ineffective—even after a sympathetic inhibitor has been added and carefully titrated to maximum dose—a vasodilator is added. Hydralazine acts directly to relax smooth muscle in the walls of the arterioles. Its effect is limited primarily to the arteries. Since its effect on veins is minimal, pooling of blood in the lower half of the body does not occur and orthostatic hypotension is not likely. The initial dose may be increased gradually in small increments.

Ordinarily, if hydralazine were to be given alone, the compensatory mechanisms would come into play and would blunt its effectiveness (Chapter 7) as discussed before. The diuretic of step 1 prevents sodium and water retention. The sympathetic inhibitor of step 2 blocks the baroreceptor reflex. Now the vasodilator is unopposed, and its full pharmacologic action is reached at relatively low doses.

However, since the responsiveness of the baroreceptor

reflex tends to diminish with advancing age in some individuals, hydralazine in small doses may be added directly after the diuretic (step 2) if the resting pulse rate is 60 beats per minute or less. If blood pressure response is good, and if there is no significant rise in resting pulse rate and no evidence of angina or abnormal heart rhythms, the sympathetic inhibitors, which are the drugs most likely to produce undesirable side effects, can be avoided. If the pulse rate does increase or if there is evidence of increasing angina or abnormal cardiac rhythms, the vasodilator is withdrawn and not added again until the traditional second step of establishing a sympathetic inhibitor base has been completed.

HYPERTENSION DE NOVO

The abrupt appearance of significant sustained hypertension in a previously normotensive elderly individual is very likely to be secondary to atherosclerotic occlusive disease of the renal artery (Chapter 4). Although surgical alleviation or bypass of the obstruction may eliminate the problem, some patients with renovascular hypertension may respond to medical therapy as well. Length of survival of patients treated surgically compared to those treated successfully by medication is essentially the same. Under these circumstances, the approach suggested by Hunt and his coworkers[5] seems reasonable. All such patients were treated medically initially. If the response was unsatisfactory after 30 to 90 days, surgery was recommended. More recently, with the early successes being attained by percutaneous transluminal dilatation of involved renal arteries (Chapter 4), a safer alternative to surgery becomes a consideration.

PURE SYSTOLIC HYPERTENSION

Isolated systolic hypertension (systolic pressure of 160 mm Hg or more and diastolic pressure of 90 mm Hg or less) is a distinct clinical entity. The prevalence remains well under 3 percent of the adult population in the United States until the age of 50 years. After 65 years, the prevalence rises sharply and includes 30 to 40 percent of that portion of our population. In most of these elderly people with isolated systolic hypertension, the elevation reflects arteriosclerotic changes in the aorta and great arteries. These vessels stiffen and lose their elasticity. When the left ventricle ejects a bolus of blood into the aorta, the latter does not stretch and accept the volume gracefully. It remains rigid, and some of the force that was absorbed by a distensible aorta in earlier years continues forward into the circulation, causing a rise in systolic pressure.

Isolated or pure systolic hypertension in the elderly has been shown to correlate inversely with survival. There is a distinct two- to threefold increase of angina, myocardial infarction, and stroke in older patients with pure systolic pressure elevation when compared to their normotensive counterparts. With any diastolic pressure, be it low, normal, or high, the risk of stroke or cardiovascular disease rises as systolic pressure rises.

Unlike essential (combined systolic and diastolic) hypertension in which beneficial results have been shown to occur with successful lowering of blood pressure levels, there have been no studies so far to help determine whether lowering isolated systolic hypertension alters the outcome in the elderly. Since severe arteriosclerosis of the aorta and major arteries is the cause of the systolic pressure elevation, it is argued by some that stroke, myocardial infarction, and death in these patients are also directly related to the arterial disease rather than to the level of systolic pressure that might be reached. However, the rigid aorta's resistance to the left ventricle's ejection of blood makes the heart muscle work harder and puts increased demands on the heart. The repeated pulsations of high systolic pressure may well hasten the progress of atherosclerotic changes.

Although studies remain to be done (some are in progress now) before a true assessment regarding the value of treatment can be made, many physicians are beginning to treat patients with isolated systolic pressure of 180 mm Hg or more. Although the decision is somewhat arbitrary, it is not unreasonable. Elderly patients do tolerate slow and cautious reduction of systolic pressure to the 140 mm Hg to 160 mm Hg range. The peripheral arteriolar bed does react with some degree of vasoconstriction (autoregulation) to the high systolic pressures attained during systole in these patients. Consequently, there is some increase in peripheral resistance and in diastolic pressure, although the latter may remain within normal limits. Experience has taught us that in these patients, any reduction in diastolic pressure is accompanied by a more substantial drop in systolic pressure. The steeper the relation between the systolic and diastolic pressures at the outset, the greater the systolic drop to be expected.

The stepped-care approach that is recommended for treatment of essential hypertension in the elderly is suitable for pure systolic hypertension as well. Even though the diastolic level is within normal limits, a minimal reduction of diastolic pressure resulting from a decrease in peripheral resistance affords an easier "run-off" for the bolus of blood ejected into the rigid arterial system with ventricular systole. This slight drop in diastolic pressure, then, frequently is accompanied by a substantial drop in systolic pressure.

It should be restated that proof that lowering solely systolic hypertension in the elderly is beneficial does not exist yet. The older individual who has pure systolic hypertension but no symptoms poses a dilemma. Until the value of treatment is established, great care must be taken to do no harm. The National High Blood Pressure Education Program Coordinating Committee[6] indicated that no definite recommendations can be made at this time, but if the decision is made to treat such patients, the goal of therapy should be to reduce systolic pressure to the 140 mm Hg to 160 mm Hg range. Obviously, the program should be a cautious one with close monitoring. If the patient develops ill effects during the process, cessation of treatment might be the better choice.

REFERENCES: CHAPTER 11

1. Veterans Administration Cooperative Study Group on Antihypertensive Agents: Effects of treatment on morbidity in hypertension. III. Influence of age, diastolic pressure, and prior cardiovascular disease; further analysis of side effects. *Circulation* 1972; 45:991–1003.

2. Priddle WW, Liu SF, Breithaupt DJ, et al.: Amelioration of high blood pressure in the elderly. *J Am Geriatr Soc* 1968; 16:887–892.

3. Beevers DG, Hamilton M, Fairman MJ, et al.: Antihypertensive treatment and the course of established cerebral vascular disease. *Lancet* 1973; 1:1407–1409.

4. Caird FI, Andrews GR, Kennedy RD: Effect of posture on blood pressure in the elderly. *Br Heart J* 1973; 35:527–530.

5. Hunt JC, Sheps SG, Harrison EG Jr, et al.: Renal and renovascular hypertension. A reasoned approach to diagnosis and management. *Arch Intern Med* 1974; 133:988–999.

6. National High Blood Pressure Education Program Coordinating Committee: *Statement on Hypertension in the Elderly*. Bethesda, National Institutes of Health, 1979.

CHAPTER 12

MILD HYPERTENSION

LARGE-SCALE trials to evaluate the effect of drug intervention in hypertension were discussed in Chapter 5. These studies indicate that successful treatment benefits even those patients with mild hypertension. Treatment slows progression from mild to more severe degrees of hypertension, and left ventricular hypertrophy, congestive heart failure, stroke, and progression to diminished kidney function are less likely to occur. It is true that the greatest reduction in death rates is achieved when mild hypertension is treated in older individuals, but the period of observation in these trials, three to ten years, may be too short to demonstrate the long-term benefits to be derived by younger patients. We should judge the success of treatment in this group in terms of preventing progression of the disease rather than by mortality rates.

IS TREATMENT BENEFICIAL?

A disappointment in the findings so far has been the inconsistency of demonstrable benefits in coronary artery disease, particularly in those under 50 years of age who have mild hypertension. In the VA study, data from the 22 subjects who were in the mild hypertension group were analyzed separately. This analysis yielded no differences in coronary artery disease between treated and untreated subjects. However, this number of subjects is too small for any statistical conclusions.

A U.S. Public Health Service study involved young subjects with mild hypertension and no evidence of target organ involvement upon entry into the study. In this study, few coronary events occurred in either group, but the incidence in the treated and untreated groups was the same. In the Hypertension Detection and Follow-up Program, however, the more successfully treated group had distinctly lower rates of death and lower rates of nonfatal coronary disease and fatal myocardial infarction (heart attack). The greatest benefit in terms of reducing the rate of death from all causes occurred in those who were 50 years and older when they entered the study. The greatest beneficial effect in decreasing both nonfatal and fatal coronary artery disease events (26 percent less), however, was found in those 30 to 49 years of age upon entry into the program who were in the more successfully treated group. Larger reductions occurred in those with moderate and severe hypertension, but there was a 12 percent reduction among the mild hypertensives in favor of the more successfully treated group.

The Australian trial demonstrated a reduction in illness and death related to coronary artery disorders in the treated group when compared to the placebo group, but the major benefit was in those whose diastolic pressures had been 100 mm Hg or greater initially. This reduction was seen predominantly in patients 50 years of age or older. In the Oslo study, however, which included only men under 50 years of age, treated patients experienced higher rates of illness and death from coronary artery disease than the untreated. The number of subjects involved, however, was not adequate to achieve statistical significance.

Finally, in the Multiple Risk Factor Intervention Trial (MRFIT),[1] an unexpected finding appeared. This study compared the effect of intensive efforts by a special intervention group in managing high serum cholesterol, eliminating cigarette smoking, and treating hypertension (if present) in a high coronary risk male population to the results obtained in a similar group of subjects under customary care by practicing physicians. The cessation of smoking, the lowering of serum cholesterol, and the reduction of blood pressure in those with diastolic readings of 100 mm Hg or higher yielded beneficial results in both study groups, but somewhat more so in the special intervention group.

After the study had been completed, results in various subgroups of subjects were compared. It was discovered that those with initial diastolic pressures of 90 to 94 mm Hg who also had abnormal electrocardiograms (EKGs) upon entry into the study and who were treated by the special intervention group (step-care strategy) had a *higher* mortality rate from coronary disease than those receiving customary care. It should be noted that many of the EKG abnormalities were those suggesting left ventricular hypertrophy. Many of the deaths that occurred were sudden, suggesting serious heart rhythm abnormalities—that is, ventricular fibrillation. Although no specific inferences may be drawn from the circumstantial evidence of these last two studies, they do raise the possibility that intensive antihypertensive therapy in men under 50 years of age with mild hypertension may be an added risk factor for coronary artery disease.

The stepped-care approach was used in both studies in which additional coronary artery disease appeared. This means that subjects with mild hypertension who were in the more intensively treated groups all received a diuretic as initial therapy. In many instances, the diuretic was the only drug required to reach and maintain normal blood pressure levels. Diuretics do have some undesirable side effects. Increased levels of blood sugar, increase in LDL cholesterol, and low serum potassium (*hypokalemia*) are particularly relevant when illness and death from coronary heart disease are considered.

STRATEGIES FOR TREATMENT

The Importance of Potassium Levels

The problem of hypokalemia with diuretic therapy and its management was discussed in detail in (Chapter 8). Several pertinent statements should be repeated here. Some patients with modest diuretic-induced hypokalemia may develop a greater frequency of abnormal ventricular rhythms. These abnormalities clear up when potassium levels are brought up to normal, even though diuretic therapy is continued. Furthermore, lack of sufficient blood flow to the heart (*myocardial ischemia*) due to undiagnosed coronary artery disease is not an uncommon accompaniment of mild hypertension. Even mild hypokalemia increases susceptibility to myocardial irritability and ventricular fibrillation, and this susceptibility is heightened if ischemia is present. Finally, left ventricular hypertrophy in itself causes increased irritability (a possible happening in MRFIT). The additive effect of all these factors may place individuals under diuretic treatment for mild hypertension in jeopardy. Obviously, hypokalemia is an important problem, but easily prevented.

Alterations in Blood Lipids (Fats)

Also in Chapter 8, lipid changes secondary to the use of diuretics are discussed. Total serum cholesterol and LDL-cholesterol become elevated and then return to the previous baseline values when diuretic therapy is discontinued. An increase in serum LDL-cholesterol levels might be implicated in more rapidly progressing coronary atherosclerotic disease. It should be remembered, though, that Grimm and his colleagues[2] showed that in mild hypertensives treated with chlorthalidone plus a cholesterol-lowering diet, cholesterol levels remained similar to those in the placebo-treated group. In a one- to three-year evaluation of 12 patients on

2.5 mg daily of indapamide, a recently available diuretic, there were no statistically significant changes in serum cholesterol or fasting blood sugar levels. A much greater experience is needed, but if these preliminary observations hold up, diuretic therapy might still be feasible without concern regarding potentially harmful lipid changes.

Alternative Therapeutic Strategies

If diuretics in mild hypertension do, indeed, pose a hazard, perhaps it would be logical to use another category of antihypertensive drugs as initial therapy, and potentially as monotherapy in some situations (Chapter 7).

Beta-Adrenergic Blockers. Since younger patients with mild hypertension are very likely to respond to beta-adrenergic blockers, and since this group of sympathetic inhibitors results in diminished compensatory responses including the retention of sodium and water, the beta-blockers are logical choices to be tried as initial and, hopefully, as sole agents in the treatment. But, as discussed in Chapter 7, the beta-adrenergic blockers, with the exception of pindolol and acebutaolol, have been shown to lower high-density lipoprotein (HDL) cholesterol levels. These lipid changes are more pronounced with the noncardioselective beta-blockers. Since HDL-cholesterol is protective against progression of atherosclerotic disease, does reducing its level cancel out the benefit of reduced pressures in mild hypertension and perhaps lead to an increased risk for coronary artery disease? If so, are diuretics and beta-blockers equally harmful?

In the United Kingdom, the Medical Research Council Working Party has completed a study[3] to determine whether drug treatment of mild hypertension (diastolic pressures ranging from 90 to 109 mm Hg) is beneficial, and to compare the effectiveness and possible adverse effects of bendrofluazide (a thiazide diuretic) and propranolol (a noncardioselective beta-adrenergic blocker). This was a single-blind study in which 17,354 patients with ages ranging from 35 to 64 years were involved. They were assigned randomly to placebo groups, a bendrofluazide group, or a propranolol group. The trial began in 1977 and the results were published in 1985.

Blood pressure levels attained were lower on average in the bendrofluazide group compared to the propranolol group. The percentage of subjects to reach and maintain diastolic pressures below 90 mm Hg was consistently higher in the bendrofluazide group. Pressure control with propranolol was less effective in the older subjects. Treatment with either of the drugs had no impact in overall mortality compared to placebo group. The incidence of stroke was reduced in those treated by each of the drugs. Bendrofluazide was equally effective in both smokers and nonsmokers, but propranolol was relatively ineffective in smokers. Bendrofluazide was not associated with any reduction in the rate of coronary events in either smokers or nonsmokers, whereas propranolol reduced the coronary event rate, but only in nonsmokers.

If one chooses to avoid both diuretics and beta-adrenergic receptor blocking agents as initial therapy, alternatives do exist. The effectiveness of other agents for initial and perhaps long-term monotherapy is discussed more fully in Chapter 7.

Central alpha-receptor agonists (clonidine, guanabenz) that decrease sympathetic outflow to the peripheral autonomic nervous system and also the peripherally acting postsynaptic alpha-receptor blockers (prazosin) either blunt the baroreceptor reflexes or the release of renin to some extent or do not provoke it. Therefore, two of the major compensatory mechanisms to maintain blood pressure at its pretreatment level do not come fully into play. Since the blood pressure–lowering in mild hypertension is not of great magnitude, glomerular filtration rate is not slowed significantly. Thus the intrinsic renal mechanism to retain sodium and water is not as vigorous as when changes of greater pressure ranges occur (as would be the case with moderate or severe hypertension). Patients, particularly those not sensitive to salt, may respond to these agents initially, and some of them are maintained in excellent control indefinitely. Frequently, however, sodium and water retention and extracellular volume expansion begin to produce a "drug-resistant" effect, usually in a matter of months to a year, and a diuretic needs to be added.

Clonidine (Catapres). In the elderly, clonidine at bedtime daily is particularly useful for monotherapy in those whose plasma volume is excessively reduced initially by diuretics. It has proved to be effective as a sole antihypertensive agent in a proportion of such older patients. If fluid expansion and blunting of the antihypertensive effect begin to appear, small doses of a diuretic at that time probably would be tolerated and will prove effective.

Guanabenz (Hylorel) is a recently available central alpha-receptor agonist that has been used as a monotherapeutic agent successfully in essential hypertension according to initial reports. A longer and larger experience is necessary before a more definitive evaluation and comparison can be made with other drugs.

Prazosin (Minipres). Another antihypertensive drug worthy of consideration as an initial agent in the treatment of essential hypertension is prazosin. Its action is directed toward the major hemodynamic immediate cause of sustained elevation of blood pressure—the constriction of the arteriolar bed. It has the distinct advantage of not affecting the lipid profile adversely. As a matter of fact, it may promote elevation of HDL-cholesterol levels. If a diuretic must be added later to maintain blood pressure control, prazosin will counterbalance the tendencies for undesirable lipid changes that some diuretics might cause (raising LDL-cholesterol).

Captopril. An angiotensin-converting enzyme inhibitor that has been used with some success as an initial agent in the treatment of essential hypertension is captopril. It has been effective as a monotherapeutic drug in some patients with mild to moderate high renin essential hypertension. If it fails to maintain control, the addition of a diuretic enhances its effectiveness considerably.

Calcium-Channel Blockers. Although only verapamil has been approved by the FDA for treatment of hypertension, all the calcium-channel blockers (Chapter 10) are emerging as possible major agents for antihypertensive therapy. Some efficacy as initial and even as sole agents is beginning to be described. Obviously, their role in the treatment of hypertension will be clarified in the near future judging from the interest that has been generated.

To summarize, in treating mild hypertension, a reasonable strategy seems to be to monitor the patient frequently to verify that diastolic pressure remains consistently at least in the 90 to 100 mm Hg range. During this time (3 to 6 months) vigorous efforts at nondrug treatment should be encouraged (see Chapter 6). If pressure continues to remain elevated and the patient is 50 years of age or older, the customary stepped-care approach may be used. If the patient is younger, monotherapy with other than a diuretic or a beta-adrenergic blocker might be considered, at least until the potential hazard of aggravating coronary atherosclerosis is resolved.

REFERENCES: CHAPTER 12

1. Multiple Risk Factor Intervention Trial Research Group: Multiple risk factor intervention trial. Risk factor changes and mortality results. *JAMA* 1982; 248:1465–1477.

2. Grimm RH Jr, Leon AS, Hunninghake DB, et al.: Effects of thiazide diuretics on plasma and lipoproteins in mildly hypertensive patients. *Ann Intern Med* 1981; 94:7–11.

3. Medical Research Council Working Party: MRC trial of treatment of mild hypertension: principal results. *Br Med J* 1985; 291:97–104.

CHAPTER 13

HYPERTENSIVE EMERGENCIES (HYPERTENSIVE CRISES)

WITH our clearer understanding, increased interest, and better management, of essential hypertension, it is rare for high blood pressure to first come to the physician's attention in the form of a true medical emergency. There are instances, however, where drastic

TABLE 13.1
Frequently Encountered Hypertensive Emergencies

Accelerated hypertension

Hypertensive encephalopathy

Malignant hypertension

High blood pressure complicating other conditions:
- Acute myocardial infarction (heart attack)
- Acute left ventricular failure
- Aortic dissecting aneurysm
- Intracerebral hemorrhage

Hypertensive crisis of pheochromocytoma

elevation of blood pressure is immediately life threatening, or the patient's symptoms suggest an impending catastrophe. These situations are summarized in Table 13.1. Lowering of blood pressure quickly takes precedence, and hospitalization for vigorous and intensive treatment is most advisable.

ACCELERATED HYPERTENSION

Accelerated hypertension is a direct consequence of severely elevated pressure within the arterial system. When elevated pressure persists at extremely high values (diastolic pressures ranging from 120 to 140 mm Hg), no matter what the cause, a severe inflammatory process involving the arterioles (vasculitis) develops. This vasculitis is the direct result of high arterial pressure in itself. It involves the arteriolar beds of the kidneys, spleen, pancreas, and brain, the retina of the eye, and other organs, including the glomerular afferent arterioles of the kidneys. They become constricted and narrow, perfusion pressure within them drops, and increased quantities of renin are released. The renin-angiotensin-aldosterone (RAA) mechanism comes into play and the hypertension is accentuated even more.

Clinically, the patient develops a generalized feeling of not being well (malaise). There may be lethargy, loss of appetite, severe headaches, and impaired vision. The arterioles can be visualized by looking into the eye. Funduscopic examination reveals marked retinal arteriolar narrowing, retinal flame-shaped hemorrhages, and fluffy irregular exudations (Chapter 3). The same changes occur in the arterioles of all other organs. In the kidney, there is leaking of protein (albumin) and red blood cells into the urine. If not treated successfully, the course is a rapidly downhill one with progressive kidney failure and death within one to two months.

The severe hypertension must be stopped quickly to prevent further arteriolar deterioration and to prevent increasing kidney damage, cerebral hemorrhage, left ventricular failure, or brain damage (encephalopathy; see later section). Each day of severely elevated blood pressure leads to additional and perhaps irreversible damage to vital organs. Reducing the arterial pressure will stop the process of accelerated hypertension and will reverse the acute vascular changes. Once the diagnosis is made, an urgent indication exists for reduction of blood pressure within a day or two. If there are no other complicating factors such as left ventricular failure, angina, or myocardial infarction, and if renal function has not deteriorated significantly, vigorous oral therapy may be attempted.

Anderson and Hart[1] found an oral clonidine-loading technique to be effective in such situations. Their study included hospitalized patients, 18 men and 18 women, mean age of 47 years, with sustained elevation of diastolic pressures above 120 mm Hg, all with evidence of target-organ damage but none with encephalopathy, acute myocardial infarction, left ventricular failure, stroke, or dissecting aneurysm (Chapter 1). The diuretic chlorthalidone was administered orally (furosemide was used if there was renal insufficiency) and a rapidly progressive dosing with clonidine was instituted. In all but two patients, this approach lowered the blood pressure. The treatment goal was to reduce the diastolic pressure to a level below 110 mm Hg or to lower it by at least 20 mm Hg. The urgency is diminished considerably when these goals are reached, and customary antihypertensive treatment is then initiated until even tighter control is obtained.

There was a significant response in 34 of these patients (Table 13.2), with none suffering excessive fall in blood pressure or slowing of the heart rate. The patients remained

TABLE 13.2
Response to Oral Loading with Clonidine in 34 Patients

Time After Treatment Started	Blood Pressure	Mean Arterial Pressure
1 hour	193/125 mm Hg	148 mm Hg
6 hours	151/103 mm Hg	119 mm Hg

in bed for eight hours after the loading, and no symptoms of orthostatic hypotension appeared subsequently. The average response time was five hours. Once the initial drop is attained successfully by this technique, the diuretic should be continued daily and clonidine titrated to an oral twice-daily dose for long-term control. If necessary, the physician may add hydralazine or minoxidil.

As discussed in Chapter 10, considerable interest is developing in the use of calcium channel blocking agents as antihypertensive drugs. Huysmans and his associates[2] treated 10 patients with severe hypertension ("crisis") and impaired renal function with nifedipine placed under the tongue. If a pinhole is punched at each end of the capsule, maximal effect is obtained within 15 to 20 minutes. The average drop in blood pressure within one hour was 30 mm Hg systolic and 27 mm Hg diastolic. There was an increase in heart rate of 15 beats per minute in response to the baroreceptor reflex. It should be noted that nifedipine also is absorbed quickly and acts within 30 minutes if swallowed. If these oral medications do not reduce blood pressure sufficiently, more vigorous intravenous therapy may be used. Intravenous therapy applied in the remaining emergency situations to be discussed.

INTRAVENOUS THERAPY IN EMERGENCY SITUATIONS

Effective agents for rapid reduction of blood pressure are relatively few. They differ in their mode of action and in the side effects they produce. The description of these methods is presented to give you some idea of the treatments your physician may order if a hypertensive emergency occurs. Three major drugs are available presently that are fast and effective when administered intravenously (IV): sodium nitroprusside, trimethaphan, and diazoxide.

Sodium Nitroprusside

As early as 1929, the therapeutic implications of the blood pressure–lowering effect of sodium nitroprusside were recognized in animal studies. Subsequently, its efficacy in human hypertension was established, and it was recommended for use in hypertensive emergencies in the mid-1950s.

Because sodium nitroprusside is *not* a stable solution, it was not available in a commercial formulation. Solutions had to be prepared "from scratch" in the hospital pharmacy whenever the need arose. Consequently, its use was for the most part restricted to major hospitals where the need to make it up was not a deterrent. Large hospitals used sodium nitroprusside not only for hypertensive crises but also to produce controlled lowering of the blood pressure during arteriography, surgery on blood vessels, and especially during neurosurgical procedures within the skull.

Recently, a commercial form of sodium nitroprusside has become available (Nipride). It may be kept in the pharmacy until needed. Then it is dissolved in 5 percent dextrose in water and administered as a continuous intravenous drip. Its availability and increasing use have confirmed earlier observations of its reliability in treating hypertensive emergencies. It is the most potent and effective drug for the treatment of all hypertensive crises, and frequently it is successful when other drugs have failed.

Sodium nitroprusside directly relaxes the smooth muscle of the arteries and veins, dilating (expanding) these vascular beds and decreasing total peripheral resistance. In addition, there is a pooling of plasma in the dilated veins, decreased return to and decreased filling of the heart, and a decrease in cardiac output. Consequently, cardiac output and peripheral resistance diminish, and blood pressure drops. There is some increase in heart rate as a result of stimulation of the baroreceptor reflex as the blood pressure drops.

When sodium nitroprusside is given intravenously, blood pressure drops within seconds. Conversely, the hypotensive effect disappears within a few minutes after the infusion is stopped. The effective infusion rates vary according to the responsiveness of individual patients. Blood pressure drops in proportion to the rate of infusion, and any level of pressure can be attained by varying this factor. Because blood pressure changes rapidly with minor changes in infusion rate, the patient is kept under constant observation. Blood pressure determinations are required every several minutes. Repeated appropriate readjustments of flow must be made to reach desired levels and then to maintain them. The usual rates of infusion and duration periods of treatment with nitroprusside in treating hypertensive emergencies produce very little toxicity. A few patients may develop nasal stuffiness, flushing, and dizziness, but all are minor.

It is true that in the metabolism of nitroprusside in the body, there is a gradual release of hydrocyanic acid. However, cyanide is converted promptly into thiocyanate. There has been no indication that there is a cyanide effect when nitroprusside is administered. If it must be used at high infusion rates for prolonged periods (more than 48 hours) serum thiocyanate levels can rise to toxic concentrations. Such a complication is more likely to occur in patients with renal insufficiency, and it may be manifested by weakness, nausea, and ringing in the ears. Thiocyanate toxicity may cause psychosis, also. If the drug is to be used for more than 48 hours, it is worthwhile to monitor serum thiocyanate levels to be sure they remain below hazardous levels.

Trimethaphan

A procedure for controlling high blood pressure surgically was developed in 1940. The continuity of the autonomic nervous system was severed so that the stimulatory impulses could not reach the peripheral sympathetic nerves. The intent was to prevent the release of norepinephrine. As one would predict, both the arteriolar and venous beds dilated and blood pressure was lowered. Unfortunately, highly undesirable side effects such as sexual dysfunction, severe orthostatic hypotension, diarrhea, and urinary retention limited use of this technique. It was the stimulus, however, to development of drugs that could produce the same effect. Such agents (ganglion-blocking drugs) did become available in the 1950s. Unfortunately, they also produce some of the severe side effects mentioned above and all but one, trimethaphan camsylate, have been abandoned.

Trimethaphan, when infused continuously intravenously, has the advantage of prompt onset of action (one to two minutes) and rapid dissipation of its action (within ten minutes) when the infusion is discontinued. Trimethaphan brings about hemodynamic effects similar to those of sodium nitroprusside, but the mechanisms of action differ. The decreased sympathetic transmission leads to both arteriolar and venous dilatation. Peripheral resistance drops, and more blood pools in the veins. Left ventricular filling diminishes, and so does cardiac output. Unlike nitroprusside, trimethaphan dampens the baroreceptor reflex when pressure levels decrease.

Once again, frequent blood pressure determinations and appropriate adjustment to flow rates are needed to obtain and maintain desired levels of arterial pressure. The rate of administration is adjusted according to the patient's blood pressure response.

Just as in any other situation in which the blood pressure is lowered, the intrinsic renal mechanism plus the RAA axis comes into play. Sodium and water are retained, plasma volume expands, and apparent drug resistance (tachyphylaxis) develops to the action of trimethaphan within a day or two of therapy. Concomitant diuretic administration enhances the antihypertensive action and prevents sodium and water retention.

Diazoxide

Of the three most effective drugs for the treatment of hypertensive emergencies, diazoxide is the easiest to handle from the standpoint that continuous monitoring of the blood pressure and close titration of the drug according to the patient's response are not required. Diazoxide exerts a direct effect on arteriolar smooth muscle to cause relaxation and a drop in total peripheral resistance. Consequently, blood pressure levels are lowered. Unlike nitroprusside and trimethaphan, it has no significant effect on veins. When diazoxide is given intravenously, blood pressure drops rapidly, the maximum hypotensive effect appearing within three to five minutes. Then the pressure begins to rise gradually, and within six to twelve hours it approaches pretreatment levels. When diazoxide is given intravenously, it tends to combine with serum albumin and become inert pharmacologically. To provide the highest concentration of unbound active diazoxide to the arteriolar smooth muscle fibers. Initially, it was recommended that the full dose be injected intravenously as a bolus within 10 to 30 seconds. A second dose may be given within 30 minutes if the pressure reduction is inadequate. Subsequently, additional doses may be repeated every three to six hours, the interval being determined by the duration of the hypotensive effect. With this technique, the patient requires close blood pressure monitoring for the first 15 minutes after administration of the bolus, since the maximum drop in blood pressure occurs usually within the first five minutes. Blood pressure may then be checked at hourly intervals until the next dose. Constant monitoring and adjustment of flow rates are not needed.

Since diazoxide acts directly on arteriolar smooth muscle, there is dilatation and drop in peripheral resistance and consequently in blood pressure. However, there is little if any venous dilatation, no pooling of blood in the veins to decrease return to the heart, and no inhibition of the compensatory baroreceptor reflex. As a result, heart rate, myocardial contractility, and cardiac output rise. These changes do blunt the hypotensive effect of diazoxide somewhat. In addition, if the patient has coronary artery disease, the increased work required of the heart muscle might precipitate angina pectoris or ventricular fibrillation.

A disadvantage to the use of diazoxide is that blood pressure levels cannot be as precisely or promptly controlled as with nitroprusside or trimethaphan. Once the single dose of drug has been given, the magnitude of blood pressure drop cannot be controlled. In rare cases, blood pressure might fall to undesirably low levels. To prevent precipitous excessive drops in blood pressure or episodes of myocardial ischemia in high-risk patients, some physicians have divided the total dose into smaller increments and administered them in 5- to 15-minute intervals. Such a form of titration apparently lowers blood pressure adequately without "overshooting."

Unlike nitroprusside and trimethaphan, diazoxide acts directly on the renal tubules so that more sodium is retained than under the usual compensatory mechanisms. Significant sodium and water retention often leads to swelling of the soft tissues (edema) after several doses. As the plasma volume is expanded by retained fluid, the original hypotensive action of the drug may be diminished. For this reason, diuretic therapy (usually employing furosemide) is usually combined with administration of diazoxide.

Diazoxide inhibits insulin secretion. Abnormally elevated blood sugar levels may result. In patients with diabetes or advanced renal insufficiency, insulin may have to be given.

Labetalol (Trandate; Normodyne)

As this chapter was being written, the alpha-beta blocker labetalol became available in the United States for the treatment of hypertension. (Beta blockers are discussed in Chapter 9.) One very desirable characteristic of this drug is its quick action. It can be given intravenously and it has already proved to be useful for treating hypertensive crises. As more experience is gained, it may well join the first three drugs discussed above as primary agents.

HYPERTENSIVE ENCEPHALOPATHY

The most urgent complication of hypertension is *hypertensive encephalopathy* (a syndrome characterized by headache, convulsions, and coma). Usually it follows a recent, abrupt onset of sustained hypertension or sudden worsening of preexisting hypertension. A sudden, abrupt increase of blood pressure over the previous level, not the height of pressure as such, triggers this dangerous condition. A sudden shift to 160/110 mm Hg from previously normal levels (such as might occur in toxemia of pregnancy or in acute nephritis) may trigger encephalopathy just as readily as an abrupt persistent elevation to the 240/140 mm Hg level in previously a hypertensive patient.

Normally, blood flow to brain tissue is relatively constant. As in other parts of the body, arterioles expand and contract to maintain a constant flow. The cerebral arterioles dilate as blood pressure falls and constricts as blood pressure rises. Like autoregulation elsewhere in the body, this process is a complex response to various hormonal (chemical) and neural (nervous system) mechanisms. It seems, however, that pressure changes in the arteries are the major triggering factors for autoregulation in the circulation of the brain.

Years ago, Byrom[3] working with laboratory rats and using "windows" produced in the skulls for direct visualization, demonstrated that reversible changes in the caliber of arteries and arterioles could be produced by inducing sudden severe hypertension. With high pressures, vessels throughout the brain constricted in an irregular pattern. Eventually, small areas of the constricted arterioles and capillaries dilated. These dilated areas became quite permeable so that plasma leaked out into the adjacent brain tissue, causing localized areas of swelling in the brain (*focal cerebral edema*). These measurable changes in the brain and its blood vessels were accompanied by the signs and symptoms of hypertensive encephalopathy. Both the blood-vessel changes and the symptoms cleared as blood pressure was lowered. Other investigators, using a radioisotope technique to determine blood flow in humans, demonstrated that beyond a certain point, continually rising blood pressure "breaks through" the autoregulation that normally controls the amount of blood reaching the brain tissue. Excessive amounts of blood reach the brain (*hyperperfusion*). In localized areas, plasma leaks through the walls of the arterioles and capillaries, leading to focal cerebral edema. The swollen tissue compresses the capillaries, ultimately reducing blood flow to the affected area of the brain.

When blood pressure levels remain high for long periods, (sustained chronic hypertension) the range of autoregulation gradually shifts so that higher blood pressure levels must be reached before breakthrough occurs. This explains why the *abruptness* of pressure rise within the arteries and arterioles is more important in the development of hypertensive encephalopathy than the total height that pressure reaches. In patients who have long-standing hypertension, much higher sustained levels must be reached suddenly before the syndrome develops than is the case in previously normotensive individuals.

Signs and Symptoms

Although hypertensive encephalopathy may progress very rapidly, with death ensuing within one to two hours, it is more common for it to begin with headache, nausea, and perhaps vomiting and then to progress over 24 to 72 hours. Gradually, the patient experiences progressive mental confusion, blurring of vision, transient blind spots within the visual fields, and focal neurologic signs signifying brain dysfunction. Eventually, there is coma, convulsions may occur, and death may follow.

In addition to the elevated blood pressure and the neurologic picture just described, funduscopic examination reveals severe spasm of the small arteries and arterioles. If there is considerable swelling of the brain, the optic nerve may swell (papilledema) (Chapter 3). If pressure elevation is of sufficient magnitude to produce inflammation of the blood vessels (*vasculitis*)—that is, if accelerated hypertension is present—retinal hemorrhages and exudates may be seen.

Treatment

Hypertensive encephalopathy requires lowering of blood pressure as soon as possible to save the patient's life. From the moment this syndrome begins, brain cells are being damaged or destroyed. Since blood pressure elevation is the triggering and maintaining factor, effective reduction of blood pressure is urgent.

Any of the primary intravenously administered drugs that have been discussed might be used successfully. If there is no history to suggest coronary disease, the physician may use diazoxide initially. Using this drug does not require waiting to admit patients into the hospital and getting them situated in the intensive care unit where they can be monitored continuously. Diazoxide may be administered in the emergency room as soon as the diagnosis is made. Once the blood pressure–lowering effect has stabilized—a matter of minutes—the patient may be moved to the intensive care unit. If good control has been attained, the physician may continue with this diazoxide. If not, nitroprusside infusion therapy may be instituted. Its rapid onset of action and rapid reversibility provides minute-to-minute control of what blood pressure level is attained and maintained.

MALIGNANT HYPERTENSION

Some confusion exists about what these hypertensive emergencies ought to be called. Some health care practitioners use the terms accelerated hypertension, hypertensive encephalopathy, and malignant hypertension interchangeably. In this book, these disorders are distinguished from one another (Table 13.3). Accelerated hypertension is defined as a vasculitis due to very high blood pressure. Hypertensive encephalopathy is a central nervous system disorder resulting from abrupt persistent elevation of blood pressure that overwhelms cerebral vascular autoregulation. Malignant hypertension is a combination of accelerated hypertension and hypertensive encephalopathy. Treatment for malignant hypertension is the same as that for hypertensive encephalopathy.

TABLE 13.3
Comparison of Accelerated Hypertension, Hypertensive Encephalopathy, and Malignant Hypertension

	Accelerated Hypertension	Hypertensive Encephalopathy	Malignant Hypertension
Disease process	Vasculitis	Overwhelmed CNS autoregulation	Vasculitis, overwhelmed CNS autoregulation
Funduscopic Findings	Hemorrhages, exudates	Arteriolar narrowing, papilledema	Arteriolar narrowing, papilledema, hemorrhages, exudates
Urinalysis Findings	Albumin, red cells, casts	None	Albumin, red cells, casts

SEVERE HYPERTENSION COMPLICATING OTHER CONDITIONS

In addition to crises that are related to high blood pressure itself, crises may occur when hypertension is associated with other life-threatening disorders.

Acute Myocardial Infarction (Heart Attack)

Ordinarily, blood pressure falls slightly or not at all when a patient with hypertension has a heart attack. Occasionally, pressure remains at 110 mm Hg diastolic or higher even after the patient has been admitted to the hospital, pain has been relieved, and the patient has received sedatives or tranquilizers. It may rise to even more alarming levels. Obviously, lowering the blood pressure will reduce the amount of work the acutely damaged heart muscle has to do. This is a logical therapeutic goal. On the other hand, blood flow to the heart must be maintained and the functioning portion of the heart must be perfused with oxygen-carrying blood. These goals require a certain amount of diastolic pressure. If blood pressure drops too low, damaged (ischemic) area within the heart muscle comes under still greater jeopardy. All this means that treatment to lower blood pressure to normal levels must not induce *hypo*tension.

If a heart attack is complicated by significant hypertension, nitroprusside may be given intravenously. This drug begins to lower blood pressure within a few minutes, and its effect is precisely controllable because it is proportional to the rate of infusion. Once the desired level of pressure is reached, it can be maintained for long periods. Of course, blood pressure monitoring must continue, and adjustments to flow must be made as needed. If pressure should drop too low, the effect of nitroprusside dissipates within a minute or two after the infusion is slowed or stopped. The dilatation of the arterial system reduces afterload on the heart, and dilatation on the venous side reduces the preload. There may be some increase in heart rate (baroreceptor reflex), but cardiac output is not increased because the volume of plasma returning to the heart is reduced.

If nitroprusside is not available, trimethaphan is a good substitute. Diazoxide, however, is best avoided, because control is lost once the bolus is injected. The resulting baroreceptor reflexes leading to increased heart rate, increased myocardial contractility, the increased cardiac output all foster increased cardiac work and an increased need for oxygen at a time when blood flow to part of the ventricle has been impeded by the infarction. In one study, intravenous diazoxide administration resulted in acute EKG changes suggesting additional damage to the heart muscle in 10 of the 20 patients with hypertension and acute myocardial infarction.

Acute Left Ventricular Failure and Pulmonary Edema

Hypertension eventually may lead to failure of the left ventricle (Chapter 1). As the ventricle becomes less able to eject all the blood it contains during its contraction (systole), the pressure remaining in the ventricle during diastole, its relaxed period when it is filling, tends to rise. When this resting pressure reaches the point where it exceeds the driving pressure in the left atrium and in the veins from the lungs, blood flow is impeded. Increasing backward pressure in the system leads to congestion of the lungs. There is swelling and "waterlogging" of the air sacs in the lungs (*pulmonary edema*), and the patient begins to drown in his own fluids.

Although high blood pressure may be the primary factor leading to left ventricular failure and pulmonary edema, it is also true that significant hypertension may be secondary to left ventricular failure due to other causes. In some individuals, the decrease in cardiac output with left ventricular failure brings about an extraordinarily vigorous compensatory baroreceptor reflex–induced vasoconstriction which results in a marked rise in blood pressure. In emergency situations, the physician may not know which condition is primary (the cause) and which is secondary (the effect). The patient is treated first for left ventricular failure.

Oxygen therapy, sedation, and intravenously administered furosemide are of primary importance. Furosemide not only has a rapid diuretic effect when administered intravenously, but it also brings about dilatation of the venous (capacitance) side of the circulation. Blood is pooled, and the return to the heart (preload) is diminished. The load on the failing heart is decreased, allowing it to gather its strength and improve its function. If hypertension persists for 30 minutes after furosemide is given, however, the elevated pressure itself is the likely culprit and therapy is directed toward it. Nitroprusside is the first choice, with trimethaphan an acceptable substitute. Diazaxide is not suitable for the same reasons it is avoided in acute myocardial infarction.

Dissecting Aneurysm of the Aorta

In hypertensives, the increased pressure on the vessel walls not only enhances atherosclerosis within the aorta but also may cause damage to the cells of the middle layer of its wall (*medial necrosis*). Atherosclerosis, medial necrosis, and hypertension combine, particularly in older hypertensive black men, to produce a *dissecting aneurysm*. A tear develops in the damaged lining of the aorta within or near an atherosclerotic plaque. The usual forward flow of blood under pressure works itself into this tear and then continues into the deteriorating middle layer, pressing the inner and outer walls apart. Bulging in of the inner wall may block the aortic lumen. Bulging out and then a tear in the outer wall produces a massive internal hemorrhage. If this complication is recognized early, the patient's life may be saved by prompt medical treatment to lower blood pressure followed by surgical intervention.

Three percent of patients die almost immediately with the onset of dissection. There is a 1 percent per hour mortality rate for the next 24 to 48 hours in untreated patients. Immediate, vigorous medical therapy is crucial in all cases. Once appropriate medical measures have begun, the physician may order aortography and may consult with a cardiac surgeon. Nitroprusside or trimethaphan are the agents of choice. Blood pressures should be dropped to the lowest level that will not impede function of the kidneys, heart, and brain. Diazoxide is less desirable since it does not allow for close titration of the blood pressure response. It also causes reflex tachycardia (rapid heart rate), increased force of myocardial contraction, and ejection of blood into the aorta. All of these result in greater tearing and dissecting forces.

Hemorrhage Within the Brain

Intracerebral hemorrhage and atherosclerotic occlusion of arteries providing blood supply to the brain (Chapter 1) may be difficult to distinguish from one another on the basis of clinical findings. Both situations benefit from careful, controlled reduction of high blood pressure levels. In patients with cerebral infarction, however, drastically reducing blood pressure might reduce cerebral blood flow to a point where the extent of brain tissue death may enlarge. Blood pressure reduction, therefore, should be gradual and controlled. A diastolic level of 90 to 100 mm Hg should be maintained for the first 24 hours. The drug of choice for such control is nitroprusside. Trimethaphan is a satisfactory substitute.

POSTCRISIS BLOOD PRESSURE CONTROL

Once the hypertensive crisis is under control, the physician generally continues IV administration of nitroprusside, trimethaphan, or diazoxide while beginning oral therapy. The first oral agent to be started is the diuretic furosemide (Lasix) at a dosage needed to prevent sodium and fluid retention. Once the diuretic is established effectively, methyldopa, clonidine, prazosin, or a beta-adrenergic blocker is started. For the first 48 to 72 hours, the dosage may be increased every six hours until the desired effect is achieved or the usual maximum effective dosage is reached. If control continues to be inadequate, hydralazine or minoxidil may be added. As the dosage of oral agents is adjusted upward and their antihypertensive effect becomes evident, nitroprusside or trimethaphan infusion or the frequency of diazoxide administration can be reduced and finally discontinued. When blood pressure is controlled by a combination of oral agents and if kidney function is adequate, furosemide may be replaced by a thiazide or thiazide-like diuretic at the usual dosage.

REFERENCES: CHAPTER 13

1. Anderson RJ, Hart GR, Crumpler CP, et al.: Oral clonidine loading in hypertensive urgencies. *JAMA* 1981; 246:848–850.

2. Huysmans FThM, Slulter HE, Thein ThA, et al.: Acute treatment of hypertensive crisis with nifedipine. *Br J Clin Pharmacol* 1983; 16:725–727.

3. Byrom FB: The pathogenesis of hypertensive encephalopathy and its relation to the malignant phase of hypertension. Experimental evidence from the experimental rats. *Lancet* 1954; 2:201–211.

INDEX

Accelerated hypertension, 16, 189–91, 200
Acebutolol (Sectral), 142, 144
Albuminuria, 16, 50, 189
Alcohol consumption, 17, 96–97
Aldosterone, 32, 35, 39, 40, 43, 46, 51, 61–64, 68, 121, 127
Alpha-receptor agonists, 105, 109–10, 134–40, 174–75, 185, 186
Alpha-receptor blockers, postsynaptic, 105, 108–9, 150–52, 173–74, 185, 186, 196
Amiloride (Midamor), 128
Angiotensin I, 32, 161
Angiotensin II, 32–33, 58, 68, 74, 161–62
Angiotensin-converting enzyme inhibitors, 110, 161–63, 186
Angiotensinogen, 31–32, 58, 59
Antihypertension drugs, 101–66
 angiotensin-converting enzyme inhibitors, 110, 161–63, 186
 calcium-channel blockers, 163–66, 187, 191
 diuretics, 34, 50–51, 104–5, 106, 109, 110, 112–29, 137–38, 151, 156, 157, 162, 171–72, 204
 for elderly patients, 169–76
 intravenous, 191–96, 199, 201, 203, 204
 stepped-care approach to, 104–6, 169–171, 178
 sympathetic inhibitors, 105–10, 130–54, 172–75
 vasodilators, 102, 103–4, 155–61, 175–76
 See also specific drugs and classes of drugs
Atenolol (Tenormin), 142, 144, 146
Atherosclerosis, 12–13, 15, 41, 44–46, 47, 51–52
 of renal artery, 68, 71, 73–75, 176

Baroreceptor reflex, 102–3, 104, 107, 108, 110, 113, 135, 156, 157, 159, 191, 200
Beta-adrenergic blockers, 105, 107, 140–149, 152, 156, 157, 159, 165, 196, 204
 bronchospastic disease and, 144
 cardioselectivity of, 143–45
 diabetes and, 145
 for elderly patients, 173

Beta-adrenergic blockers (cont'd.)
  after heart attacks, 147–48, 173
  intrinsic sympathomimetic activity of, 142, 143, 146–47
  for mild hypertension, 184–85
  peripheral arterial disease and, 144–45
  side effects of, 143–48
  water solubility of, 146
  withdrawal from, 148–49
Birth control pills, 39, 40, 41–42, 53, 57–58, 68
Blood pressure:
  aging and, 168
  diastolic, 4, 5–6, 9–10, 16, 101, 189
  high, see Hypertension
  low, 46, 48, 62, 66, 170, 174, 201
  measurement of, 4–6, 46–47
  normal fluctuations in, 4, 102–3
  normal vs. abnormal values of, 6, 7, 8, 9–10, 168
  physiological factors relevant to, 2–4, 19–37
  systolic, 4, 5, 6, 176–78

Calcium-channel blockers, 163–66, 187, 191
Calcium supplements, 97–98
Captopril (Capoten), 110, 161–63, 186
Chlorothiazide (Diuril), 82–83, 113
Chlorthalidone (Hygroton), 115–16, 132, 172
Cholesterol, serum, 12–13, 50, 51–52, 128–29, 182, 183–84
Chromaffin cells, 42, 64
Clonidine (Catapres), 83, 105, 109–10, 137–39, 149, 175, 185, 186, 190–91, 204
Coronary artery disease, 8, 11, 13–14, 41, 51–52, 75, 81–82, 123, 173, 180–81
Cortisol, 58–59, 60–61
Creatinine, serum, 50, 114
Cushing's syndrome, 39, 40, 43, 49, 51, 58–61

Diabetes, 51, 121, 145
Diastolic pressure, 4, 5–6, 9–10, 16, 101, 189
Diazoxide, 194–96, 201, 203, 204
Digital subtraction angiography, 72–73
Diltiazem (Cardizem), 165–66

Diuretics, 34, 50–51, 104–5, 106, 109, 110, 112–29, 137–38, 151, 156, 157, 162, 204
  for elderly patients, 171–72
  lipid changes associated with, 115, 128–29, 183–84
  loop, 117–18, 121
  for mild hypertension, 182, 183–84
  potassium depleted by, 51, 114, 121–28, 182, 183
  smallest effective dose of, 123
  side effects of, 114, 120–29
  sites of action, 117, 118–20
  sulfonamide derivatives, 114–18, 121

Elderly patients, 167–79
  antihypertensive drugs for, 169–76
  hypertension de novo in, 176
  pure systolic hypertension in, 176–78
Enalapril (Vasotec), 163
Epinephrine, 22–23, 42, 64–65, 68
Excretory urograms (rapid sequence IVPs), 53–54, 70–72
Exercise, 94–95
Eyes, funduscopic examination of, 44–46, 189, 200

Fibromuscular dysplasia, 48, 68, 69, 70–75
Furosemide (Lasix), 117–18, 128–29, 159, 202, 204

Glucose, serum, 50, 51, 62, 66, 114, 121, 145
Gout, 52, 120–21
Guanabenz (Wytensin), 105, 110, 139–40, 175, 185, 186
Guanadrel (Hylorel), 105, 152–53
Guanethidine (Ismelin), 105, 106, 153

Hexamethonium, 77–78
Hydralazine (Apresoline), 83, 155, 157–158, 175–76, 191
Hydrochlorothiazide (Esidrix; Hydrodiuril; Oretic), 84–85, 118, 171–72
Hyperaldosteronism, 39, 40, 43, 46, 51, 61–64
Hypercholesterolemia, 12–13, 51–52, 128–29
Hyperglycemia, 51, 62, 66, 121, 145
Hyperkalemia, 125, 128

Hyperplasia, 62, 63
Hypertension:
  accelerated, 16, 189–91, 200
  in blacks, 7, 9, 167, 168, 203
  in elderly patients, 167–79
  emergencies associated with, 188–204
  malignant, 199–200
  mild, 180–87
  prevalence of, 7
  pure systolic, 176–78
Hypertension, essential, 10–55
  alcohol consumption and, 17, 96–97
  central nervous system and, 21–25
  diagnosis of, 38–55
  dietary supplements and, 97–98
  diseases resulting from, 12–16
  drug treatment of, *see* Antihypertension drugs
  early stages of, 11–12, 25–26
  in elderly patients, 168–76
  exercise and, 94–95
  hemodynamic patterns in, 20–21
  heredity and, 17, 92, 112
  high-renin, 33–34, 54, 74, 110
  life-style and, 17
  low-renin, 33, 34, 104, 161–62
  mid-renin, 33, 34, 161
  nondrug treatment of, 90–100, 102
  physiology of, 19–37
  salt intake and, 17, 25, 34, 91–93, 94, 112
  secondary vs., 10–11
  symptoms of, 12
  tobacco and, 97
  and vasodepressor mechanisms of kidneys, 34–35
  weight reduction and, 93–94
Hypertension, secondary, 10–11, 19
  aortic arch disorders and, 39, 46–47
  Cushing's syndrome and, 39, 40, 43, 49, 51, 58–61
  diagnosis of, 38–55
  essential vs., 10–11
  hyperaldosteronism and, 39, 40, 43, 46, 51, 61–64
  oral contraceptives and, 39, 40, 41–42, 53, 57–58, 68
  pheochromocytoma and, 39, 40, 42–43, 46, 48–49, 51, 64–68
  renovascular, 39, 40, 42, 48, 53–54, 68–75, 161, 176

Hypertension de novo, 176
Hypertensive encephalopathy, 196–99, 200
Hyperuricemia, 52, 120–21
Hypoglycemia, 145
Hypokalemia, 51, 62, 63, 121–28, 182, 183
Hypotension, 46, 48, 62, 66, 170, 174, 201

Indapamide (Lozol), 115, 117, 123, 171–72
Intravenous pyelograms (IVPs), 53–54, 70–72

Kidney disease, 7, 8, 11, 16, 51
  secondary hypertension caused by, 39, 40, 42, 48, 50, 53–54, 68–75, 161, 176
Kidneys, 25–35
  RAA axis and, 31–35
  sodium transport in, 29–31
  structure of, 27–28
  vasodepressor mechanisms of, 34–35

Labetalol (Normodyne; Trandate), 105, 152, 196
Loop diuretics, 117–18, 121

Malignant hypertension, 199–200
Medicine. *See* Antihypertension drugs
Methyldopa (Aldomet), 83, 84–85, 105, 106, 133, 134–36, 149, 174, 204
Metolazone (Zaroxolyn), 115, 116–17
Metoprolol (Lopressor), 142, 144
Metyrosine (Demser), 68
Minoxidil (Loniten), 155, 158–61, 191
Monotherapy, 106–11, 184–87

Nadolol (Corgard), 142, 146
Natriuretic hormone, 29–31
Nephrosclerosis, 16, 50
Nifedipine (Procardia), 164–66, 191
Norepinephrine, 21–23, 33, 42, 64–65, 68, 97, 108, 131, 141, 150

Obesity, 17
Orthostatic hypotension, 46, 48, 62, 66, 170, 174

Pancreas, 65
Parathyroid gland, 65

Percutaneous transluminal dilitation, 75, 176
Pheochromocytoma, 39, 40, 42–43, 46, 48–49, 51, 64–68
Physical fitness, 17
Pindolol (Visken), 83, 105, 142
Pituitary gland, 59, 61, 65
Postganglionic sympathetic inhibitors, 105, 152–53
Postsynaptic alpha-receptor blockers, 105, 108–9, 150–52, 173–74, 185, 186, 196
Potassium, serum, 50, 51, 62, 63, 114, 121–28, 182, 183
Potassium-sparing drugs, 127–28
Potassium supplements, 97–98, 122, 124–27
Prazosin (Minipres), 105, 108–9, 150–52, 173–74, 185, 186, 204
Propranolol (Inderal), 33, 34, 83, 84–85, 105, 133, 142, 144, 145, 146, 148–49, 156, 159, 173

Rauwolfia, 82–83, 131–34
Renal angiography and arteriography, 53–54, 70, 72–73
Renin, 31–34, 54, 110, 135, 156
 high plasma levels of, 33–34, 54, 74, 110
 low plasma levels of, 33, 34, 54, 62, 104, 161–62
Renin-angiotensin-aldosterone (RAA) axis, 31–34, 35, 43, 58, 68, 73–74, 103, 104, 108–9, 110, 156, 189
Renovascular hypertension, 39, 40, 42, 48, 53–54, 68–75, 161, 176
Reserpine, 105, 106, 131–34, 172–73

Salt intake, 17, 25, 34, 91–93, 94, 112
Salt substitutes, 126–27
Saralasin test, 74
Serotonin, 131, 133
Sodium, intracellular transport of, 29–31, 121–22, 127–28

Sodium nitroprusside (Nipride), 192–93, 201, 203, 204
Spironolactone, 127–28
Strokes, 7, 11, 14–15, 51–52, 80, 81, 168, 169, 177
Sulfonamide derivatives, 114–18, 121
Sympathetic inhibitors, 105–10, 130–54
 beta-receptor blockers, 105, 107, 140–149, 152, 156, 157, 159, 165, 173, 184–85, 196, 204
 centrally acting alpha-receptor agonists, 105, 109–10, 134–40, 174–75, 185, 186
 for elderly patients, 172–75
 for mild hypertension, 184–86
 postganglionic, 105, 152–53
 postsynaptic alpha-receptor blockers, 105, 108–9, 150–52, 173–74, 185, 186, 196
 side effects of, 131, 132–34, 135–36, 138, 139, 140, 143–48, 151–52, 153, 172–73, 174
Systolic pressure, 4, 5, 6, 176–78

Thiazides, 84–85, 113, 115, 116, 117, 118, 128, 171–72
Thyroid gland, 65
Timolol (Blocadren), 142, 148
Tobacco, 97
Triamterene, 128
Trimethaphan, 193–94, 201, 203, 204

Urea clearance test, 6, 77
Uric acid, serum, 50, 52, 120–21
Urinalysis, 50, 61, 62–63, 66–67

Vanillylmandelic acid (VMA), 66–67
Vasodilators, 102, 103–4, 155–61
 for elderly patients, 175–76
 side effects of, 156, 157–58, 159, 160–61
Verapamil (Calan; Isoptin) 165–66, 187

Weight reduction, 93–94